Praise for the novels of Heather Graham

"The paranormal elements are integral to the unrelentingly suspenseful plot, the characters are likable, the romance convincing, and, in the wake of Hurricane Katrina, Graham's atmospheric depiction of a lost city is especially poignant."
—*Booklist* on *Ghost Walk*

"Graham expertly blends a chilling history of the mansion's former residents with eerie phenomena, once again demonstrating why she stands at the top of the romantic suspense category."
—*Publishers Weekly,* starred review on *Phantom Evil*

"An incredible storyteller."
—*Los Angeles Daily News*

"A fast-paced and suspenseful read that will give readers chills while keeping them guessing until the end."
—*RT Book Reviews* on *Ghost Moon*

"Be sure to read Heather Graham's latest.... Graham does a great job of blending just a bit of paranormal with real, human evil."
—*Miami Herald* on *Unhallowed Ground*

"Graham's rich, balanced thriller sizzles with equal parts suspense, romance and the paranormal—all of it nail-biting."
—*Publishers Weekly* on *The Vision*

"Mystery, sex, paranormal events. What's not to love?"
—*Kirkus Reviews* on *The Death Dealer*

Also by HEATHER GRAHAM

AN ANGEL FOR CHRISTMAS
THE EVIL INSIDE
SACRED EVIL
HEART OF EVIL
PHANTOM EVIL
NIGHT OF THE VAMPIRES
THE KEEPERS
GHOST MOON
GHOST NIGHT
GHOST SHADOW
THE KILLING EDGE
NIGHT OF THE WOLVES
HOME IN TIME FOR CHRISTMAS
UNHALLOWED GROUND
DUST TO DUST
NIGHTWALKER
DEADLY GIFT
DEADLY HARVEST
DEADLY NIGHT
THE DEATH DEALER
THE LAST NOEL
THE SÉANCE
BLOOD RED
THE DEAD ROOM
KISS OF DARKNESS
THE VISION
THE ISLAND
GHOST WALK
KILLING KELLY
THE PRESENCE
DEAD ON THE DANCE FLOOR
PICTURE ME DEAD
HAUNTED
HURRICANE BAY
A SEASON OF MIRACLES
NIGHT OF THE BLACKBIRD
NEVER SLEEP WITH STRANGERS
EYES OF FIRE
SLOW BURN
NIGHT HEAT

* * * * *

Look for Heather Graham's next novel,
The Unseen,
available from MIRA Books
in April 2012.

HEATHER GRAHAM

GHOST WALK

Recycling programs for this product may not exist in your area.

ISBN-13: 978-0-7783-1303-8

GHOST WALK

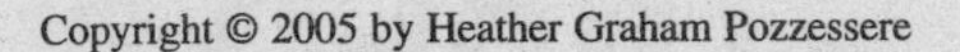

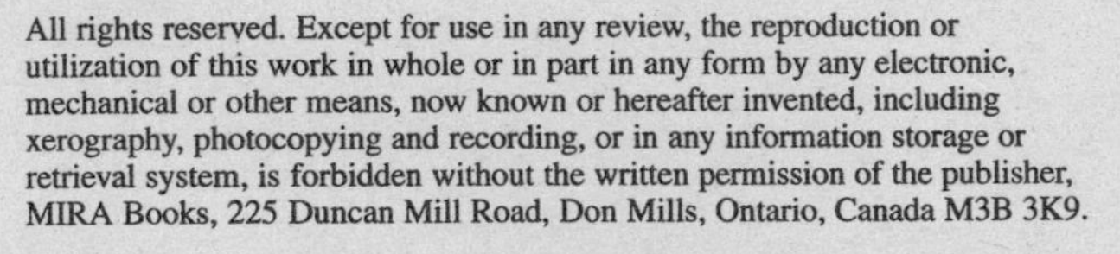

For questions and comments about the quality of this book please contact us at Customer_eCare@Harlequin.ca.

www.Harlequin.com

Printed in U.S.A.

For Molly Bolden, with all the love in the world.
Also, for Bent Pages, and the girls,
Kay Levine, Michelle Bergeron, Bonnie Moore,
Jolene Leonard and Betti Basile.

And for Connie Perry, Al, Scott, Stacy, Josh
and Me Maw, and the Ladies of Louisiana,
Brenda Barrett, Lorna Broussard,
Karin David Debby Quebedeaux and Mary Lomack.

There's nowhere like New Orleans, but people
always create the heart in the why we love a place!

Prologue

The child awoke, not sure why. He could hear voices from the living room, but they were hushed, and though he immediately sensed a strangeness in their tone, he knew they hadn't been loud enough to wake him.

He lay there, wondering.

Then he felt it.

Exactly what "it" was, he didn't know. But it wasn't frightening. It was just a sense of being comforted, like a blanket, like the soft brush of a feather, entirely pleasant. He felt enveloped by gentleness, care and concern. Even strength.

All the different tales that had been told to him seemed to blend together. There was a mist in the room that echoed the stories of the Great Spirit. He thought he heard a cry on the air, barely discernible, a soft keening. Perhaps it was only in his mind, but it might have been the distant cry of the banshee.

He wasn't frightened.

Whatever it was…a mist, a shape, nothing concrete, but yet…it was there and it touched him, reassured him. The bathroom light was on; the little night-light was always kept on for him, even though he was five and already quite grown up.

But he knew that the mist or whatever it was had nothing to do with light or dark. It was simply there. It was a kiss on the forehead, a promise that everything was all right. It wasn't a something but a some*one*, he thought. Someone who loved him and needed him to know that he was loved in return. *Someone who had entered...*

The kiss again, and the feeling of love, somehow deeper than anything real. And there were words, but not words that could be heard. They were words he simply felt.

Another world...

When the door opened quietly, he lay still. He could hear the tears in his grandfather's voice as he whispered to his uncle, "He's sleeping. There's no need to wake him."

He wanted to rise, to wrap his arms around his grandfather, to tell him that it—whatever it was—was going to be okay. But something held him silent, eyes closed, pretending he was sleeping. They were whispering again.

He was a strong child. He would be fine.

But he was an only child. He would be so alone.

No. It would be all right. He would have the rest of his family. And he was one of a great Brotherhood. He would be all right.

He definitely didn't want anyone to know that he was awake, listening, and that in their words he had already grasped the sense of tragedy that was tearing them apart.

He was afraid that if he made the slightest sound, he

might lose the precious sense of the light, the touch… the love that surrounded him.

Finally they left, the door closed.

It was in the morning that his grandfather spoke with him, stoic as always, firm in his belief in the Great Spirit, God, the Creator. There would always be an end to life here on earth, his grandfather told him, and it was how each man lived it that mattered, not the length of his lifespan. There was a world beyond, and it did not matter what a man called that world; it was simply there. His parents were gone from this place, and they could not be with him, not in the now. Nothing could hurt them anymore, ever. All they would know in the future would be the tender grace of their Maker. He—no matter what one chose to call him—would watch out for them.

His grandfather was wise, and yet the boy couldn't help but wonder if he himself wasn't more at peace than the man who would now raise him. His grandfather's eyes were filled with pain. He didn't fully feel the truth of his own words; he hadn't felt the gentle touch.

The boy slipped his hand into his grandfather's, then touched his face. His grandfather offered him the wisdom of the native peoples; his mother had brought him the fanciful mystery of a faraway country and the beliefs of the Old South. "It will be all right," he said simply, knowing his parents were still alive in his heart and would always watch over him from above.

"My boy." His grandfather wrapped him close.

Yes, the boy thought, his parents would be fine, in

a world past all pain, all strife. But all the same, they were gone.

His father would never throw him up in the air again, play ball with him, teach him, tell him tales of the Great Spirit. And his mother would never match those tales with her own Gaelic whimsies. The soft tinkle of her laughter would not come again, nor would she tell him that he was a big boy, yet tuck him into bed anyway.

They would never offer him their deep, unconditional love again…

No, that wasn't true.

He knew that love as deep and abiding as theirs had been was eternal. And there was comfort in that, a comfort that could ease loss and pain.

But there were other elements in the world that were also eternal.

Just as there was love, there was hatred.

Just as there was gratitude, there was vengeance.

He believed that he had a gift, and that his gift was special. But it wasn't long before he learned that he was destined to face far more than the soft touch of love in the night.

1

"Six, please," Nikki DuMonde said. "Six." She was smiling, but firm as she emphasized the number, indicating the tray where there were only five cups of café au lait. She and Andrea Ciello were in line at Madame D'Orso's, as they so often were. Madame herself was wonderful, but apparently she was busy, and the young woman behind the counter seemed overwhelmed. It seemed quiet enough right now. Though many of the little terrace tables were taken, there was only one other person inside the café at the moment, and he was slumped against the far wall. She glanced toward him. He had looked up once and had an attractive face, eyes that were intelligent, cheekbones hard and sculpted. But his clothes were ragged, with a slept-in look; he was unshaven, and his hair was shaggy and unkempt.

"Six coffees, six orders of beignets," Andy added, flashing a smile as the girl added a cup to the tray along with plates filled with the delicious pastries so famous in New Orleans—and better, in the minds of the locals at Madame's than any other place in the world. *"S'il vous plaît,"* she added.

As the girl turned to ring up their order, Andy assessed Nikki with her exotic dark eyes. "My treat today," she said.

"Don't be silly."

"No, ever since I came aboard, you've been wonderful." She had only been a tour guide for Myths and Legends of New Orleans for about four weeks. For Nikki, it was old hat.

"Hey, we all rely on each other, since we always work in pairs. And you're doing just fine."

"Oh, I don't know," Andy said, tossing a length of her sleek dark hair over one shoulder. "I know all the stories, and sometimes I get chills, like there's someone looking over my shoulder. But you… Nikki, it's like you see ghosts."

Nikki shrugged, glancing around the café. "Maybe it's just ingrained," she said. "I went to school with half the palm readers and voodoo queens working the Quarter these days. I guess it's like…well, walking into any place that's really historical…and…"

Nikki frowned and floundered, looking for the right word.

"Creepy?" Andy suggested.

Nikki shook her head. "Where deep feelings existed, where trauma occurred—like Westminster Abbey in London. When you walk in there—"

"The place is like one giant cemetery," Andy said dryly.

Nikki laughed. "Yeah, it is. But you can get the same feeling at a Civil War battle site—even with all the bodies removed. I guess it's a way of feeling the past, of history, people, the emotions. Remnants of the lives that were lived there, lost there."

"You see ghosts," Andy said, nodding sagely.

"I do not *see* ghosts."

"You have an affinity for them."

Nikki was growing uncomfortable. "No. I told you. It's just a feeling of...history and the human condition, that's all," she said firmly. "Everyone gets it at some point, at some place."

Andy reflected a moment. "Well, I do feel something in several of the cemeteries. And now and then in the cathedral, there's a kind of...vibe."

"Exactly," Nikki agreed. She reached for the tray, but Andy was getting it, so she turned to head back to their table and nearly screamed.

The derelict had risen. He was in front of her, his mouth working, as he reached for her.

She couldn't help but recoil, but even so his hands touched her shoulders. She thought he was going to collapse against her, but he straightened, his mouth still working as if he was trying to say something.

He needed money, she thought.

"Here," she said quickly, reaching into her purse. She pulled out a bill and, pity replacing her feelings of revulsion, said, "Get yourself a real meal, please. No alcohol or drugs, please. Get food."

She felt his touch again as she went quickly past him, Andy in her wake, hurrying with the tray.

The others were outside, but before they could reach the table, Andy said softly, "Nikki, that was really kind of you."

"He'll probably just drink it or shoot it up his arm," Nikki said.

"No, maybe not. Actually, he didn't look like a junkie."

"Just a bum."

"There but for the grace of God go I," Andy murmured beneath her breath. Nikki turned to look at her, but Andy shook her head. She had been in trouble with drugs; she'd been dead honest with Nikki when the two had first met. She'd been clean for years, however. She seldom even drank now, unless it was a special night out, a celebration.

At the moment, however, she clearly didn't want to say any more, not in front of the friends waiting for them: Nathan, Julian, Mitch and Patricia.

They all worked for the same tour company, and they were making a success of it, despite the competition in New Orleans. Maximilian Dupuis, the founder of the business, had taken Nikki on board first. Max had found her through the articles she'd been writing for one of the local tourist papers.

Max himself was really something. Tall, dark and bony, he resembled a vampire and could have haunted New Orleans just fine himself, though the cigars he loved to chomp on kind of ruined the impression. Nor was he really interested in ghostly occurrences himself.

Max was out to make a buck.

His brilliance was in putting together what the public wanted and in the art of delegating, he had told Nikki. He'd had the cash to start up the business, she'd had the ability and the knowledge. When he'd hired her, she'd suggested bringing in Julian, who'd been her best friend forever. As they'd prospered, they'd added the rest.

Nikki was Max's number two. She was responsible for hiring new guides, then for training them. It worked out well, since Max didn't particularly like to stick around and run the business. Max liked his money and having other people work for him, so he could travel the globe. At the moment he was hiking in Colorado.

"That took long enough," Patricia said as they approached the table.

"Nikki was flirting," Andy teased.

"Oh?" Patricia Broussard had been born and bred in Cajun country, and, like Andy, she had long dark hair. Her eyes were equally dark, and her grin was entirely impish. "Nikki's got a guy?"

"Very mysterious," Andy said.

"I gave a bum a dollar," Nikki said, shaking her head.

"She gave him a twenty," Andy corrected.

"He looked like he needed it," Nikki said quickly as Julian stared at her in surprise.

"Actually, he looked like he might be pretty handsome if you cleaned him up a bit," Andy said.

"You gave a bum a twenty?" Mitch, their out-of-towner, a blonde from Pittsburgh, demanded. "Wow... you're making a lot more in tips than I am."

"She's cuter," Patricia told him.

"He just seemed really needy," Nikki explained. "So let's get past this moment, shall we?"

"No, I like this conversation. All work and no play, Nikki..." Nathan, who was living with Patricia, teased.

"Actually," Patricia said, eyeing Julian and then Nikki, "most people think you two are a couple."

"Ugh," Julian said.

"Thanks," Nikki told him.

"No, no, that wasn't about you," Julian protested quickly.

"I know," Nikki assured him. She stared at Patricia. "It's just that we've known each other forever. It's like a brother/sister thing. Now can we get down to business?"

But Nathan grinned, leaning forward. "Nikki, forget business. We've got to get you set up with someone."

She sighed deeply. "I do not want to be set up with anyone."

"Her last excursion into *amore* didn't go so well," Julian said with a dramatic sigh. "But, then, I did tell her not to date the creep."

"I've never seen you date," Patricia told her.

"That's because she hasn't in nearly a year," Julian informed them.

"What? Why, that's...un-American," Mitch protested.

Nikki groaned, clenching her teeth. "He wasn't a creep. He just wanted to go off to Hollywood and get rich and famous."

"And he wanted Nikki to come along and support him while he did," Julian said dryly.

"We had different agendas," Nikki said firmly. "I love this business and I love New Orleans. I like California, but I want to live here. He really wasn't a jerk."

"Not a total jerk," Patricia interjected. "He was really good looking, and he could be really sweet."

"Sweet?" Mitch queried politely.

"Flowers, opening doors…the little things. But in the big things, he wanted his own way."

"See, I just don't think that she felt that *thing* for him, you know? Good-looking guy, charming…but when it's just not there, it's just not there," Nathan said.

"Yeah, but if you always had to wait for *it* to be there," Mitch laughed, "I'd spend a lot more nights alone than I already do. No wonder you're so tense, Nikki."

"I'm not tense," Nikki said.

"Yeah, and if you don't get off it, she'll talk to Max and see that your ass is fired," Patricia warned sweetly.

"Ouch!" Mitch said.

"Guys, please," Nikki said. "I'm busy, and I'm discerning, and I take my time, okay? And right now we need to worry about work, okay?"

Julian turned to Andy. "Just how decent would this bum of hers be if we cleaned him up?"

"Pretty decent," Andy said thoughtfully. "He just looked…down on his luck."

"Okay, guys, playtime over," Nikki said firmly. "Julian, Greg wasn't that much of a creep, just a little self-centered. I had no intention of going anywhere with him, so it was fun, but it's over. And thanks, but I don't want to date the bum. I'm fine. I love my apartment, love my work and enjoy my friendship with all you guys. I'm normal, not tense, and when I want to date, I will."

"Maybe she's working the strip clubs at night under an alias," Mitch teased. She shot him a glare from blue-green eyes. He lifted his hands. "I'm going to behave now. Really."

"Okay, guys, I've got notes from Max. Mitch, you're welcome to introduce any new story, as long as you validate it first. Julian, if anyone makes you feel uncomfortable on the walks, tell them you're married."

"What?" Julian said, startled.

Nikki shrugged. "That's what Max said to tell you. He said it works for him all the time."

"Oh, really? Who would be trying to pick up old Max?" Julian demanded.

"Oh, come on," Patricia protested. "Max is cute—in a creepy kind of way."

"Great. I say I'm married, then when the right person comes along…they think that I'm married or a liar," Julian said. "There goes my social life." He groaned. "I'll end up like Nikki."

"Oh, come on, will you guys please, please leave me alone?" Nikki demanded.

"That bum is looking better and better," Julian said to Nathan.

"You didn't even see him," Nikki protested, irritated.

"We're just trying to help," Nathan said.

"I don't want to be helped," Nikki snapped. "Hey—work on Andy for a while, huh?"

On cue, they all turned to stare at Andy. She laughed. "Nikki, they don't know me as well. I won't be nearly as much fun to torture."

"Besides, Andy is a flirt," Nathan said with a dismissive wave of his hand.

"Really?" Andy said.

"Yeah, really," Mitch assured her.

Andy giggled. "Okay…I am a flirt. I admit it."

"You can flirt with me anytime," Julian teased.

"And if he's not around, and you're looking for a good solid Yankee boy..." Mitch suggested.

"Never play where you work, that's what Mom always said," Andy told them with a sad shake of her head.

"Well, you could just sleep with me," Mitch said. "We wouldn't have to play at all."

"Hey! Go back to torturing Nikki, will you?" Andy demanded.

"If you all don't quit, tomorrow night's off," Nikki said.

"The tour is off?" Julian asked, puzzled.

"Of course not," Nikki said patiently. "If you'd all just behave like adults and listen... We had a record month. Max is going to pay for a celebration at Pat O'Brien's. Dinner and drinks on him, tomorrow, after the night tour."

"All right!" Mitch cried happily.

At that moment Madame D'Orso made one of her sweeping appearances, bearing her elegant coffeepot, chatting with her guests.

And they were special guests. Their tours met in front of her place, bringing her lots of business.

"It's calmed down out here some, huh?" Nikki asked her.

"Yes. Not that I complain about business, but we had a busy late lunch crowd today," she told them, pouring them more coffee. At her place, it was premixed. Café au lait meant café au lait.

"Hey," Mitch said to her, setting a friendly hand on her back, just above her waist. The gesture wasn't flirtatious, just affectionate. Mitch was in his late twenties. Madame was in her late…well, hard to tell, but she was a few decades older. "Should Nikki date the bum who was in your place?"

"What bum?"

"You didn't see him?" Andy asked.

"Honey, I wouldn't have noticed if Robert E. Lee stopped in. It was busy in there today. As if this parish isn't nutty enough, it's election time. Campaigners, do-gooders and politicians everywhere, thick as flies. There's those trying to clean up the place, make New Orleans a 'family' destination. And then there's those trying to keep her wild, wicked and free." She removed Mitch's hand, grinned and moved on.

"Damn. Wish I'd seen the bum. Then I'd know if we could clean him up enough or not," Mitch said with a wink.

"Drop it. Or there will be no free meal for you tomorrow night," Nikki warned him.

"It's dropped," he assured her.

Nikki rose. She could see a tour group gathering out front. "Julian, it's showtime. Andy, you're following along. Patricia, Nathan, don't forget you're on tonight."

With a last long swallow of her café au lait, Nikki started off with a smile to meet the growing crowd. Twenty minutes later, she was standing in front of the Bourbon Street bar, once a blacksmith's shop, that the pirate turned patriot Jean Lafitte was said to haunt. She found the story of the man a fascinating puzzle, and focused her speech on his enigmatic history, along with a mention that there were definitely "spirits" of all sorts to be found there—many of them behind the bar.

Her smile was as inscrutable as her story. She was certain that Jean Lafitte's ghost loved to have his story told. She could feel the mischief in the air, something a little wicked, and yet benign.

She always told the story of the man with affection, and she knew that she always gave her audience a few delightful chills.

Ghosts filled the streets here, between the neon lights that advertised *Girls! Girls! Girls!* and the shop fronts offering voodoo charms, the ever-present music, the mimes on the street, the antique shops, the boutiques and the T-shirt shops that also sold pralines and potions.

It was New Orleans, and she loved it.

Tom Garfield fought to retain his senses, fought because that was what a man did. It was simple instinct. And so many times before, it had served him well. But this time?

The girl. Had he gotten to the girl? He didn't know. No matter how he struggled, his mind was deeply fogged.

There had been a chance.

But he hadn't been able to talk.

And then…

Then it had been too late. He had been followed.

Well, it had been a good fight. And he had done as much good as he could. Maybe someone would come after him, someone who knew the truth. He had tried so damn hard to talk…

He felt a jostling, and he knew. He was being "taken care of." It no longer mattered, even to him. Dreams were taking over reality. And he could see…

The woman. Like a fairy-tale princess. Long blonde hair, eyes both blue and green… And that face, porcelain, and the look of pity…

The…money.

More money than anyone ever gave a bum.

Not a bum. Once…

In his mind's eye, in dreams, all that remained, he could see himself in a suit. No, in a tux. Clean. Walking across a room. And there, the woman…

He was jostled again, the dream broken. It was her kindness, he thought, that had most moved him.

He felt the needle.

Dreams…

Dreams were good.

He was dying. And as he died, one regret tore at him.

They would never know the truth.

Unless she realized just what she had, what she had received, what he had slipped to her in that instant when they touched…

It was over. Had he lost? No, he had to die for a reason! God help him, he had to have counted. She had to realize…

Fading. Fading, fading, and then…

Death.

2

The afternoon French Quarter tour wound up being a long one. They always allowed for questions after the tour, and it turned out they had a lot of people with questions. When they finished, Julian decided to head home, but Nikki wanted to do some shopping, so she and Andy headed off.

In addition to suggesting the party, Max had given Nikki a bonus. There was a corset shop on Royal Street and a certain piece of clothing she had been coveting for quite a while. On the way they stopped by Andy's place to check on an old woman, Mrs. Montobello, Andy seemed to have adopted. The woman was full of tales about her younger years in New Orleans. She was an Italian immigrant who'd come to marry a fellow Italian, sight unseen, but now her husband was long gone, her one son had also passed away, and her grandchildren were sweet but living their own lives in New York City.

That day, she was on a kick about the many voodoo queens, and tarot and palm readers in the French Quarter.

"All shysters," she said, shaking her old gray head

with animation. "Once upon a time voodoo was a way for the slaves to have something of their own—and to get back at their masters, eh? But I can tell you this—there were women once who really had a special gift."

"Mrs. Montobello," Nikki said, "Marie Laveau supported her 'powers' by eavesdropping."

"Dear child," Mrs. Montobello protested. "Don't you go doubting things just because they can't be seen. I hear that you give the best ghost tour out there. That people believe they've seen ghosts when they get back from a walk with you. That's because you see them, don't you?"

Nikki shook her head. "I think it's just a matter of seeing history, feeling the emotions that must have played out. But I'm a girl who sees the real picture. We lead tours, we make money. I don't fall for the shyster palm readers. Oh, I believe there are people who give 'good' readings, but I think that's because they would have made fabulous psychologists. They know how to read people."

"Nikki's good. No matter what she says, I've stood next to her and felt chills," Andy said.

"So you really do talk to ghosts, huh?" Mrs. Montobello said, rheumy blue eyes studying Nikki in far too serious a manner.

"No. I have a feel for history, and I think I'm a good story-teller," Nikki said. "I do not talk to ghosts."

"So you don't talk to them, but do they talk to you?" Mrs. Montobello asked.

"Good heavens, no!" Nikki said. "I'd have a heart attack on the spot if that happened. And if they're out there," Nikki said mischievously, "they apparently know that."

"Maybe they will talk to you one day," Mrs. Montobello murmured. "I suppose, just like plain folk, ghosts need to have something to say. But you believe they're out there—I can tell."

Nikki felt a sudden chill. *Yes, she believed in ghosts, or if not ghosts, per se, in a memory that lingered in certain places.*

It sure as hell wasn't something she was going to share with anyone.

Not even Mrs. Montobello.

"At my age," the old woman said, "you come to know a difference in this world, perhaps because you're so close to the next."

She was still studying Nikki closely. Nikki found herself staring back for a long moment.

For a moment she found herself thinking, I *can* see a fog. And I can feel the cold, an essence, a feeling... when someone is lost, when they're frustrated. Looking for something. They're benign, meaning no harm, and they are no more than mist, something in my heart, or imagination.

Then she shook off the feeling, and they continued to chat as Nikki and Andy picked up the tea they had made for Mrs. Montobello, washed and dried and straightened, and then headed out.

At the door, Mrs. Montobello stared at Nikki strangely again. "Go shopping. Listen to the music. But stay away from shysters."

As they walked along the streets, past neon lights,

garish come-ons, charming boutiques, and bars and clubs that wailed with blues and pop and everything in between, Andy suddenly stopped. "Isn't it funny? I feel like a little kid. Mrs. Montobello just said we shouldn't stop by a voodoo shop, so now I'm itching for a palm reading."

"Andy, come on, they're just silly."

"Okay, how about a tarot card reading?"

Nikki hesitated, staring at her. "Just let me buy that corset I want and I'll take you to a good place."

"Yeah?"

"We won't tell Mrs. Montobello."

Nikki liked the boutique where she purchased the corset. Everything was unique and handmade. But since Andy seemed restless, she didn't take the time to look around, just made her purchase, and then they headed for Conte Street.

The name of the place was Contessa Moodoo's Hoodoo Voodoo. Not promising, Nikki admitted as Andy stared at her, but she knew the woman who owned the shop fairly well. She was large, of mixed ancestry, African, Native American, white...maybe even some Asian, and whatever her real name might have been, she didn't use it. She just went by Contessa. She had long ago told Nikki that her potions were just what they said on the bottles—vitamins, with maybe a few herbs thrown in. And in her readings...well, she told people what they wanted to hear.

After purchasing a love potion, a bottle of vitamin E and a few sachets, Nikki introduced Andy.

"And," she said, "my friend wants a reading."

Contessa had remarkable eyes, like marbles, so many colors it would be hard to describe them in any customary way. Hazel was the best Nikki could summon, but they sometimes looked almost blue, sometimes gray, and sometimes they seemed very dark and mysterious.

She stared at Andy with a shrug. "Come on, then." Contessa had a little nook, filled with the pleasant scent of incense, and blocked off from the rest of the room by a bead curtain. They walked by voodoo dolls, more potions and curios to reach it.

Contessa took a seat behind a table with a beautiful crystal ball in the middle—she had long ago told Nikki it was just for looks. She indicated that Andy should take the chair opposite her.

She picked up her deck of cards and asked Andy to hold them. Then she took them and dealt them out.

But as she flipped the first over, she paused. Andy touched a card, and this time, Contessa swept up the deck, shaking her head. "The cards aren't talking tonight, I'm sorry," she said.

Nikki stared at her, puzzled. She brought people here because she knew that Contessa would find something uplifting to say to her clients. *A decision looms before you, think long and carefully.* Or *There has been a division of sorts in your life and you must consider the past and remember that forgiveness is something we all must feel, if we are to be happy with ourselves.* Or even, *The future is bright, go for it.*

"Okay, how about a palm reading?" Andy suggested.

Contessa stiffened, lowering her head. Nikki saw

Andy smile, as if she were applauding the act. But Nikki knew this was no act.

With a sigh, Contessa held Andy's palm, looking very serious. At last she looked up at her. "You be careful, young woman. Very careful."

"Why?" Andy demanded.

"When you're home, you lock yourself in. Don't go talking to no strangers. And..."

"And?" Andy demanded.

"There's something..." Contessa muttered.

"Oh," Andy said lightly. "I lived a pretty hard life for a while. Drugs," she admitted. "But I'm clean as a whistle now. Honestly."

"You lock your doors," Contessa said. "And you keep away from those no-accounts, you hear?"

"Yes, ma'am. And thank you. What else? Am I going to fall in love?" Andy demanded.

Contessa kept her strange mottled eyes on Andy; she didn't look at her hand again.

"We all fall in love, don't we?" she asked. Then she added, "Okay, shoo, now. Off you go. And keep those doors locked!"

Nikki was surprised when Contessa all but hustled them out the door.

"But I didn't pay you!" Andy protested.

"Honey, you don't owe me a thing. Now git. There's a world out there to be lived. You go live it quick."

The door closed behind them with a soft ringing of bells.

Andy burst into laughter. "Well, you and Mrs. Montobello are right. She sounds more like a mother than a psychologist. Go home, lock your doors. Watch out for strangers. Well, she was fun, anyway. Thanks, Nikki."

Nikki nodded, not knowing why she was feeling disturbed when Andy was amused.

"Strange, though, huh? I'll bet she could tell I'd been a junkie once upon a time." Andy sighed. "Hey…you don't think, if Max knew about my past, that he'd fire me, do you?"

"No. And who knows about Max's past, anyway?" Nikki joked. Then she turned serious. "Andy, you had a hard life, but you've risen above it. Contessa gave you good advice. Watch out for anyone who might want to drag you down again. That's it."

"She warned me to watch out for strangers. Let me tell you, there were some damn strange people in my past, that's for sure."

"So leave them in the past."

"Yeah, well…sometimes I wonder if they'll come back to haunt me, no matter where I leave them." She hesitated. "Did you ever smoke, Nikki?"

"Smoke…you mean cigarettes?"

Andy laughed. "Yes, I meant cigarettes!"

"In high school and college. Then I quit."

"Yeah, but were you ever really addicted?"

"You bet. I went to a hypnotist, and I chewed the gum like crazy."

"They say cigarettes are the hardest addiction to break," Andy said. "But you know how it is. You quit smoking—you may have given it up for years—but sometimes you'll see someone with a cigarette, and you just want one so badly you can barely stand it. But you know you can't have that one cigarette because you'll wind up with the addiction all over again, no matter what you tell yourself. Do you know what I'm saying?"

"Yes, I know I can't have one cigarette."

"It's like that with other stuff… Every once in a while, you think, man, I'd love to have that high, just one more time. But you know you can't do it."

"You're not afraid you'll be tempted, are you?" Nikki asked her, worried.

Andy shook her head. "No. Because I know what could happen. And I've seen far too many lives destroyed. I'm straight as an arrow now."

"Good for you," Nikki said.

"And I love my job."

"That's great. Hey!" Nikki said suddenly. She lowered her voice. "Speaking of drugs and addictions… look."

"What?"

"There's that guy again."

"What guy?"

"The one we saw today, at Madame D'Orso's."

Andy turned, looking across Conte. There was a crowd around the popular bar on the corner, which was supposedly haunted by a cool jazz guitarist. "Where?" she demanded.

"Right there. Great. I gave him a twenty, and he used it to go drinking," Nikki said in disgust.

"I don't see him," Andy said, craning her neck and frowning.

"There…right there." Nikki pointed. The man was

there, staring straight at her. He still looked as if he longed to reach out, touch her…talk to her.

Then the crowd moved. People laughing, talking. A sad trumpet lament began to play. And he was gone.

"Well, go figure. No more twenties to junkies, huh?" Andy said. She walked on.

And Nikki followed, trying to shake off the sudden chill that seemed to wash over her like ice from a not-so-distant past.

Another day.

Another corpse.

A junkie, lying beneath one of the highway overpasses, nearly covered by newspapers and other debris, needle by his side.

Detective Owen Massey and his partner had been called in after the patrol cops had cordoned off the scene. The ME had arrived, too, and agreed that this was just another life wasted, tragic but simple.

Not dead too long. At least the poor sucker hadn't rotted and decayed like a misbegotten rat. By the ME's estimation, this particular John Doe had only been a goner for a matter of hours. Cause of death seemed obvious. Heroin overdose.

Nearly quitting time, and he was tired. He loved the French Quarter like he might his child, if he'd ever had one. But there were days…

A few more lines to fill in, and he could go home, he thought, sitting at his desk.

Massey had nearly finished with the paperwork—not

a homicide, death by misadventure—when his partner came striding across the room.

"Hold the presses," Marc Joulette said.

"You got an ID?" Massey asked. "A match on the prints?"

"Yeah. Tom Garfield. FBI. Under cover for the last three months."

"What?"

"FBI," Joulette repeated.

Massey groaned, nearly letting his head fall on the table.

It would be one hell of a long time before he'd be going home that night.

"The feds will be sending someone."

"Oh, great."

He let his head crash to the desk.

No one noticed. A bunch of uniforms were heading out, talking as they went.

Massey looked up, frowning. "Politics," Joulette told him. "Going to provide security for some rally."

Massey arched both brows. Joulette shrugged. "It's a hot race for that senate seat," he explained. "I haven't seen this much activity in a coon's age."

"Politics. In Louisiana. There's a cesspool for you."

"Hey!" Joulette protested. "There are a lot of good guys out there, trying to make a difference. Not to mention right here in the department."

Actually, Massey agreed. There were plenty of good men in the department. And he hated the fact that Louisiana politics had too often been on the shady side. It was a good state. He loved New Orleans with a passion.

He shrugged. "Problem is, no two guys seem to have the same opinion when it comes to what constitutes the greater good."

"Well, we're not politicians. We're cops. And we've got a dead fed on our hands."

"Right," Massey said.

"Hey, Massey, Joulette." It was Robinson, a street cop who had spent some time in forensics.

"What's up?" Joulette asked.

"Purse snatcher," Robinson said. Young and wiry, he was a good cop, capable of running down perps who were convinced they could outrun any of the parish's beignet-eaters.

Massey cleared his throat. "Um…wrong fellow to get after a purse snatcher," he said.

Robinson grinned. "Hey, I know."

"You mean you didn't run the guy down?" Joulette asked him.

"Naw, I got the call too late."

"So…?" Massey prompted.

"This is just curious. Maybe nothing. But I thought that I'd show you."

Robinson produced the small sketchbook he'd been carrying. He was a good artist, and the sketch he'd produced appeared to be a likeness of Tom Garfield, their dead FBI agent.

Frowning, Massey stared hard at the picture. "What's this?"

"The woman whose purse was snatched told me that she never saw the man who swiped her bag, but she said she'd seen a suspicious-looking down-and-outer right before it happened. On Bourbon Street. I asked her to describe the guy. And this is what I got. A picture of your corpse."

"Robinson, you've seen the pictures of Garfield. You just drew him 'cause those images were in your mind," Joulette said.

"No. The woman told me this was the guy she saw—to a T."

"Couldn't have been. If this purse snatching just happened, Garfield was already dead," Massey said more gently. He liked Robinson.

"The woman swears up and down that this is who she saw."

"So our fed is dead but snatching purses?" Joulette scoffed.

"Maybe he's got a look-alike running around the city, that's what I'm suggesting," Robinson said. "Who knows how or why, but it could mean something. I just thought you two should know."

"Did you show the boss?" Massey asked.

Robinson nodded. "Weird, huh?"

"Thanks," Massey told him. "Hey, can I keep the sketch?"

"I'll make you a copy," Robinson assured him. "The boss already has one." He gave Joulette an aggravated stare and moved on.

"Everybody's just got to get in on the act, huh?" Joulette said.

Massey shook his head. Robinson was a bright officer, and the sketch was disturbing.

He sighed.

It was going to be a hell of a long night.

Brent Blackhawk fought the dream, because he knew what the dream meant. But it was too strong for him.

First there was the mist.

Then there was his grandfather.

Finally he was back on the day when they had gone to the battlefield where Custer had made his last stand. Where the combined forces of many tribes had conquered.

As a child, he had seen them.

There had been awful moments when he had felt sheer terror. He had seen the soldiers and the warriors. Heard the savage war cries. The shouts of the cavalry.

The cries for mercy.

He had seen the agony and fear, tasted the acrid scent of gunpowder.

He had kept silent, had not corrected the tour guide. It would be wrong for a little boy to correct his elders, even though he knew what they did not. He had listened to the tours; he had gone to the encampments. He had sat with his grandfather in a sweat lodge, and the old men and the younger ones had discussed how Custer's last stand had in reality been the last stand of the American Indian.

Later his grandfather had talked to him. He had known.

"It's all right," he had assured him. "It's all right."

"Is it because I'm a quarter Indian?" he had asked.

And his grandfather had taken him into his arms.

"Well, boy, I don't know. Your mom, now, she was what they called a truly lovely lass from the old country. And her people are known for being what they call a bit 'fey.' What matters is that you have a gift, and you have it for a reason. Perhaps in time you'll see that it's not frightening, and you'll know why it's been given to you. And that it's good."

Sometimes, he still wondered when the "good" would kick in. He had learned to use it, just as a policeman learned to use his weapon. There were times when he knew that his help changed lives, even made them bearable again.

But as for himself…

In the dream, he groaned.

It's time again, his grandfather told him.

I know, he replied. *I've felt it coming.*

His grandfather nodded.

So they stood together again in that valley near the Black Hills, and the mist began to swirl around them.

Those who thought that native peoples were stoic, that they did not show their emotions, were wrong. He felt, in the deep recesses of the dream, the love that came to him through time, through space. Through the darkest boundary of death.

He woke. And when he did, he sighed, looking at the rays of sun that streaked through his bedroom window.

Nothing to do about it. Go along with his life as it had been planned.

When he was needed, Adam would find him.

* * *

Nikki awoke in the morning, feeling oddly exhausted.

She felt as if she had barely slept at all, and she knew it was because she had tossed and turned in a series of weird nightmares.

She couldn't remember her dreams; she just had the lingering sense of having spent the night in a whirl of very strange sensation. It left her with an odd feeling.

A foreboding.

Oh, man!

She tried to shake it off. It was a beautiful morning. The sun…she could just see it peeking in through her drapes.

She rose, thinking it must have been the conversation with Mrs. Montobello and then Contessa's reading.

This sense of unease wasn't something she usually felt. Even when the "ghosts" were around. The ghosts were benign…faint indentations upon the present that simply lingered. There was a sweet nostalgia to what she saw and felt, something that made her feel even more affectionate toward her home, reassured her that New Orleans was special.

But there had been something about the dreams last night. Something…

Something that was malignant rather than benign.

Something that seemed to be a warning.

"Hey, it's a beautiful day," she said aloud, and went into the bathroom, where she splashed her face with cold water.

Suddenly she was afraid to look up. Afraid to look

in the mirror above the sink. If she looked into the mirror…

Would someone else be looking back at her?

She had to look up, of course. She couldn't remain in her bathroom forever, bent over the sink.

She looked up. And felt like a fool. There was nothing there but her own reflection.

She gave herself a shake, got ready quickly and left the house.

And still…

That sense of foreboding clung to her, like a gray mist, damp and chill against her flesh.

3

"At first man wandered the earth with little thought as to the great beyond, to right or wrong, and the way that he should live. Then came the White Buffalo Woman. Two hunters were out one day, and she appeared. She was very beautiful, dressed in white skins, and she carried something in a pack that she wore on her back. Now, when I say beautiful, she was stunning. And one of the hunters thought, 'Hmm, now there's a woman I would like to have in my tepee,'" Brent Blackhawk said, scanning the eyes of his audience.

"Have in his tepee?" one of the older boys teased lightly.

"Do you mean date?" asked one of the girls.

"Something like that," Brent said dryly. "But, you see, she was the White Buffalo Woman, and not to be taken lightly. She saw that the hunter had designs on her, so she crooked her finger toward him, and thinking himself the big and mighty hunter and warrior, he approached her. But as he did so, white fog rolled out around the both of them. And when it dissipated, the great and mighty warrior had been turned to bone. And as the bones fell to the earth, they were covered with snakes that writhed and crawled among them."

"Ugh!" cried one of the younger girls.

"What happened then?" asked the older boy who had heckled him before.

"Ah, well, the other hunter was naturally amazed—and more than a little afraid. But the woman told him to hurry to his village and tell the elders, chiefs, shamans and all the people that she was coming, and that she had a message to give that all must heed. The hunter hurried to the village and relayed his story, and everyone—from the great chief to the smallest child—dressed in his and her best and gathered in the great tepee as if for a council, and awaited her. She came, beautiful in her white, carrying the bundle that she had previously worn on her back."

"And what then?" asked a boy of about eleven.

"First she took a stone from the bundle and set it on the ground. Then she took out a pipe. It had a red stone bowl, the color of the earth, and she said that it stood for the earth. There was a calf carved upon it, and the carving stood not just for the calf but for all the creatures that walked the earth. The stem of the pipe was wood, and that stood for all things that grew. There were beautiful feathers attached to the pipe, and they stood not just for the hawks and eagles, but for all the birds that flew in the sky. When she had explained all this, she said that those who smoked the pipe would learn about relationships—first, with the Wakantanka, had come before them, grandfather, grandmother, father, mother, and those who would follow, sons and daughters. All relatives were bound as one and meant to be honored. All the earth was sacred and to be cared for. All were to be respected."

The boy of eleven looked troubled.

"What is it?" Brent asked.

"We're not supposed to smoke," the boy told him solemnly.

Brent smiled. "You're Michael?" he asked, trying to remember all the names.

"Michael Tiger," the boy said proudly.

"Michael, you're right. Smoking isn't just very bad for your health, it's an expensive and annoying habit."

"Then how can anyone smoke the sacred pipe?" the girl at Brent's side asked.

Brent lowered his head, smiling. "The sacred pipe is now part of a ceremony. There are very specific times when the pipe may be smoked among the Lakotas, you see."

"You never finished the story," another of the girls pointed out.

"Ah, yes," Brent said. "Well, the rest of the story relates to what we're saying now. The stone that the White Buffalo Woman put down at first had seven little cuts in it. They indicated those very special times when the pipe might be smoked, ceremonies to honor all that she was teaching. They would be part of the relationships that the people must learn so that they would not be like animals, wandering the earth, without care for it or those around them. When she had taught them a bit more, she walked a few steps away. Then she turned into a brown and white calf. Again she walked, and this time she became a white calf. After a few more feet, she became a great black buffalo. She left the council tepee and walked up a hill and there she bowed to the four corners of the earth, north and south, east and west, and then…"

"And then?" Michael Tiger demanded.

"She vanished," Brent said.

"But…why did she come, if she was only going to disappear?" Michael asked.

"She came to teach the people to respect and care for one another, for the earth itself, and for all creatures, and for all the gifts that were given to man, even the stones and the river and the ground," Brent said. He smiled, rising. "That is the Lakota legend of the White Buffalo Woman." He swept an arm out, indicating the many people who were attending the festival, a gathering of tribes deep in the Florida Everglades. It wasn't a reenactment of the old days—vendors sold soda, popcorn, tribal T-shirts, corn dogs and other non-native foods, while rock bands filled the air with sounds that would certainly have shocked the White Buffalo Woman. He'd come with a group called the Wild Chieftains, and since he had something of a reputation as a storyteller, he'd been asked to tell a few legends to the children. They weren't all Indian, and that pleased him. The children represented local tribes, such as the Miccosukee and Seminole, along with Cree, Creek, Cherokee and others. There were also a number of African-Americans, Hispanics and whatever mix the so-called "whites" might be. He'd heard British and

German accents in the crowd, so even the tourists had come out for the festival.

"The truth is, every group has its own legend. The Great Spirit is God to some and Allah to others. There are many paths a man—or woman—might take to reach the same place. The important part of the story is that we all need to respect and take care of one another, and respect the earth, as well," Brent said, grinning.

Then his grin faded as he looked past the children, and saw, in the group of adults standing behind them, a familiar face.

A too-familiar face. That of a man he knew well.

But hadn't he been expecting him?

"Are you really a Lakota?" one of the little girls asked him. "Your eyes are green."

"Oh, Heidi," Michael Tiger said, sighing, as if he were possessed of a great deal more wisdom than she, a younger child, and a *girl*. "My sister's eyes are blue, because my stepmother is mostly German. People mix up."

"Was your mother mostly German?" the girl asked.

He grinned. "Irish," he told her.

"But your father was all Lakota?" Michael asked hopefully.

"How about this—my grandfather, Chief Soaring Blackhawk, was all Lakota," Brent said. He could feel the eyes of Adam Harrison boring into him as he spoke. He could also see the man's smile. Adam was very much enjoying the way the children were putting him on the spot.

"Is it easier to be only half Indian?" Susan asked, her tone serious.

Brent ignored Adam for a moment, hunkering down in front of the little girl. "Let's hope that very soon it won't matter whether we're red, black, tan, yellow, white...male or female. Or whether we believe in the White Buffalo Woman, the teachings of Buddha, Allah or God."

"Yeah!" The little girl turned to stare at Michael.

"She is really smart," Michael told Brent grudgingly. "She makes the best grades in school. Especially in math." He made a face.

"I said I'd help you," the girl protested.

Brent had a feeling he was watching a budding romance. "Take her up on it, eh, Tiger?" he said, and smiling, he waved a hand, starting away from the group that had gathered around him. His departure was acknowledged with a nice round of applause. He smiled, waved again, and Adam caught up with him.

"You've got quite a talent there," Adam told him.

Brent shrugged. "Kids like fables from any land, about any people." He stopped walking and stared at Adam. "All right, why did you track me down?"

"I need you to go to New Orleans."

Brent groaned inwardly as a wave of dread washed over him. He avoided New Orleans like the plague. Not that he disliked the city. It was full of wonderful people, great food, incredible music.

But it was one of the places a man such as himself should never go.

"New Orleans," he muttered bitterly. He stared at

Adam, shoving his hands into his pockets. "I'm supposed to be back at the Pine Ridge Reservation on Tuesday," he said.

"You're needed?" Adam said.

"Every man is needed," Brent told him.

Adam smiled, looking away from the area where the festival was taking place, out to the rich areas of sawgrass that seemed to stretch forever, though the road, the Tamiami Trail, was really within a few hundred feet.

"Your eyes *are* green," Adam commented, looking at him again.

"And what is that supposed to mean?" Brent asked.

"Well, I just listened to you give the most marvelous speech to those children. About acceptance."

"Yes?"

Adam smiled. "Heritage is a wonderful thing. The Irish arrived after a potato famine. Italians poured into the country in the 1920s. Cubans and South Americans and immigrants from the Caribbean all came to South Florida. You know what happens after we're all here a while? We become Americans."

Brent had to smile. "And…?"

"My point is the one you were just making. We're all many things. You're more Irish than you are Lakota. You're just an American."

"So?"

"So you should support your heritage—all of it. You teach, you counsel…and then you have your special gifts. Your mother was full-blooded Irish, you know."

"Is that a comment on my 'gift'?" Brent asked.

"It's a comment on the fact that you're a mongrel, like

most people. And right now the mixed-up all-American part of you is needed," Adam said.

"In New Orleans?"

Adam looked away for a moment. "Look, I know how you feel about New Orleans. I wouldn't ask you if I didn't believe this was important."

"It's where Tania died," Brent said quietly.

"I know. I said that I wouldn't have asked you if it weren't important."

"A lot of things are important."

"I need you, Brent."

"You have other people."

Adam hesitated. "You know I always weigh what I need to do very carefully. And in this circumstance, I need you."

"I assume you're going to explain?"

"The government lost an agent."

Brent was still puzzled, and he said softly, "I'm not without sympathy, Adam, but agents put their lives on the line. And sometimes they die."

"This agent was seen walking around—after he'd been killed," Adam said.

Brent arched a brow. "All right," he said after a moment. "I guess you're going to tell me all of it?"

"I'm going to tell you everything I know," Adam assured him solemnly.

"And I'm going to guess that I already have a plane ticket?"

"You leave tomorrow."

"The new Storyville district is a great place to visit," Nikki assured the crowd around her. "As in the past, there's music and great food, but you won't find the same...business that flourished years ago. Alderman Sydney Story knew he couldn't get rid of the oldest profession as it's been called, but he was hoping to control it. I can't imagine he was happy when the red light district he worked so hard to contain was named Storyville, after him. The district limited prostitution and, in time, other vices to the area from the south side of Customhouse Street to the north side of St. Louis Street, from the lower side of North Basin Street to the lower side of Robertson Street.

"There are endless tales to go with the area. The bordellos ranged from the poor and ragged to the rich and classy, the girls from young and green to long in the tooth. But the true reigning queen of Storyville was Josie. She was born just about the end of the Civil War, raised by a very religious family, and seduced at an early age into the arms of a fancy man. But at heart, Josie was an entrepreneur. In her early days, she was red-haired and wild-tempered, and her place was known for some of the fiercest and most entertaining catfights to be seen anywhere. Then, when the brawling became too much even for Josie, she reinvented herself and ran ads for ladies of the highest rank. She managed to make a fortune and buy herself a splendid home in an affluent quarter of the city. Eventually she became obsessed with death. Not that she seemed to be terribly worried about her immortal soul. She was consumed, however, with concern regarding her physical remains. She wanted to be as grand in death as she presumed herself to be in life. So she had a tomb built, a truly magnificent tomb. It incorporated pilasters and urns and torches. And a beautiful sculpture of a woman, one foot on a step, her hand reaching for the door.

"In time Josie died and was entombed. But an heir squandered away her money. Her house was sold, as was her tomb. The new owners did not want her remains, so they were removed. In New Orleans, after a year and a day, that's no problem. Where they lie today…it's one of the best-kept secrets of the cemetery. But it's often said that Josie's spirit slips into the statue of the woman that still stands at the entry to her former tomb. Is she trying to get into heaven? Or merely beckoning others to follow her? If you happen to see the elegant statue moving, don't be afraid. Josie had a temper, but she was also a social creature, and it's said that she's merely visiting gentlemen callers who happened to have ended their days in the same cemetery."

"Where is the tomb?" a slender woman called to her.

"Metairie. It's featured on another of our tours, and we hope you'll join us for it," Nikki replied. "Well, folks, that's it for the evening, except that my colleagues—the tall, dark handsome fellow there, Julian, and the beautiful young woman to my right, Andrea—will join me in answering any questions you might have. And thank you so much for joining us. There are many tour groups here in New Orleans, so we hope we've fulfilled your expectations, and enlightened and entertained you."

The usual round of questions followed. Nikki never minded, but that night, she knew, she was glancing at her watch. At last she was able to extricate herself from the last family eager to learn more.

It had been a good evening. In fact, it had been a good

day. Her ridiculous sense of foreboding hadn't meant a thing. When she finished with the family, she waved to Andy and Julian, and they headed off for Pat O'Brien's.

"Man, I have never seen so many posters up before an election," Julian commented as they passed the wooden barricade around a construction site. The posters advertised the current sensation, an older man named Harold Grant. "He looks like you, Nikki. Far too serious," Julian teased. "Maybe we need new blood running the place. Have you seen all the posters for what's-his-name?"

"Billy Banks," Andy reminded him. "Yeah, and he's a cutie. Have you seen him, Nikki? Vibrant guy, lots of charisma. Poor old Harold probably doesn't have a chance against him."

"Some people don't vote for a candidate because he's cute," Nikki said.

Julian shrugged. "They're both swearing they're the one who can clean up crime in the parish," he said. "Politicians. Who do you believe?"

"None of them," Andy said.

"Hey...lots of people out tonight," Julian said, forgetting politics as they neared their destination.

Despite the popularity of the place—an absolute must for tourists—they were able to garner a table. It was almost as if Max could see them in his mind's eyc from wherever he was, because they had just started on their first round of Hurricanes when Nikki's cell rang.

"Drunk yet?" Max asked her.

"Funny," she told him.

A soft chuckle came over the phone. "Come on, kid.

Celebrate. Let yourself go. Drop down among the mortals and do a little sinning, huh?"

"Who is it?" Mitch asked, over the din.

"Is it Max?" Julian demanded.

She nodded, pressing the phone closer to her ear and mouthing, "He wants to know if we're drunk yet. He's telling us to celebrate."

"Tell him I'm on my way to happily inebriated—since he's picking up the tab," Nathan yelled, slipping an arm around Patricia's shoulder. "And Tricia's doing fine, too."

"Hot time tonight, huh?" Julian asked.

Patricia laughed. "Like he needs to get me drunk at this point."

"Just...perky," Nathan teased, hugging her.

"Would you guys quit with the sex thing? At least until you see the rest of us coupled up for the night, huh?" Mitch said. "By the way, Nikki, make sure you're hearing Max correctly. He's telling you to celebrate, not to be celibate."

"Funny, Mitch," she mouthed.

"What was that Mitch said?" Max asked. He said something else, but the music was playing and there were voices all around.

Nikki waved a hand at them, frowning. "I can't hear you, Max," she said.

The others ignored her.

"You won't see me coupled up—not in the near future," Andy said. "A voodoo queen warned me to watch out for strangers," she assured them

"Max?" Nikki said, narrowing her eyes fiercely at the others.

"I'm here, Nick," he said. "I just called to say that you're doing a great job—one of the travel magazines just rated us as the top tour bargain in the Big Easy. So tell Nathan to drink himself silly. And you do the same."

She realized that the idea actually appealed to her. What had it been? The weird junkie at Madame's yesterday? That sense of foreboding this morning? The back-to-back tours she had done that day? She needed to take it a little easier. Once Max got back, she was going to tell him that they needed to hire more people.

The Hurricane she had assumed she would nurse all night was already empty. A waitress replaced it without being asked.

She smiled her thanks and spoke to her boss.

"Max, thanks, that's great. I'll tell the others."

"Tell us what?" Patricia demanded.

She waved an impatient hand again, trying to get them to shut up while she was still talking.

"When are you coming back?" she asked Max. "I need to ask you—"

"Do what you need to do. I'm not sure yet when I'm coming back. You've got my cell—call me with any problems. And for tonight, let loose. Eat, drink and be merry. We'll talk soon."

"Max—"

He'd hung up.

"What did he say?" Julian demanded.

She told them about their ranking in the tourist mag.

A cheer went up, and then a toast. "Did we order food?" Nikki demanded.

"Our little China doll is getting tipsy!" Patricia teased.

Nikki groaned. "Hey, for real."

"Hey, for real," Julian assured her. "We've got a shrimp and crawfish appetizer coming, gumbo and a special thing, pork, red beans and rice…succotash, darlin'!" he teased, managing to sound just like Max.

"Thank God," she murmured.

"Indeed. Another toast," Nathan said, raising his glass. "We're the best. And congrats to Nikki, our blonde beauty."

"Hey, don't look now, but that guy over there is looking to be a couple tonight," Patricia said, nodding toward the other side of the room.

"He's looking at Nikki, not me," Andy said.

Nikki twisted around. The guy in question was nice looking, sandy-haired, either a businessman letting down his hair, or maybe a college student.

"No, I think he's looking at you, Andy," she said.

"Ladies, ladies, I hate to disappoint you, but I think he's looking at me," Mitch said.

Another round of drinks came to the table. Nikki's head was beginning to buzz, but it was a celebration, and she did need to let loose now and then.

So she ate crawfish and had another Hurricane, and laughed at the banter around the table.

The plane rose, angling into the air.

Below, there was light.

And darkness.

Along the coast, the highly populated sections were ablaze with artificial light. Housing and commercial development were pushing the boundaries, eating up great chunks of the Everglades.

And yet the great area of no-man's-land remained, thick with grass and slow-moving water—and darkness.

South Florida. From the air, it was easy to see just how much of the landscape was still taken up by the "river of grass," since, technically, the Glades weren't swampland at all.

Brent loved it, loved the festivals held by the Seminole and Miccosukee Indians. He loved playing guitar with his friends. Loved the seemingly endless expanse of the Glades, even with the mosquitoes, snakes and alligators.

The Everglades made a great place to dump bodies, too. When someone went missing…well, the police knew where to look.

This was his home now, the place he'd chosen to live. But there was also the home of his childhood.

After the deaths of his parents, his grandfather had been his legal guardian, so he'd spent a great deal of time, school vacations, holidays, summers, in South Dakota. But his mom's family had been among many Irish immigrants to the Deep South, and until recently, they'd lived in the parish of his birth. Most of the time when he'd been growing up had been spent with that side of his family, in Louisiana.

New Orleans. The French Quarter. Where he'd been born.

He knew the area far too well.

New Orleans. And beyond the Vieux Carré, the bayous. Endless canals. Alligators, shrimp and shrimpers, crawfish, Cajun food…

There were bodies there, too. And strange events that went beyond the accepted norm…

It was what he did, he reminded himself.

But not always by choice.

New Orleans.

Damn, but he hated to go home.

4

"Help me! Nikki, wake up and help me!"

Nikki woke groggily from a deep sleep. She forced her eyes open.

"Nikki, please, for the love of God...there's nothing. I have nothing. Tell them—you've got to tell them!"

She blinked. There was a soft glow of green light emanating from her clock, and a thin gleam coming from the bathroom, from the night-light she kept on. She had failed to fully close the draperies across the sliding doors in her bedroom. Though she faced the small garden area at the rear of the house, enough light made it into the back that a gentle glow came in through the window. Though the light seemed pale and misty, she could see the basic shapes of the furniture in her room.

And the woman at the foot of the bed.

Andrea was standing there, clad in a long T-shirt advertising the New Orleans Saints. Her long dark hair was tousled, as if she'd just gotten out of bed.

"Andy, what are you doing here? What are you talking about?" she asked, glancing over at her bedside clock. Almost 4:00 a.m. They had only parted at two, and after all those Hurricanes, Nikki felt as if her mind was moving on a very slow track. In fact, her head was pounding. She had to be dreaming, but it was unfair for her head to hurt so badly in a dream.

"Go away, Andy. You're the one who kept ordering the drinks," she grumbled miserably.

"The bum in the coffee shop, he's dead, Nikki."

Nikki shook her head, which made it hurt even more. "Andy, we didn't know the guy. We couldn't know if he's dead." She stopped to think for a minute, but between the liquor and exhaustion, she knew she wasn't doing too well.

"How did you get in here, anyway? If you guys are trying to scare me… Did Julian put you up to this? Hell, I don't really care right now. Go away. And lock the door behind you when you go."

"Nikki! Please…help!"

"I understand a joke, Andy, but I really feel like hell. So…ha, ha, go away."

"Nikki, for the love of God," Andy implored. "Wake up…I think…I think it's you they're after."

"Andy, go away. Go home. What the hell are you doing out dressed like that, anyway? Look—I'm closing my eyes. When I open them, you're going to be gone. And if those other idiots are with you, tell them to get out, too."

"Okay, I'm going to open my eyes, Andy, and you'd best be gone!"

She opened her eyes. To her amazement, Andy was gone.

"Make sure my front door is locked when you go!" she called.

She sighed. She needed to get up and make sure that the door had been locked. She should close the drapes—and avoid the sun that was going to tear into her eyes in the morning. But none of them had to work tomorrow morning. Not until night…the eight o'clock tour. Ample time to recover, and so, to get in all the healing sleep she needed. She should get up…

She couldn't quite do it. Couldn't quite make herself get up.

She closed her eyes, and went back to sleep.

When Nikki woke in the morning, she didn't even remember at first that she'd opened her eyes to see Andrea in her room. Her head was still thudding. She managed to crawl out of bed and into the bathroom, and down several aspirins. In the kitchen, she decided toast would be a good thing. Coffee first, because she couldn't bear life without it, then toast and orange juice.

Walking back into her bedroom, she unlatched her glass doors and walked out on the little balcony that looked over the small courtyard in the back of the house where she lived. The antebellum grande dame had been restored beautifully—into six apartments. She had chosen her own when the work had barely been completed because of the two upstairs bedrooms, hers, that she slept in, with the windows that faced the garden, and the spare bedroom, that she used as an office, that overlooked Bourbon just beyond the small front yard and brick fence. Then, to make it all the more wonderful, downstairs her front entry wasn't through the main hall, but was a separate entrance, a one-time servants' door. It opened to the far end of the broad porch, an amenity accessible to all the tenants, but convenient to her. The porch looked on to grass and flowers and the swing that fell from a huge old oak. Downstairs, the street was blocked from view—and vice versa—by the brick fence. From the front, all the music and mayhem of the city could be heard, but in the rear, all was quiet.

A slight breeze filtered in. Fall was coming, and with it, days and nights that were beautiful, still warm, but relieved of the drop-dead humidity that could plague the city.

She determined to shower quickly and dress. That might help.

It did. Her hair still damp, in jeans and a knit shirt, she walked out to pour her coffee. The headache was beginning to recede. She took her coffee outside.

It was at the front door—where she discovered both her bolt and the chain lock still in place—that she remembered the dream. She smiled to herself.

Hurricanes.

She'd never have another.

So—the crew hadn't sneaked in on her last night, determined to play the world's most annoying practical joke.

She really had dreamed it all up!

Andrea would be amused when she heard about it. No…she wasn't going to say anything to Andrea at all. That would only bolster the teasing concept that she had no life other than her work, that her life would be much more fun if she did submit to more alcohol upon occasion, and that she was…well, something of a workaholic.

She took her coffee outside, sat in one of the big wicker chairs on the porch, and looked out at the lawn and the eternal flowers there. Pretty. The breeze was pleasant.

A few more cups of coffee, her toast…and she might feel like living again.

She closed her eyes, letting the air caress her cheeks, ease away the night of living it up a bit too much—well, for her, anyway. But she was very serious about her work for Max. She might be underpaid for the amount of responsibility she was taking on now, but she knew that Max had big plans. He wanted to go around the country with his tours. Nikki had always loved to travel, and once Max got going, she wanted in on the whole thing. People simply loved this kind of tour. And no matter where a city might lure lots of tourists, there were surely ghosts to be found!

All right, this was her special turf. She'd spent her life here, right here, in the French Quarter. If there was a story out there, she'd heard it. The history of the city was something she could recite in her sleep. And she loved it. Funny, that made her think of Andy.

When she'd first met the girl, her friend had been amazed that she still loved living in New Orleans. In fact, she'd burst into laughter when Nikki had urged her to tell her why she was grinning like an imp.

"It's just…well, you're not a drinker. And it seems you always want to go somewhere without crowds… so, why live in and love New Orleans?"

The question had startled Nikki. "It's home. It's all I know. And, okay, so I'm not a big boozer. I love jazz! I love the artists on the street, and the performers…and even the people who pass through!"

And she did.

"What on earth do you do during Mardi Gras?" Andy had demanded, still laughing.

"Visit friends in Biloxi," she said dryly.

It was true. There were always tourists in New Orleans. She liked tourists. She just didn't like the melee that came along with Mardi Gras in New Orleans.

Well, she thought, yawning and stretching, she would stay in New Orleans for Mardi Gras next year. They all wanted a party. She'd do it—for Andy, and the others, as well, she figured. Julian was Mr. Party himself, a good friend, and she loved him—even if she was ready to clobber him right now. She'd known him her whole life, and he'd taken the job when she'd asked him on Max's behalf because of her, not because he'd originally thought they could really do something new and special. He was wickedly tall and good looking, and great at this work, even if he was overly dramatic. Didn't matter—those who went on the ghost walk with him were always thrilled.

Sure, this year, she'd have a party. Patricia, who had grown up not too far away, in Cajun country, longed to have a really good Mardi Gras party, too. She'd grown up close—but far enough away so that she longed to be part of the real heart of the celebration, too—from the above-the-vomit line, as she called it. Mitch, of course, was from Pittsburgh, and he was dying to get into the dead center of it all. As he had told Patricia, he didn't care what evils lurked on the street; he wanted to see it all. Of course, he'd prefer a nice party place, but…

Nathan was more like her. He was shy, except with friends, unless he was on, and then, like Julian, he was on. Now, he was madly in love with Patricia, and he was comfortable with their close group of workers. Though Nikki was certain Nathan would just as soon head for Biloxi during Mardi Gras, too, he would want a party because Patricia would want a party.

And, of course, it would be an important time for them to be working.

They were doing so well.

Nikki felt a real sense of pride—despite her pounding headache. A lot of the time, tourists thought that costumes and makeup on tour guides was just schmaltz.

Not so with their group.

They were good. They knew their subject matter. They could answer questions. They didn't just give a tour—they were an event.

And though the whole thing had been created through Max's plan, vision—and money—Nikki felt as if it were her own dream child finding real fruition. She had been there with Max at the very beginning, when there had been just the two of them, working hard, footing it all over the place by herself. Befriending the concierge staff at the hotels, begging store managers for flyer space. She had been the one to give the free tours to travel agents, thanking God that Max had saved up enough to be able to bring the people in. After the first go, Max had told her to bring Julian in. He hadn't been convinced that he'd ever really get a substantial income from the enterprise, but he'd been willing to take a chance because she was so impassioned.

And he was a total ham.

They had begun to thrive, and so, Max had told her to increase the program, and the staff. She had found the others later—they'd had to "audition," both for historical accuracy, and for their ability to tell a damned good and eerie story without getting into outright lies. No one in their group ever said that such things as vampires, ghosts, or any other metaphysical creature existed. They told the stories that had been told. The legends. They were still known as the "ghost" walk, though officially, the company was called "Myths and Legends of New Orleans."

Nikki ran her fingers through her hair, trying to let it dry in the breeze.

A newspaper came flying over the brick wall. The newsboy—late as he was!—had cast it over the brick with amazing accuracy.

It landed in front of her. Staring down at the headline, she let out a sigh. There were two pictures on the front page. One of the statelier Harold Grant and one of the more charismatic Billy Banks.

"Billy Banks," she muttered aloud. "Who the hell votes for a guy named Billy Banks?"

As she leaned down to pick up the paper, she heard the front gate opening.

As it did, she felt a vicious cold sweep through her, as if an arctic blast had suddenly hit her entire bloodstream. Her breath caught.

Her sense of foreboding… It was coming true.

She looked up, remnants of her dream flashing through her mind's eye like a chaotic movie trailer.

She knew, though he was in plainclothes, that the man who approached her was a policeman, and that he was about to tell her something terrible.

She stood up, her mouth working, no words coming.

"You—you're a cop. Something's happened," she finally gasped out.

The officer nodded. He cleared his throat. "I'm Detective Massey, Owen Massey, Miss DuMonde."

Nikki stared at him, hating the wave of knowledge that filled her, muscles constricting as she denied everything rushing into her mind.

"No, no…there's a mistake."

"I'm so sorry."

"Someone is…hurt?"

"I'm here about Miss Ciello, Miss Andrea Ciello."

He looked helpless—big, kind and helpless. Cops like him must have to give people bad news all the time, but it looked as if it had never gotten easy for this guy. "We were referred to you. A Mrs. Montobello is the one who called us…insisted we go in, swore that Miss Ciello would have come to see her first thing in the morning. She said that you were Miss Ciello's best friend? I'm sorry, so sorry. I wish there were an easier way to do this. Um…should we go inside?"

"What's happened? Tell me what's happened!"

"Perhaps—"

"No! Talk to me, tell me, what's happened?"

"Overdose, I'm afraid. We believe it was accidental,

but you know, we have to go through procedure.... The thing is, we need someone to make a formal identification of the body."

"Body?" Nikki gasped.

"Yes, I'm afraid—"

"No!" Nikki stared at him in disbelief. No. It had to be an elaborate joke. Andy—vivacious, fun-loving, rowdy Andy—couldn't be dead.

"I'm truly sorry. It appears that she—"

"Andy was clean."

"I'm sure she wanted to be clean."

"No! She *was* clean." Nikki realized that she was backing away from the man, denying everything that he was saying. But it couldn't be true. "She was clean. She knew not to touch the stuff. It's impossible that she did this to herself. It's impossible that..."

But from the way he was looking at her, she knew it was true.

Just as the dream had been true. She wanted to black out; she wanted the world to go away. Yes, she had always had a sense of the past, of spirits that remained, but never, never, had she felt...*seen*...anything like...

Last night. Andy had been dead. Or dying. And she had come to Nikki for help. She had failed her friend somehow.

She shook her head again. Her words were fierce. "Andrea Ciello was off drugs. I know it. If something's happened to Andy, it was not self-inflicted, and it was not accidental. She was murdered."

Murdered.

The officer was staring at her, troubled, frowning.

"I'm telling you, she was clean. And if you don't believe me, I'll raise a stink in this parish the likes of which you've never seen. She can't be…oh, God."

No. This was impossible. She was still dreaming. Imagining this cop just the way she'd imagined Andy last night.

"I'm sorry, Miss DuMonde. Look, is there someone I can call? Are your folks here…a sister, brother, friend?" he asked.

She ignored him, shaking her head, anger keeping her standing. "She did not overdose. If she had drugs in her system, someone else put them there. I am going to demand an investigation. I want to see a homicide officer."

"I handle homicide cases," he said gently. "We have to look into any death that's questionable in any way."

"Oh?" She stared at him anew, heart racing.

"It wasn't a natural death," he said. "So they call us in."

"What time was she killed?" Nikki managed to ask.

"What time did she die?" he countered gently.

"Please. Yes, whatever. What time—did she die?" Nikki gasped out again.

The detective looked wary, as if he wasn't sure why that information should be so pertinent.

"The ME only had an estimate, but it would have been around 4:00 a.m.," he told her.

She reached out, grasping for a railing…for help…for something that wasn't there. Too late, the detective realized what was happening.

Nikki crashed down on the porch as the world faded before her, Andy's words suddenly echoing in her ears.

"Help me!"

"Sorry," the taxi driver told Brent as they slowed to a near halt on entering the French Quarter.

"No problem," Brent told him.

It was usually a slow process, maneuvering the tourist-filled streets. Delivery vans could block a narrow byway, and any little snarl could close things off, though in the tight confines of the place—with many streets blocked off for pedestrian traffic only—most people preferred to walk. Still, vehicles were sometimes necessary, and delays were just a fact of life.

Brent breathed a deep sigh as he looked around. *Charming.* That was definitely a word to describe the architecture, the handsome wrought-iron railings the locals called iron lace. The sound of the music, the colors, the architecture itself. Yes, the place had charm.

And once upon a time he had loved it.

But that was then, and this was now, and if he'd never come back, it would have been just fine.

"What the hell is going on?" he asked as a patrolman in the street brought the traffic to a stop.

"Debate," the taxi driver said.

"Debate?" Brent said, and frowned.

"Politicians, and I'm not sure what they're debating. They both claim to have the same platform. Working to keep the history and unique quality of the place while cleaning up crime. I guess the old guy is saying that he knows what he's doing, that his record is great, and we're already on the way, while the younger guy is claiming the old guy hasn't done a thing, hasn't moved fast enough…well, you know. It's politics. Everyone swears to move the moon, and everyone out there is a liar, just the same." He winked at Brent in the rearview mirror.

"The crime rate has come down, though, hasn't it?"

"Crime rate goes down, crime rate goes up. Hey, no matter who wants to run what, nothing changes. Those that have want to keep what they have. Those that don't have want to get. We have real poverty in some areas, some pretty rich folk in others. Same old, same old, the human condition. Unless you change the conditions… well, that's what both our boys say they mean to do, so…you know how you usually vote for the guy you dislike the least? Well, both these guys are likable, so I guess we can't lose."

"That's good."

"I think so. But then, I love this place. You visit often?"

"No."

"Where you from?"

Brent started to say, all over.

But he didn't. He told the truth.

"Here. Right here."

"Yeah? Well, welcome home!"

The traffic began to move again.

They passed the police station on Royal.

At last they came to the bed-and-breakfast where Brent was planning to stay, after crashing at a hotel out by the airport the night before.

He paid the driver, met the hefty man who owned the place, paid and found his room.

And crashed down on the bed. New Orleans.

Arriving here was like having his blood drained from his body. Like being on the wrong side of a bout in a boxing ring. The pain in his head crashed like hurricane waves on the shore.

Drapes were drawn, door was closed…darkness.

All he needed was a little time. And he could adjust.

He didn't want to adjust.

But he would.

5

A year and a day.

That thought kept going through Nikki's head as she stood in the graveyard. Andrea hadn't hailed from New Orleans, but she didn't have any family left anywhere else, either. She'd been orphaned, like Nikki, and had grown up in a series of foster homes.

There had been no one to call. Andrea had been out of school for two years, traveling and taking odd jobs along the way. She'd left no names to contact in any kind of an emergency. She had gone to Tulane and probably still had friends in the area, but who they were and how they could be reached, Nikki hadn't had the faintest idea.

And because there was no place Andrea had called home and no one she had called family, Nikki had decided that she would take care of all the arrangements.

So Andy was being buried in Nikki's family vault, since there was plenty of room and no one left to fill it. The DuMondes had lived in the area since the late 1700s. Where her very early ancestors had been buried, Nikki didn't know. But in the 1800s they had acquired a plot in the Garden District. Someone at some time had put some money into the family mausoleum. Giant angels guarded the wrought-iron doors to the elaborate family tomb that boasted the name DuMonde in large chiseled letters.

The last interment had been her parents, killed in an automobile accident when she had been a toddler, and her grandparents, gone just a few years ago.

As she stood in front of the door, she realized that it was truly sad, but she barely remembered either her mother or her father. She had pictures, of course, and because of the pictures, she had convinced herself that she remembered much more than she really did.

A year and a day…

The time it took for the fierce New Orleans heat to cremate the earthly remains of a once-living soul. Then the ashes could be scraped back into a holding cell in the niche within the vault, and a new body could be interred. There were actually twelve burial vaults within the family mausoleum. Nikki had decided that Andrea should be buried with her own folks. She certainly didn't believe that corpses or remains could find comfort with one another, but it made her feel a little better to know that they would be interred together.

Of course, funerals were for the living.

Julian wrapped an arm around her shoulder. They all thought she was in serious shock. She was. They all thought it was because she and Andy had bonded so quickly. It wasn't.

She had liked Andrea, really liked her. But none of them had known her more than a few weeks.

It was partly because Nikki was convinced Andrea had been murdered, no matter what anyone else said or thought. But there was more.

It wasn't the fact that a monster was out there, still at liberty, unknown by the police, that was the greatest horror.

It was the dream....

"Sweetie, it's over," Julian whispered to her. "Set your flower on the coffin."

She nodded, swallowing. And set the flower on the coffin.

The funeral had cost a mint, a mint she didn't really have. But the rest of the group had been wonderful, contributing what they could, and Max had told her to take whatever she needed from the corporate account.

After she set her flower down, she turned. The glass-enclosed, horse-drawn hearse, empty now, remained on the dirt path that led from the street to the vault. The band began to play—a typical New Orleans band, a small group that Nikki was convinced would have meant a great deal to Andrea. It hadn't exactly been a full-blown New Orleans jazz funeral, but it had been close.

Andy had wanted to be a part of the real New Orleans.

Now she was.

Andrea had been dead for four days. Despite the fact that an autopsy had been not only demanded by Nikki but required by law, nothing the ME had been able to tell them had shed any light on the situation. Nikki had continued to insist to Massey that there had been a killer.

To her relief, he didn't try to convince her that she

was simply in denial, grieving for the loss of a friend. Perhaps he didn't believe her, but he had at least gone through the motions of an investigation.

All they knew was that Andrea had gone to Pat O'Brien's with her friends, and at 2:00 a.m. they had parted company.

What had happened after that, none of them knew.

The police had found her—forcing the door of her apartment at the insistence of Mrs. Montobello—at nine o'clock in the morning. Andy had checked in with Mrs. Montobello with such regularity that the woman had been worried, and rightly so.

Andy had no longer been clad in the short sassy skirt and bandeau top she had been wearing when they celebrated. She had been in a New Orleans Saints shirt and nothing else.

Just as Nikki had seen her.

She had been found with a needle and other drug paraphernalia at her side. The only prints found in her place could be traced to her friends, and even those had been sparse. Many surfaces had been wiped clean. Nikki knew that some of the officers involved in the case believed that was because Andy had recently cleaned the apartment. Thankfully, Massey seemed to find it a bit suspicious.

But…other than that…

There had been no forced entry, nothing to show that anyone else had been with her that night. There was nothing.…

Nothing. Nothing at all. Or, if the police did have anything, they weren't sharing.

Nikki didn't think any of her own friends believed her. They had tried, however, to help her cover any possible angle. They had all spent hours in the police station, trying to remember if they had seen anyone, anyone at all, looking at Andrea oddly or threateningly. Hard to decide, though they did remember the sandy-haired guy who might have been looking at Nikki herself. Admittedly, they had all been smashed.

Even Andy.

Oh, God, please let it be that she didn't feel fear and pain, Nikki thought.

Had Andy been followed home? By someone who had been watching her at the bar? Or by someone who had seen her on the streets as she walked home.

Were the others right, when they looked at her with sympathy, thinking that she just couldn't accept the fact that Andy had fallen back into using? God knew, it was easy enough to buy whatever drugs you might want.

No. There had been someone else, someone who had forced the drug on Andy.

Mrs. Montobello hadn't heard a thing, which wasn't surprising. She couldn't hear a bomb go off without her hearing aid, which she wouldn't have been wearing at four o'clock in the morning. She was here now, softly crying into an embroidered handkerchief. Andy had always been so good to her, checking up on her, bringing her gourmet treats and other little presents. Poor Mrs. Montobello was really going to miss Andy. But as to being much help when it came to the investigation… well, she wasn't any.

The account executive who lived above Andy had

been in New York on business. The single mother of two next to him had taken her toddlers to her mother's house. So there had been no one in Andy's quaint Victorian manor who might have heard anything, or have any clue as to what had happened.

The police had posted an appeal in the newspaper seeking anyone who might have seen Andy that night. And people had come in, trying to be helpful with stories about any strange character they might have met.

In New Orleans, that could be practically anybody.

The police were at a loss. As far as Nikki knew, the crime scene investigation department had gone over Andy's apartment with the best forensics available. They hadn't found as much as a hair that might help unravel the mystery of her death. Not a single clue.

Naturally, Nikki had kept silent about her strange dream. She could barely remember it, anyway—other than the fact that Andy had been there at the foot of her bed. But she hadn't been there. She had been either dead or dying by that time.

She was pretty sure, though, that even as they went through the motions, the police believed that Andy's death had been self inflicted, even if accidentally so. Still, Massey had assured Nikki that, as tragic and frustrating as it was, finding a murderer could take a long time. Months or even years. Though Detective Massey didn't say it, she knew that far too often a killer was never discovered and walked away free.

That made her think that maybe she should mention her dream to someone. The only person she had told was Julian, and he had looked at her with such incredulity that she had immediately felt foolish. Julian had gone on to warn her that telling her bizarre tale would either make the police think she was a kook who had been giving her own tours for too long or a suspicious individual herself.

But the dream bothered her on a daily basis. No. Hourly. Constantly.

She felt a pang in her heart that was so sharp it might have been delivered by a knife.

Oh, God, Andy, I can't stop believing that you came to me for help.

And I failed you.

She closed her eyes tightly as she stood near the coffin, desperately trying to remember everything that she had seen that night.

"Nikki."

It was Patricia, looking at her with dampened eyes. "Come on, now. Let them finish."

Nikki nodded and looked around. The funeral had been small, but a few people had made it. There were her neighbors, and even Madame D'Orso from the coffee shop, and a few other local business owners.

As always, there were the curious, tourists, who happened to be at the cemetery and slipped in to join the crowd at the service.

A stretch limo awaited their group, and Nikki knew it was time to walk away.

She looked back. The cemetery workers were in the tomb, getting ready to slide the remains into the appropriate vault.

The band played to the end.

They drove back into the French Quarter, and then went through another ritual, the after-service gathering at Madame D'Orso's.

Madame was in her element. Tall and buxom, with her silver hair swept high on top of her head, she took charge naturally. She had liked Andy. Besides, it was her place. Nikki realized that she was one of the few people who knew that Madame's real name was Debra Smith and she'd actually had ancestors come over on the *Mayflower.* But a pretense of being French was a good thing for business in the French Quarter.

She had come through today, closing her café in the morning, then opening in honor of Andrea in the afternoon.

Julian, Nathan, Mitch and Patricia were trying to do what was usually done on such occasions, remember the person with affection and a smile.

It wasn't easy, when some people clearly thought it was her own fault for being a junkie.

People cared, but Nikki knew, too, that most of them would not think about that day much after they had returned to their regular lives.

At last, as the hour grew late, people began to leave.

Madame, who had truly been the perfect hostess, settled tiredly into a chair by Nikki. She patted her hand where it lay on the table. "Come on, child," she said. "Andy wouldn't want you to be morose forever."

Nikki nodded. "No, of course, you're right."

Madame smoothed a stray lock of hair from Nikki's face. "You're plumb ashen, girl. Pale as if you'd seen a ghost."

Nikki's brows arched. Julian, who was standing nearby, turned and stared at Nikki.

She frowned back at him, then turned to Madame.

"Hey…do you remember that last day when Andy and I were in here?" she asked.

"Well, vaguely," Madame said. "You all come in most days, you know."

"I know, but that day, there was a…kind of a bum hanging around. He looked as if he'd be good looking if he had a bath and a haircut."

Madame looked at her blankly.

"You must have seen him," Nikki persisted. "I asked you about him, so I figured you would have noticed him when you went back inside."

"Honey, I see lots of folks. And we get our share of bums. If one passed out on my floor, I'd have the police in so fast he wouldn't even get to exhale. Other than that, I doubt I'd notice."

"He must have come and gone while you were busy," Nikki murmured.

Madame smiled. "Do you know what I do remember? Andy teasing you about the fact that you needed to get yourself a fellow."

"That's when the guy was in here," Nikki said triumphantly.

"Honey, I'm really sorry, I don't know why it's so important, but I really didn't see him."

Julian, frowning, took a chair at the table. "Nikki… do you think the guy followed you and Andy? Maybe that's something you should report to the police."

She shook her head, aware that Julian's gray gaze

was intense and serious. "You guys were sitting out here when Andy and I brought out the beignets and coffee, and you didn't see him—did you?"

"No...but we weren't paying any attention. We weren't paying any attention that night, either," Julian said ruefully.

Patricia came over and slid into another chair. She, too, patted Nikki's hand. "You holding up?"

"I'm fine," she murmured. "Patricia, you did make sure that any tours for tonight were rescheduled, right?"

"Yes, I did. I spoke with Max, just as you told me, and he apologized again for not being here, by the way," she said, offering Nikki a weak smile. She shrugged. "We had no problem rescheduling—there was a mention about the funeral in the paper. People—" she glanced dryly at Julian "—even tourists, tend to be sympathetic—still curious, yes, but sympathetic...."

"Did everyone reschedule?" Nikki asked.

"Oh, yeah," Patricia said.

"Those sympathetic tourists are sure we'll be the best tour out there now," Julian said, and flashed a stern look at Patricia.

"What was that look all about?" Nikki demanded.

Patricia stared at Julian, then shook her head with a sigh. "Oh, one woman said that she was certain the spirit of our departed comrade would remain with us on our tours, making them even better," she murmured.

"How awful," Madame breathed.

"Some people are just heartless that way," Mitch said, sliding into another chair at the large round wrought-iron table. "Hey," he said pragmatically, "some of the stories we tell are pretty grim. It's just that now...well, now Andy's part of it, whether we like it or not."

"We will never, ever mention Andy on a tour!" Nikki said fiercely.

"Of course not, but, Nikki, in our business, you know that this will come up," Mitch reminded her. He offered her an ironic smile. Mitch wasn't as dramatic a guide as either Julian or Nathan, but his knowledge of the area was inexhaustible. He had a wonderful all-American, corn-fed look, ash-blonde, flyaway hair, bright blue eyes, handsome face. He was very popular with the younger crowd. Nikki was certain that they often had repeat local customers just because a certain teenage crowd loved to follow him around the city.

He frowned, looking at her suddenly. "We will never, ever mention Andy," he agreed. He hesitated, clearing his throat. "I'm sorry, you knew her much better than we did. She was only with us a few weeks.... Nikki, are you doing all right?"

She nodded.

"I think one of us should come stay with you," he said firmly.

She shook her head. "Thanks, Mitch. Julian has been hanging around for me." She stared at them all. "Okay, I'm telling you, and I mean it. I'm convinced that someone forced that heroin on Andy. Whether it had to do with her past or not, I don't know. But also, I'm okay, and I don't need my friends to babysit me. But thanks."

"Well, I don't know how you're living alone," Patricia said, flipping aside a length of her long dark hair. She glanced sideways at Nathan, who was saying goodbye to the last of their comourners. She grinned suddenly. "I was wondering if maybe Nathan and I weren't making a mistake…rushing to live with one another. Now I thank God every minute that we're living together. Because those drugs came from somewhere. From someone. I just think I'd be pretty miserable and scared right now, if I were alone."

"Hey, you two are just right for each other," Nikki commented. "And that's why it's good that you're living together. Anyway, I'm going to shake this off. It's just that it's only been a few days. But I'm not going to turn into a coward. I'm going to be proactive and bug the police until they discover her murderer—don't look at me like that. There *was* a murderer. That's the least I can do for her."

"One way or another, I agree with Nikki. Whether someone just pushed the purchase on the streets or plunged the needle into her vein, someone caused Andy's death. And for the sake of everyone in the parish, we need to know who. We'll all work on that, right, guys?" Mitch asked.

They all nodded.

"And by the way," Julian said, "I *am* staying with you tonight, Nikki."

"Julian, I'm all right."

"And so am I. But I think we ought to be all right together."

"The bed in the guest room is as hard as a rock. You said so yourself," Nikki reminded him.

"Honey, I'm all in. Tonight, I could sleep on a real rock just fine."

She was about to protest again, then sighed. "Okay, thanks. I guess, tonight, I'll be glad of the company."

The two of them were the last out of Madame D'Orso's. Julian decided they should walk Madame home first. It was around midnight, which in New Orleans, in the Vieux Carré, wasn't all that late. Madame said that they really didn't need to walk her anywhere, there were plenty of police about and the streets were crowded.

Julian, however, told her that they could use the walk anyway. The night was beautiful, with fall just beginning. The oppressive humidity that could press down on the city had lightened.

"Hey, it's a nice night just for being alive," he said cheerfully, then winced.

Nikki slipped an arm through his. "Hey, don't worry. I don't want to spend my days walking on eggshells, worrying about every word that comes out of my mouth. It *is* a beautiful night—and a great night to be alive."

They walked Madame the few blocks to her place, then turned and started back toward Bourbon Street.

"Want a nightcap or anything?" Julian asked, a brotherly arm around her shoulder.

She shook her head. "Honestly, you know what's strange? I've never been much of a drinker, and I had such a bad hangover the day we found out about Andy that I just haven't wanted anything since."

"Maybe you need a hair of the dog that bit you," Julian said.

"Actually, I'd like to get home. I haven't been sleeping much."

"Hey, it's okay. Lots of people in your position would be on sedatives, you know. I mean, you hired her. You two bonded right away. And you had to deal with trying to find out if there was someone to contact, and then arrange the funeral and all...well, that's a tough load. And it's tough just to have known someone who was... murdered."

"The rest of you seem to be doing all right."

"Like I said, you two kind of bonded. You and Andy, well, you were both orphans. You had that in common."

"I had my grandparents, at least," Nikki said. "Cousins, aunts and uncles...though they've mostly moved pretty far away these days. But I had family. Andy didn't have even that."

"She had us. We were family," Julian assured her. "Well, we would have been," he said.

They reached the iron gate in the brick wall that surrounded Nikki's place. "What is the trick to this damn thing?" he muttered.

"The latch is under and over. It's not a lock, it just keeps the curious out," Nikki said. She bit her lip, wanting to reach over and open it herself, but Julian seemed determined. She folded her arms across her chest, looking around.

It was always amazing how life went on.

A couple, arm in arm, strolled leisurely down the street, leaning toward one another. He was ebony. She was ivory. Nikki smiled, loving the ease with which people lived their lives in New Orleans now. There had been a time when old "Beast" Butler had ruled the city, but that was long ago. They were on the move here now.

A rowdy group of young men walked along the street, then paused nearby, drinks in hand, talking about a sax player who was working down on the square.

More couples strolled along.

A larger group of young men joined the first.

"Damn this thing, but I will get it," Julian said, determined.

Nikki barely heard him. She straightened against the brick wall.

There was someone in the midst of the group in the street, but he wasn't one of them. He was shaggy-haired. Clothes wrinkled, worn. He turned toward her.

Handsome face…

Beneath the scraggly growth of beard.

He stared at her as if he recognized her.

And she stared back, certainly recognizing him.

She swung around, tapping hard on Julian's shoulder. "Julian…*Julian.* Turn around quick. I just saw him."

"Him, who?"

Julian turned to her, confused.

"The bum who was at Madame's that day."

"Where?"

"He's there—in that group of college guys," she declared.

Julian stared out to the street and searched the clean-shaven faces. So did she.

"Where?" Julian said.

"There, in the middle of them," Nikki announced. She ran into the street, into the midst of the ten or so young men.

"Hey!" said one, almost falling into her.

"Hi, there, babe," another slurred. He cast an arm sloppily around her shoulder.

"Hey, get your hands off her," Julian demanded forcefully.

Nikki was barely aware of their exchange.

"He…he was here," she said, puzzled.

"Who was here, honey? I'm available," a blonde kid with a New York accent said, smiling stupidly and coming up on her other side.

"Leave her alone," Julian said angrily.

"Yeah? And who are you? Her daddy…pimp daddy, something like that?"

Julian hauled off, catching the young man beneath the jaw. He sucked in his breath, staggered back and fell.

"Julian…shit!" Nikki breathed, her attention wrenched back to their current situation.

"Hey, asshole, there was no call for that," the blonde from New York said. He dropped his plastic drink cup and strode menacingly toward Julian.

Others began to follow suit, circling him as their friend staggered to his feet.

"Everyone!" Nikki announced loudly. "Stop it right now. I'm going to scream, I'll get the police. Just calm down."

No one seemed to hear her. The first kid reached Julian. He dodged that blow, but another one of the youths was to his right, and he took a swing.

"Stop!" Nikki jumped onto the back of one of them. He didn't even seem to notice her weight. She banged a fist on the top of his head. "Stop it right now!"

He still didn't seem to notice her. She slid off his back, landing on her rump.

In a fair fight, Julian could handle himself. Against ten or so…

He didn't stand a chance.

Nikki opened her mouth to start screaming. The police had to come, and come quickly.

"Hey!"

The voice that suddenly thundered through the crowd was deep and resonant, and had a note of such pure authority that everyone, including Nikki, suddenly went dead still.

A man came striding into the frozen tableau. From her position on her butt in the street, he seemed extraordinarily tall, dark, broad shouldered and well muscled beneath a casual knit polo shirt and jeans. He caught hold of the kid who was about to deck Julian.

"What the hell is going on here?"

"He started it." The college boy sounded like a gradeschool kid in trouble.

"They were coming on to Nikki," Julian said.

"Just break it up, all of you," the man said irritably.

"Or what?" ventured one of the drunker college boys.

The man stared at him. That was it; he just stared.

"Just asking," the boy muttered. He turned and started down the street. "Come on, guys, let's get out of here."

They all followed suit, heading down the street.

The man turned toward where Nikki was still sitting on the street. He strode toward her, offering her a hand up.

She saw his face.

His complexion was a deep tan, almost bronze, his eyes a startling, brilliant green. The hard chiseled angles and planes clearly denoted a Native American background somewhere. His hair was pitch dark and dead straight, just a little long. It wasn't so much that he was typically handsome, but he was one of the most arresting individuals she had ever seen. He seemed to emit confidence and authority, and not just because of his imposing height or the breadth of his shoulders. There was a sleek agility about him for a man of his size, and his features were hard cut, seeming to exude an essentially masculine sensuality mixed with stark assurance.

His hand, outstretched to her, was large, the fingers long, nails neatly clipped, clean—and powerful, she quickly discovered.

But it wasn't the strength of his grip, bringing her easily to her feet that so disturbed her.

It was his touch.

Energy, almost like a fire, or a current, streaking from him to her.

And then…

His eyes.

They looked into hers.

And they saw something.

What, she didn't know. He released her instantly, stepping back, surveying her, not in a sexual way, and not with disdain or disinterest.

As if he recognized her.

"Are you all right?" he asked politely.

"Um…fine," she murmured.

He nodded. "You?" he asked Julian.

"Yeah, thanks to you," Julian told him, eyeing the stranger curiously. "Hey, we kind of owe you. Can we buy you a drink or something?"

The man shook his head. "You don't owe me anything." He cracked a slight smile, which transformed his face. He was suddenly striking. Still hard, but striking.

"I just wouldn't mess with large crowds in the future, huh?" he suggested.

With a wave, he turned and left them.

6

Brent walked down the street, shaking his head.

New Orleans.

America's most European city. A mixture of architecture and mood, sultry heat and shifting shadows. It was as if time had cast a mood over the city that had sunk into the very bones of its man-made structures. History piled upon the passions of those who had lived before.

It held the remnants of days gone by, mixed with the new, the lively, the present-day city, with its love of gardens, jazz, good times and voodoo.

There was unbelievable talent to be found with the turn of a corner, like the old black man two streets over who had played a banjo better than he'd ever heard before. The man had just been sitting there, playing and smiling and, Brent hoped, making a fair amount of money from the passersby who were dropping bills in his instrument case.

Brent passed a closed shop with a storefront announcing "Dolly's Dolls," and next to it was a neon light advertising "Girls, Girls, Naked Girls."

People laughing, drinking, admiring artists, musicians, mimes…

People drinking themselves silly, picking fights.

The encounter he'd just had was disturbing, and he didn't want to think about it.

He could still feel her hand in his.

And he'd walked away. Which had been smart. Still, he couldn't help but wonder about the woman. She had the biggest, brightest eyes he'd ever seen. Green. Blue. Aqua. Something like the sea, somewhere in between. Fairly tall, nice figure, obvious even in the long black dress she'd been wearing.

A Goth? Hell, everybody in this city seemed to think they were a voodoo queen, a long-dead duchess, a vampire or a tarot reader.

No, maybe not. The guy with her had been wearing a somber black suit.

Funeral, he realized suddenly.

He shook his head, stopped in the street. From the corner to his right, a rock band hammered out a Stones tune. From the other corner, he could hear jazz. Somewhere down the street, a blues guitar was belting out an indiscernible tune.

He swore softly.

New Orleans.

Hell, welcome home.

Oh, yeah. It was just great to be here.

"You're going off the deep end, Nikki," Julian said. "That was just great. Throwing yourself into a group of drunks. What were you expecting? And don't even think about giving me a lecture on how no one deserves to be attacked. You went flying into a sludge of inebriated testosterone in its sweet young prime, so what were you expecting?"

"I saw him!" she said, finding the catch on the gate and pushing it open herself. Julian's words made her feel guilty—he was a good friend, and he would have defended her to the death, which, considering the drunken mood of the rowdy gang, just might have been the sad finale if it hadn't been for their strange savior—but he couldn't begin to understand how she was feeling. "Julian, I'm sorry, but…I saw him," she repeated.

"Yeah, and I saw him, too, whoever the hell he was, and I have to admit, it was a damn good thing he showed up when he did. I'm not much brighter than you are, apparently, since I got it into my head to defend you from a pack of wolves."

She waved a hand in the air. "Not *him,*" she said, though the "him" to whom Julian was referring had been almost as disturbing as the man she had first seen. "Not…not the guy who came along and broke the whole thing up. I mean, I saw the man who was in the coffee shop that day. The day before Andy was killed."

"Okay, okay, so you saw him," Julian said, hurrying behind her to the door. "Some bum who was in the coffee shop. You saw him. Great. But…so what? Nikki, I'm sorry to say that we have tons of drunks and addicts in this city. You saw a loser in a coffee shop, and tonight you saw him again. Hell, I run into the same people I don't really know day after day. And as to this guy—you can't really think that he followed you all day, through a tour, into the night…and then went after Andy?"

She had reached her door and was suddenly so irritated that she nearly twisted her key in half unlocking the door. Before letting Julian in, she spun on him. "You don't understand. Julian, Andy said something about him."

"When? At Madame's?" he demanded. "Was he someone she knew? What exactly did she say?"

Fiercely, she shook her head. "She didn't know him, or at least I don't think she did. And she didn't say anything about him in the café. It was…in the dream. Julian, she said something about him being dead. And I…I think it's important somehow."

He stared at her wide-eyed for a moment, then caught her by the shoulders and pushed her forward, into the parlor of her apartment. Once they were inside, he closed and locked the door, then looked at her sternly. "Nikki, you had a dream. A nightmare. Weird? Yes. The mind plays tricks, but I think you're just feeling guilty about the fact that Andrea was murdered. People do feel that way—why her, why not me? Nikki, what happened was terrible, tragic things happen on a daily basis. It's just that usually bad things don't occur so close to us. So think about it—under these circumstances, it's a very normal thing that your mind might play tricks. People don't remember their dreams in detail, so you don't really know what you dreamed. Listen to yourself. You're telling me that Andy said the guy was dead, but now you're certain you saw him on the street. It's one or the other, Nikki. You've got to get a grip."

"Julian, what if—"

"I know a doctor, Nikki. A good one."

She stared back at him, her mouth open, no sound coming out. At last she found her voice. "I don't need a doctor, Julian. I need some faith here."

"Nikki, I'm sorry, but..." He stopped with a sigh, then walked into the living room, hit the light switch and sat down on the Victorian sofa. "Okay, you really believe that you had a dream, and Andy was in it—right when she was dying."

"Or being killed."

Julian sighed. "Or being killed. She was talking about the guy you'd seen at Madame's. Now, tonight, you saw the guy. What you need to do, logically, is go to the police. I think you'll feel better if you stress to Detective Massey the fact that you've seen this guy, this kind of scary bum or junkie, on the street again. Massey can hunt him down and question him."

She had been standing angrily, her arms crossed over her chest, frowning. But his words made sense.

"Well?" he demanded.

"All right. I'll go see Detective Massey. I think I can describe the man fairly well. Maybe they can do a sketch of him. And if they find him and question him... well, I'll feel better."

She was startled to realize that Julian was frowning.

"What's wrong?" she asked.

He shook his head, stared at her. "Nikki...say that the guy in the coffee shop was a junkie. Hard up. And maybe a psycho to boot. And...what if he did follow us around all day?"

"What are you getting at?"

"Nothing," he replied quickly.

"What do you mean, nothing?" she demanded. "Dammit, Julian, I know you. Tell me what you were going to say."

"I'll only worry you."

"I'm worried now."

Still, Julian hesitated. She didn't intend to let him off the hook. "Julian, what?"

He sighed. "All right, you saw this guy...and who knows, maybe he did know Andy from before."

"No, she didn't recognize him."

"She didn't *admit* that she recognized him."

"No, I really don't think she recognized him."

"But he might have recognized her."

"You mean...from sometime before in her life?"

"Or even from the flyers."

"You mean, the business flyers we hand out?"

He nodded. "The minute you saw Andy, you called Max about using her for a new flyer, remember?"

"I'm at fault in this somehow," Nikki whispered, sinking down on the sofa beside him.

"Don't be ridiculous," Julian said firmly. "Only the killer is at fault. What I'm saying is...well, we might have a psychotic who had a thing for Andy and had been watching her. Or knew about her past. And maybe he knows that you're suspicious and won't stop hunting. And if so...well, you could be in danger, too."

She glared at him, feeling as if her flesh were beginning to crawl.

"I told you, I didn't want to worry you. And it's not

like you were ever a junkie, but still, you should be careful."

She groaned, leaning back. Then she jumped up and ran around the house, checking every window to see that it was latched, and making doubly certain that the glass doors that led to the balcony from her bedroom were secured.

Julian followed her, double-checking everything.

They met in the living room and stared at one another.

"I told you I shouldn't have said anything," he told her.

"No...no, it's good to be careful," she said.

"I'm really sorry, Nikki," Julian said, running his fingers through his hair. "Most likely what happened to Andy was...random. I mean, seriously, think about it. All that's happened is that you saw a guy the day before she died, and you've seen him again. That doesn't mean anything at all. The police will probably just humor us when we go in—I mean, it's so far from any concrete evidence that anyone could base anything on. You'd have to suspect just about everyone in the city."

Nikki nodded. "Right." But she didn't agree. She couldn't shake the dream. "All right, well, it seems that we're locked up tight for the night. I'm going to bed," she told him.

She leaned over and kissed his cheek, and started for the stairs.

"You want to leave the lights on down here?" Julian asked.

"Hell, yes," she told him.

Upstairs, he headed toward the guest bedroom, and

she headed toward her own. She paused at the door. "Hey, Julian."

"Um?"

"Thanks for staying."

"Not a problem," he assured her.

In her room, Nikki quickly changed for bed. No sooner was she under the covers, with the light out, than she jumped up and turned it back on. She was angry with herself, and maybe even a little angry with Julian. The first nights after Andy's death, he'd stayed with her. But she hadn't been afraid.

She hadn't thought that she might be stalked.

Now…

She turned the television on. The first show that popped up was about forensic files. She switched stations. The next show was about cold cases that investigators were going back into.

She tried the news, but it was no better. There was a local politician on, the man with the improbable name of Billy Banks, and he was crusading against violent crime in New Orleans, swearing that he would clean it up. He was young, in his early thirties, with the kind of personal charisma a politician prayed for. He talked about cleaning up the image of New Orleans, making it a better destination for families. The man had something, Nikki thought. Not the kind of self-righteousness that people would find offensive, but a determination to make the city better. He might well win the election, she thought; he seemed to have what it would take to breathe excitement into city government. He was a good speaker, and Nikki found herself intrigued by his speech. But then he went on to say that if he were elected, he would see to it that drugs were taken off their local streets, and then they wouldn't have tragic deaths, like that of the young woman Andrea Ciello.

Nikki hit the button on the remote and changed the channel.

The next channel she came to was playing a biography of Ted Bundy.

She swore, and at last found a kids' channel that ran old sitcoms at night.

Topper came on, and she groaned, but it was just ending. Next up was *Leave it to Beaver.* That would do. With the lights and television on, she closed her eyes.

She didn't know how much time passed, but she dozed. Then she woke again as June Cleaver said something to Ward. The sound of a soft laugh alerted her to the presence of someone in her room, and she opened her eyes, blinking.

A scream rose in her throat, but she was so completely terrified that sound wouldn't come.

Andy was there again.

Now she was wearing the handsome black pantsuit in which she had been buried that afternoon.

Her hair was brushed back, shimmering, as it had been…in her coffin.

But her face was pale. Horribly pale, ashen…gray. Dead gray.

Nighttime, prime time.

Whether he liked it or not, it was his city, and Brent knew it well.

The main problem with New Orleans was…

…the ghosts. The damn ghosts.

He hadn't been many other places where he felt such a barrage of sensation, the presence of the dead but undead, or the dead but unaccepting. The cemeteries were far more alive at night than most people could imagine, and the grievances that moved the spirits ranged from bitterness left over from Civil War days to prostitutes who had been done wrong in old Storyville. Victims of more recent murders sought ways to avenge the gang members who had put them in their graves. One old black man in St. Louis Cemetery Number 1 was still seeking the cruel master who had beaten him into an early grave. Years ago, Brent had tried to assure the man that his master was long gone, as well. It hadn't stopped the old man from seeking his revenge, and Brent had to admit that neither had he done very well in convincing the haunt, who he knew only as Huey, that the times, they were a-changing.

New Orleans was simply sensory overload. Brent didn't try to explain that to many people. He never freely spoke about his peculiar "calling." When Adam brought him in on a case, he spoke honestly, if somewhat anonymously, with those involved. He had never agreed to a newspaper or magazine interview, since they without fail attempted to be either sensationalist or mocking. He usually worked under a pseudonym, since information about hauntings and exorcisms had a habit of leaking out, sometimes because the victims were relieved, and sometimes because someone wanted their fifteen minutes of fame. Adam Harrison had never been interested in press.

He always came here, to New Orleans, however, under his real name: Brent Blackhawk. Grandson of the son of an old-time war chief, but also, just as Adam had said, a mongrel. Irish with whatever else thrown in, as so often occurred in the country and this city.

Even in the graveyards.

He had a hunch he would be visiting a lot of them. Tonight he thought he would start at St. Louis Number 1. See what Huey knew, if anything.

People loved the cemeteries in New Orleans, and with good reason. They called them "Cities of the Dead," and they were just that, cities of the departed, a microcosm of New Orleans at the present and in the past. The very sight of them touched an inner human core that spoke of man's tragic knowledge of his own impending demise. Broken angels held sacred vigil over the departed. Weeds grew through cracks in masonry. Tombs stretched in haphazard array, silent, staunch. In the moonlight, stone and marble told of both immortality and decay.

The cemeteries were considered dangerous—all the tour books warned visitors to go only in daylight and never alone. They were great places for a mugging, and many an unwary traveler had been deprived of his goods over the years.

Worse had happened in the cemeteries, as well. The great tombs and mausoleums allowed for darkness and shadows, dozens of places for evil intent to lurk. The gates were locked at night, and with good reason.

Brent definitely wasn't afraid of the ghosts. He did have a tremendous respect for the living and the evil they could get up to. He hated firearms, but he respected them, as well. He didn't like carrying a gun, but he was licensed, though generally, he chose not to have a weapon when walking around the city.

But there were places where being armed wasn't just a precaution, it was a necessity, so his little snub-nosed Smith & Wesson .38 went with him whenever he went into the cemeteries.

Brent hesitated at the wall of the cemetery. As he had expected, the gate creaked open. He lowered his head and smiled, knowing that it was mischief and not evil that lured him.

He stepped in.

The gate creaked closed behind him.

For a moment he closed his eyes, steadying himself against the level of unearthly noise that filled his ears. When he opened his eyes, all was dark, caught in eerie shadow. Then a rock went flying by his ear.

"You're not going to scare me, Huey," he said softly.

The old black man came into view, though his color was now decidedly gray. He was in old work pants, a white shirt and sneakers.

He seemed a bit disappointed to see Brent, as if he had been hoping for an errant schoolboy bent on vandalism who he could frighten up the wall. Over the years, Huey had perfected his abilities to work his spectral energies upon that which was tangible. Stories were rife about "experiences" here in the graveyard. Some were nothing more than the ripe imaginations of those who told them. Some of them had a grain of truth. Huey loved to touch the long hair of the ladies who teased his fancy, and to taunt those who arrived here to do harm or carry out a fraternity prank. Despite his enduring anger against his old master, he seemed to take quite a bit of pride in the old cemetery.

Huey hadn't been buried with shoes. Brent had provided the sneakers many years ago, in hopes that the shoes would send him on to his eternal reward.

Huey hadn't gone.

"What you doing here again, half-breed Injun boy?" Huey demanded. Huey called it as he saw it—there was no thought of political correctness in any of his speech.

"I need some help."

Huey shook his head. "You want help, boy? New Orleans ain't the place to be."

Beyond Huey, the darkness seemed to have eased. Brent could then see them all…spectral images, moving about, mostly looking at him impassively. Their presence was faint, a mere line of white against the haze, casting a soft, ethereal glow. A gentleman in a high hat argued with another in a Victorian business suit, the two of them ignoring Brent. A waiflike beauty sat on one of the lower-platform tombs, staring at him curiously, as if she was glad for any break from the tedium of death.

"Huey, you like to be an old tough guy," Brent said. "But you were decent in life, and I know you're a damn decent fellow still. I need some help."

Huey lifted his hands with a shrug, his head cocked to one side.

"Ain't no burials here gonna help you, boy," he told Brent. "Not if you're looking for something specific."

"Yes, I know, but sometimes spirits wander."

"Who you lookin' for?"

"A man. He would be in his mid-thirties. Looked like a junkie when he died."

"He buried in New Orleans anywhere?"

"No, his family was all up in Kentucky. They took him home for his burial."

"So why would he be wandering around here?"

"He was killed here."

"How?"

"A massive overdose of heroin."

"So you looking for a junkie?"

Brent shook his head. "He'd never taken the stuff before in his life. He was a cop, here undercover, slipping in with some of the bad boys out of Algiers, and exploring the bars and clubs in the Vieux Carré. He's been seen walking about. His name was Tom Garfield."

"I ain't seen him," Huey told him, still watching him speculatively. "You sure your boy didn't come here and go bad himself? I've seen it often enough."

"I don't believe so."

Huey shrugged. "Tom Garfield. I'll keep my eyes—and ears—open, Injun boy." Huey turned his head slightly. "Gotta go."

"Go where?"

"You hear that?"

"What?" Brent's hearing was usually fairly acute, but he had heard nothing except the night breeze.

"Get on out of here now," Huey told him. "There's

someone crawling the walls in the back. Around here, that usually means a mugging, if there's some fool white boy around to mug." Huey glared at him.

"Huey, there you go again," Brent said with a sigh.

"All right, all right, but you can't tell me that the world has really come right, not after all these years," Huey said, annoyed. "Don't matter what you are. You got money on you? We got toughs in this city who want it. You go on and get out of here. Tend to your business, and I'll tend to mine."

"All right, but keep an eye out for me, will you, Huey?" Brent asked.

"Yeah, sure, me and the others," Huey told him. To Brent's surprise, Huey paused for a minute. "You're not a bad guy," he told Brent. He wiggled his toes in his sneakers. "Maybe you could find out what happened to the old master."

Brent arched a brow.

"Give me a name," Brent told him.

"Archibald. Archibald McManus," Huey said.

"I'll do my best," Brent told him.

"Yeah, yeah, you do that," Huey said, still studying him.

By then, even Brent could hear the noise coming from across the graveyard.

"Huey?"

The voice calling the old man was soft, barely a whisper on the air. It was coming from the pretty little waif sitting on the tomb.

"What is it, Emmy?" Huey asked.

"Can I help you tonight?" she asked eagerly.

"Sure, sure, sweet thing. Soon's I get this flesh-and-blood boy outta here, we're on it."

He glared angrily at Brent, who lowered his head, smiling. "I'm going, Huey."

In a minute, he was back on the street.

Huey was right. It wasn't a good time to be wandering around any housing projects. He started back into the Quarter, heading toward the small bed-and-breakfast where he had opted to stay.

He walked slowly, though. The living in certain areas were certainly far more dangerous than the dead, but he was hoping that the spirit he was seeking would find him.

As he walked, though, he couldn't get a picture in his mind's eye of the dead agent.

Instead, he saw the girl. The "flesh and blood," as Huey would have said. There was something about her eyes, something about the feel of her hand when they had touched, that haunted him.

She was extraordinary to look at, but the world was full of pretty people.

There was something different about her, though. Even the fear that had touched her eyes had not been fear of the rowdy crowd or of him.

She had been afraid of something else.

Of something she was seeing…

He took his time, walking around a bit rather than taking a straight track back. Some areas were dark and deserted, others remained alive and busy. At Harrah's, gamblers played all night, and lots of establishments remained open until the wee hours.

There were a few old sots and young kids sleeping on the streets.

There was one guy who looked as if he was weighing the idea of an attack when Brent walked by him on a dark corner.

Something stopped him, and he looked away when Brent stared back at him.

Brent reached his B&B without incident and decided sleep would be in order, since he meant to be at the police station early.

Lying in bed, though, he remained awake.

And he wondered about the girl, then knew, with certainty, that he would see her again.

Andy's laughter sounded softly again.

Nikki thought she herself was dying. She was choking…frozen with absolute terror. The lights were on. This was no trick of night or the moon. Andy was there.

Nikki couldn't breathe.

Andy was there. She'd drawn the dressing-table chair over by the bed and was watching television, laughing softly at the old jokes.

The words that rushed through Nikki's head did nothing to dispel the illusion.

Andy was dead. Dead and buried.

Yet she was there. Andrea Ciello, dressed in her funerary finest, turned to see Nikki gasping, staring at her, frozen to the core.

"I always loved the old *Beaver* reruns," Andy murmured. "Hey…it's just me. And thanks…this is the exact outfit I would have chosen. Thank God you didn't choose a silly frilly dress…something I'd never really wear." She sounded wistful suddenly. "It was a lovely service, wasn't it? A real New Orleans funeral. Thanks, Nikki. I had no one, and you were there for me."

That did it. Andy, speaking as if she were really there, casually, throwing in a thank-you, just as she would have done.

The scream tore from Nikki's throat at last.

She was vaguely aware of a thumping sound. As if Julian had fallen out of bed.

"Nikki," Andy protested reproachfully, hearing the thud, too.

Nikki knew she was gasping again, staring.

Then Julian burst into the room.

And Andy evaporated as if she had never been there.

"What the hell…?" Julian demanded. He was in a pair of too-short sweatpants he'd borrowed from Nikki, hair disarrayed, eyes bleary. He was blinking madly and rubbing his left elbow.

"She…she was here!" Nikki got out. "Julian, didn't you see her?"

He sighed, looking down. "No, Nikki, I didn't see anyone." He shook his head, looking at her again, fighting a wave of anger, she thought. "Nikki, there's no one here. The doors are locked tight."

"She was here," Nikki whispered.

"Um. Great. Well, she's gone now. And you really need to see that doctor."

Nikki let out a long sigh from between clenched teeth. "All right, Julian. But after we talk to the police."

Julian walked out. Goose bumps formed on Nikki's

arms. She swallowed, afraid again. But a minute later Julian was back, a pillow and comforter in his arms.

"Julian..." she murmured miserably.

"Go to sleep," he said.

"You take the bed, I'll take the floor."

But Julian was already lying down. "Just go to sleep," he repeated.

Easier said than done...

Yet sometime before morning came, she drifted off.

And when she dreamed, it was not about Andrea, or the strange man she had seen before Andy's death and again that night.

She dreamed of the man who had come to their rescue. He was across a crowded street, staring at her.

His lips weren't moving. He was just staring at her. High cheekbones, dark hair, rugged set to his chin. Green eyes locked on her.

And she could hear what he was thinking.

I can help you.

His words made her more afraid.

No one can help me. It's all in my mind.

He was so improbably good looking, the mixture of cultures so evident in his striking features.

He smiled...

And turned away.

When she awoke in the morning, Nikki tripped over Julian.

As he groaned, she bent over and kissed him on the forehead, and promised him the best cup of coffee he'd ever had.

She didn't remember the dream, and she didn't wake

afraid. She was determined to take decisive action and head straight for the police station.

It was what she didn't know that was haunting her, she was suddenly certain.

7

"Television isn't helping us in the least," Owen Massey complained, setting a cup of coffee in front of Brent.

It was evident already that Massey wasn't the kind of cop to place much store in psychics, so Brent had been very careful about anything he said. With Adam's connections, his introduction to the police department had been a no-nonsense one, and he didn't want to do anything to jeopardize his standing.

Massey might suspect that he was a psychic, but they had hit it off well when Brent asked questions about hard evidence, then commented that it was a seasoned policeman's hunches that kicked in on the streets.

Taking his seat behind his desk, Massey shook his head again. "I mean, some of those forensics shows. In one night, one crew handles everything and comes up with the killer. Don't get me wrong, I'm not knocking forensics. Crimes have certainly been solved because of a hair or a fiber, and DNA typing is the greatest gift since fingerprints. But most of the time, even if you're lucky enough to find a hair or a fiber, it's like looking through a haystack to find what the hell to compare the damn thing to. Okay, domestic crimes…you can usually trace those suckers. Drugs? You're looking for another thug. But then you have the random crime, the woman who looks like the girl who rejected the perp back in high school, and happens to be at the wrong place at the wrong time. Serial killers. Strangers killing strangers. That's when it gets hard."

Brent nodded sympathetically, wondering just what Massey's frustrated speech had to do with the matter at hand. "Tom Garfield was onto something, and we know that he didn't inject himself with heroin."

Massey, who had been frowning and distracted, focused on Brent suddenly, and his large ruddy face flushed darker. "Sorry…I've got another case that's equally frustrating. Beautiful young woman, same kind of death. Except she had been a junkie, and we'll probably discover she just fell back to her old ways. Her friends are insisting she was murdered, though."

Brent arched a brow. "Heroin?"

"Yep."

"Her friends claim she was clean?"

"Yeah, but you know, friends see what they want to."

Brent leaned forward. "But the deaths were similar otherwise?"

"Like I said, the girl had a past history of drugs. She nearly got herself kicked out of Tulane because of her habit."

Brent decided he had to be careful. He didn't want to irritate his contact. Still, since the deaths were so alike, it seemed evident to him that they should be investigated for a connection.

Of course, the dead girl hadn't been a government agent.

"Where did she die?"

"Her own apartment."

"Anybody see anything or anyone unusual?"

"Nope."

"Crime scene investigators went over the apartment and found nothing?"

"You know, we're not idiots here."

"I wasn't suggesting you were. It's just that…since she'd been a junkie, I was wondering if the death was being investigated with the same rigor as a case that might not be self-induced."

"We searched the apartment. Not so much as the hint of an unknown fiber or hair," Massey said coldly. "Nail scrapings—nothing. The ME went over the body with a fine-tooth comb. Again, nothing."

"Sorry," Brent said.

Massey shrugged. "Well, I guess I went off on you first, venting my frustration," he said. He leaned toward Brent across the desk, lowering his voice as if he was suddenly worried about being heard by others in the busy precinct office. "Actually, right now a couple of the dead girl's friends are here, going through mug shots, looking. The kids had been drinking together the night before. I asked them about anyone suspicious lurking around. Of course, half the people in New Orleans look suspicious. Anyway, it's just one of those times when being a cop kind of makes you ill, you know? When you see the haunted eyes of those left behind."

Massey's gaze slid past Brent, indicating a small conference room.

Brent knew before he turned to look that he was going to see the couple from the night before.

The guy, tall, dark and good looking, was standing protectively by her side. He'd been protective the night before, too.

She was seated. He couldn't see her eyes, but he could remember the color. Not blue. Not green. A true aqua, like the waters of a Caribbean reef. Her hair was long, of a golden, honeyed color. And she had a great face. Classic bone structure. Perfect nose, not too small, straight, and just right for the width of her cheekbones.

Great mouth. Full, sensual lips set against a firm chin. He couldn't see any of that at the moment. It was simply ingrained in his memory.

She was seated at the table, a massive book in front of her. An officer at her side was slowly turning pages.

She shook her head, looking up at the assisting officer.

Haunted eyes, Massey had said.

Good description. Her friend was dead, but there was more than just fear, anger and frustration in her gaze. There was something like desperation. A feeling she undoubtedly loathed, since it was apparent that she'd been blessed with determination and no lack of courage.

Brent gazed down at the desk in front of him. Massey had given him a nice clear shot of Tom Garfield in his last disguise. Garfield had been good at his work. He had infiltrated cartels in South Florida, Texas and California, fingering those who needed to be fingered, then getting away clean. He'd been a good-looking, hardened man in his mid-thirties, and not even the scraggly beard and dirty countenance he'd taken on really hid his inner strength. That would have worked well for him, trying to get close to the big leaguers. He'd had the ability to bluff his way through the toughest situation.

Brent's gaze shifted from the photo before him on the desk back toward the conference room.

"She's looking for people she might have seen the night before her friend's death?"

"She's got a 'hunch,'" Massey said wearily. "She saw some guy when she was with her friend, and says she saw him again last night, out on the street. I tried to tell her that she might see the same tourist types over and over again. Even the same bums. And that it doesn't matter how many times she might have seen the guy—it wouldn't make him guilty of murder. But what the hell, I got nothing else. So she's looking through mug shots."

"For a bum?" Brent said a little sharply.

Massey frowned, looking at him. Not angry, just curious. "Yeah, someone she saw begging at a café."

"Would you mind?" Brent asked Massey, indicating Garfield's photo.

"You're going to show her a dead guy?" Massey said.

"Hey, you got nothing else, right?"

"She couldn't have seen a dead guy on the street last night," Massey said.

Brent shrugged, smiling dryly. "How many of those books have you got? This could go on a long, long time."

"But that's a dead guy."

"Humor me."

"Hey…go ahead. Knock yourself out."

* * *

Nikki was tired. Faces swam before her.

New Orleans had quite a photo gallery of suspicious types. She was glad they hadn't asked her to go through all the mug shots on the computer. She would have an even worse headache by now.

They'd even narrowed down the choices for her, looking specifically for a white guy in his late twenties to early forties.

Scary…to see all the possible perps!

"Nothing?" Julian asked a little tensely.

She shook her head. Julian was growing impatient. He'd gotten her an emergency appointment with his shrink, and he was clearly anxious to get going.

"I'm sorry," she murmured.

"No one even close, huh?" That question came from Marc Joulette, Owen Massey's younger partner. "People can change, you know. Minus a beard, dyed hair, that kind of thing," he pointed out helpfully. Whereas Massey was a big solid guy with a ruddy complexion, Joulette was taller, leaner, darker. Of mixed race, he was neither white nor black but a striking golden hue. Though he was too striking ever to blend into a crowd, Nikki assumed he must be one hell of a detective, because he had great people skills. His voice was gentle and melodic. Soothing, comforting. His manner was equally gentle. She had a feeling he could garner a confession before the suspect even knew he'd been talking.

Nikki sat back, rubbing her temples, shaking her head again. "I'm sorry. I really want to find this guy. I know you can't arrest people on feelings, but I can't help but believe he's involved somehow. But I can't find him, and I feel like I'm wasting your time," she apologized.

Julian made a grunting sound. She ignored him.

Detective Joulette smiled. "Hey, this job is pure tedium at times, and you're not wasting my time. It's the little things that sometimes get the job done, huh? We can go to the computer, or..." He paused, turning.

Nikki and Julian both looked toward the door, as well.

She barely swallowed back a gasp.

The man standing in the doorway was the same man who had come striding into the fight the night before.

Like Joulette, he would never blend into any crowd.

He stood about six-two, with a solid, yet lean, agile-looking build. His dead-straight black hair was tell-tale, though Nikki vaguely remembered someone telling her once that hair couldn't really be black, only a very dark brown.

Could have fooled her. This man's hair was so dark it wasn't just black, but jet.

Then there were his eyes. A deep and startling green against the bronze of his skin.

She met those eyes with surprise. And as her eyes touched his, she felt a strange tremor deep inside. Just as she had when their hands had met the night before.

"You," Julian breathed.

"You all know each other?" Massey, who was behind the unnamed man, demanded in surprise.

"We met at a minor street brawl last night," the man said, smiling. "Well, actually, we didn't meet formally."

The guy had a truly great face, Nikki thought. Full

of character. A chin like concrete. High, broad cheekbones. Bone structure to die for…

Die for...

Not a term to use these days.

"Thanks again for the help," Julian said, striding around the desk to shake hands.

"I'll make the formal introduction, then," Massey said. "Nikki DuMonde, Julian Lalac, this is Brent Blackhawk. Brent, Nikki, Julian…"

"Pleased to meet you," Brent said, smiling in acknowledgment.

"Are you a cop?" Nikki asked.

His smile deepened. He shook his head. "Kind of a troubleshooter," he murmured vaguely.

"Here as a guest," Massey said.

Marc Joulette rose, stretching. "This is a good break. Nikki, you want a soda? A coffee? Julian? Anyone…? I've got to go get another book."

"Nothing for me, thanks," Brent Blackhawk said. "Sorry, I didn't mean to interrupt. I kind of came in on a…well, I'm curious. Thought you might have run into this guy."

He strode to the desk, setting down a picture.

Nikki gasped, stared at the picture, then back at Brent Blackhawk. His eyes were strangely knowing. She looked around at the others.

"That's him!" she exclaimed. She looked around at the others, triumphant. "That's him," she repeated.

"Good. We know who it is, then," Julian said, pleased.

But the others didn't say a word. They were staring

at her strangely. Massey and Joulette looked stunned. Brent Blackhawk seemed to be seeing something beneath the surface that brought a pensive look to his eyes as he studied her.

"What's the matter? Who is he?" Nikki asked, feeling a headache coming on strong.

"You have to be mistaken," Joulette said softly.

"No, I'm not," Nikki said firmly.

"Nikki, you've been through a lot," Massey said.

"This is the man I saw," Nikki said indignantly. "I know it. So what's the problem?"

"You couldn't have seen him," Massey said. "Not last night."

"And why not?"

"Because he's dead," Joulette explained very softly.

The room spun. Nikki was suddenly afraid she was going to pass out. Fear washed over her in terrible, sweeping waves.

She fought the sensation furiously.

She gritted her teeth hard and rose.

"He has a double, a twin or something, then. Or you've been deceived. I saw this man last night. I *saw* him. I have excellent eyesight. Twenty-twenty." When no one said anything in response, she went on, "Excuse me, it's obvious you don't intend to believe me."

She started out of the room. Brent Blackhawk was watching her just as intently as the others. And he was in her way.

It suddenly seemed to be all his fault. After all, he'd brought in the picture.

"Excuse me," she said, trying to get past him.

"Miss DuMonde," he said, "I'd really like to talk to you—"

"Not now." Julian was behind her. Both Joulette and Massey were silent.

"Not now," she agreed icily. She had to get out of there. She had to get away from the police station, out onto the street.

For a moment she was afraid he was going to stop her. That he was going to take her bodily by the shoulders and insist on speaking with her.

But he stepped back. Suddenly she was aware only of his eyes, and she had the most bizarre thought.

He didn't have to stop her physically. He knew, *knew,* that he would find her, that he would speak to her.

"I have to get out of here," she insisted, and she pushed blindly past him.

She fought for control as she pushed her way outside, back to the busy street, the tourists and the vendors, the ever-present music.

Julian was close behind, and when she stopped on the sidewalk, he was right beside her.

Control. She took a deep breath and tried to sound completely casual. "We should have lunch, or something."

"We should head straight to Dr. Boulet's," he said, and taking her firmly by the elbow, he led her along the sidewalk, past a voodoo shop, an antique shop, a toy store…and a strip club.

It was New Orleans, after all.

"They're mistaken," she said. "That guy has to be alive. Or there's someone who looks just like him."

"Yeah, and Andy's alive, too?" he asked softly.

She fell silent and didn't say anything else the rest of the way to the doctor's office, which was above a souvenir shop, next to another strip joint. Yup, this was New Orleans.

"Who exactly is Nikki DuMonde?" Brent asked the detectives.

Massey snorted. "A wacko, that's what it's beginning to look like," he said, shaking his head.

Joulette shrugged with a wry grin. "Damn gorgeous wacko. I think she was serious, though. She really believes she saw this guy. Hey," he said to his partner, "you've spent more time with her than I have, but she's never seemed to be anything less than intelligent."

Owen Massey let out a sigh. "Yeah, yeah. But she's high-strung."

"She's convinced her friend was murdered, what do you want?" Joulette asked.

And she's probably right, Brent thought.

"What does she do for a living?" Brent asked.

"She works for one of the tour companies, unofficial manager for an absentee owner. They're good, I understand. They do history tours, with an emphasis on ghosts and spooky stuff. And she's a native," Massey told him. "Of New Orleans, I mean," he added hastily. He frowned suddenly. "What the hell made you show her Tom's picture, anyway?"

"Just a hunch," Brent said.

"Tom was dead. She couldn't have seen him last

night," Massey said. "Tell me you don't really believe she could have seen a ghost?"

"She saw something," Brent said evenly.

"You really are one of those psychics, huh?" Massey said.

"No. I'm not a psychic," Brent told him.

"Then…?" Joulette asked.

"A researcher."

"Yeah?" Joulette pressed. "What kind?"

Brent smiled, shaking his head. "Let's just say 'different' for now, huh? I don't want to alienate you before we get started. I get the feeling you're both good at what you do. I'll bet your CSI folks are good at what they do, too. I just come at things from a different angle."

"We've got plenty of voodoo in New Orleans already," Joulette drawled, challenging him.

"I don't practice voodoo," Brent said evenly.

Both detectives studied him, and Massey said, "Whoever or whatever you are, your boss is apparently in with the bigwigs. We have the FBI in on this, too. Lots of agents, one main liaison between the departments. Guy's name is Haggerty. And he says you're definitely not a fed. In fact, he has his panties in a knot about you being here."

"Oh?" Brent said. He wasn't surprised that the FBI had men on the case—they'd lost one of their own.

"Yeah, Vince Haggerty isn't into mumbo jumbo," Massey responded.

Brent ignored the mumbo-jumbo part. "You're conducting separate investigations?" he asked.

"Not really," Joulette said. "Haggerty has access to

everything we've got. But the guy is a real loner. He wants to work on his own, and doesn't want to share what *he* has. He *will* give us whatever he's got eventually. If we can find him. You'd think Owen and I grew up in the bayou and never went to school, the way he acts. Or," he added bitterly, "that I should still be saying 'Massuh' when I talk to the guy."

"So, here we are," Massey said. "Marc and I working two cases…and in neither case do we have so much as a semisolid lead to anything. At least in Garfield's case we can hit the clubs, get some help from the narcs. As to the Andrea Ciello case, well, I'd hoped Nikki DuMonde would be able to give us something solid. All she did was hand us a ghost."

Brent was silent for a moment, then lifted his shoulders and let out a sigh. "I think I'll take one of Miss DuMonde's tours," he said.

"That's how you're going to find a killer?" Joulette said skeptically.

"I think your murders have something to do with one another," Brent said flatly.

"We don't even know that the girl's death was a murder. What makes you think the two deaths are connected?" Massey said. "A fed, undercover, and a former junkie. What motive could connect them?"

"I don't know. But you're looking at two heroin overdoses."

"Hey, he's a psychic," Joulette told Massey.

"Look, guys—" Brent began.

But Joulette started to laugh. "Hey, go for it, man."

"Yeah, you do what you have to do," Massey said.

Brent arched a brow.

"We actually kinda like you," Joulette explained. "'Cause you're not some superior fed."

"Next to him, hell, you can bring in all the ghost busters, voodoo priestesses, palm readers...whatever. You want 'em, you bring 'em on," Massey said.

"Great. Well, then, gentlemen, let me get to it. And I swear, what I know, you'll know," Brent promised.

Brent left the station thinking the two of them were probably laughing at his expense.

But what the hell, they liked him.

Things could be worse.

Dr. Boulet was a man of about forty. He was pleasant, nicely dressed and comfortable to talk to.

He did have a couch, but he also had an easy chair.

"Am I supposed to lie down?" she asked.

"If you like. Or just take a seat."

She chose the chair.

"So what's the problem?" he asked.

"I'm seeing dead people."

"Do you want to give me a few details?"

She waved a hand in the air. "Ghosts."

"Have you always seen ghosts?" he asked, not blinking.

She smiled, lowering her head. "Only since my friend died. Or maybe right before she died."

"Why don't you tell me the story from the beginning."

She did, and he paid rapt attention, his expression grave. He took notes.

When she had explained it all—starting with the man in the café and ending with her recent shock at the police station—he quit writing and waited.

"That's it," she said.

"Do you really believe in ghosts?" he asked.

"I must—I'm seeing them now."

His smile deepened. "But you didn't—before all this?"

"Um…no."

"Even though you give ghost tours for a living?"

"I've always had a…sense, I guess you'd call it."

"A sense?"

She waved a hand vaguely in the air. "I don't know how to explain it. When…I'm in certain places, I can feel past events…even see something like a mist."

"Aha." He started to write.

"No, it's not an aha!" Nikki protested. "I've never actually seen a ghost before, and sure as hell, one never talked to me before."

"Someone important to you died tragically," he reminded her softly.

"Yes."

"Well, the mind is far more incredible than any computer. You might have imagined your dream, you see. It might have been implanted when you heard what happened, or even when the policeman came up to you. Take déjà vu for instance. We go somewhere, and we know we've never been there, but it's familiar. So… were we there in another lifetime? Or has the brain given us a memory that doesn't exist?"

"You're asking me?" Nikki said.

"I'm giving you suggestions. When someone close to us is killed, there's often a matter of guilt. Survivor's guilt, it's called. She's dead, I'm not."

"But I don't feel guilty. I don't feel that I should be dead. I'm horrified that Andy died, and I'm angry. I'm furious that someone could do that to her."

At that point, he looked at his watch.

The sigh he gave then was everything she would have imagined, as were his next words.

"I'm afraid we're out of time. You might want to think about the things I've said. And schedule an appointment for next week with my secretary. Do you want something to help you sleep?"

"Pills?"

"Yes."

"No."

"Are you sure?"

"Positive, thank you."

"Then we'll meet again. And we'll get to the bottom of this," he assured her cheerfully.

"So…I'm not exactly…crazy?" she asked pleasantly.

"The mind, as I said, is incredible. You've been through a terrible trauma. You want answers. You want an explanation for how something so terrible happened. There could be many reasons."

"Maybe ghosts really exist," she suggested.

"In our minds, of course they do. When we love someone and lose them, they're always with us, in a way."

"I don't love a stranger I never saw before," Nikki said.

"No...but the memory of having seen him not long before Andy's death might be confusing the picture."

"A logical explanation for everything," Nikki murmured.

"It can take some time to get all the ghosts out of our minds," he said, glancing at his watch again.

Nikki rose. "Thanks," she managed to say.

Julian was pacing the waiting room when she came out. He rushed quickly to her side. "Well? Do you feel better?"

"No, not really."

"Did he say you were having delusions or...well, what the hell did he say?"

"He didn't call me crazy. He talked about the mind playing tricks, and how I might be dealing with survivor's guilt."

"There you go."

"Right—and that explains why I saw a dead *man?* I still don't even know who he is—only that the guy who showed up at the right time showed me a picture of him. I'm hungry. Let's get something to eat."

"Nikki, you *are* going to see the doctor again, right?" He sighed. "You need help."

"Sure. I'll see him again. Can we eat?"

A little later, over po'boys at Madame D'Orso's, Julian said, "Maybe you should take some time off."

"Why?" she demanded, staring at him.

"Well, we actually do ghost tours, no matter what we call them."

"We talk about history, and history includes the superstitions and rumors that have sprung up through the years."

"Yes, but don't you think that may be bad for you right now?"

"No!"

He sighed, sitting back. "Well, you're on for the eight o'clock tour tonight. You sure you're up to it?"

"Of course. Who's on with me?"

"Me. We can rotate, you know. I can lead the tour."

She smiled, shaking her head. "I'm not going to let the monster who did this to Andrea ruin *my* life, as well."

Julian was silent.

"What?" she demanded.

"No, I still think…maybe you should take a vacation."

"I can't take a vacation. We just lost a guide, remember? And everyone else was shaken up, too."

He leaned forward, speaking softly. "The rest of us aren't seeing ghosts, Nikki. And Max could get his ass back from wherever he is to help out."

"I'm fine," she insisted.

They were seated in the courtyard, and Nikki wasn't surprised when Madame came out with more coffee, pausing to fill her cup.

"You doing okay, Nikki?"

"Yes, thanks, Madame."

"No, she's not doing okay at all," Julian said.

Nikki kicked him under the table.

"She's seeing ghosts," Julian said, grimacing and rubbing his shin.

"Ghosts?" Madame said, not appearing shocked, just concerned.

"Andy comes and talks to her at night."

"Julian!" Nikki could have kicked him again.

"Oh, Nikki," Madame said with soft sympathy. "This has been really hard on you, huh?"

She sighed. "I'm not ill, guys. I'll be fine."

"Well, you know I'm here for you, Nikki, if you need me," Madame said. She glared at Julian. "Sometimes… well, grief and trauma can do strange things. Anytime you need to talk, you just come to me."

"You going into palm reading, picking up the tarot, Madame?" Julian asked.

She scowled at him. "What Nikki doesn't need is for her friends to make fun of her."

"Ouch. Sorry," Julian said.

Madame gave him a superior stare and moved on to the next table.

"I'm going to strangle you," Nikki hissed to him.

"Well, sorry, but you *are* seeing ghosts."

"It's not something we need to share. Not till I know what's really going on."

"So you admit you may not really be seeing ghosts?"

She groaned. "Julian, I'm seeing them. Whether that means that ghosts exist or that I'm losing my mind, I'm not sure. The point is, one way or another, I'd rather not share my state of confusion with the world."

"Sorry…sorry," he murmured quickly. "I just thought that if I said it out loud like that, it would make you… well, make you see that it's kind of crazy."

She glanced at her watch. "Meeting here, in ten minutes."

"Ten minutes?"

"It's almost three."

"Wow, the day just kind of went, huh?"

"Time flies when you're talking to the cops, thinking you've seen dead men walking around and explaining it all to a shrink," she assured him.

"Hey, you know what we didn't do?" Julian said.

"What?"

"Get the real lowdown on that guy...Tommyhawk or whatever."

"Blackhawk."

"Yeah, yeah...he came up with that picture, you recognized it, we were told the guy was dead...and you freaked."

"I didn't freak."

"You did."

"All right, all right, so?"

"So we didn't really find out anything about him, either. The dead guy or Blackhawk. We really should find out everything there is to find out about both of them. The entire story about the dead guy." He looked around, as if he was suddenly afraid of being overheard. "Okay, point one. You may suddenly have the ability to see ghosts. Point two—my personal choice—the mind *does* play tricks. Because there's something in your mind that can't quite get to the front burner but should."

"What does that mean?" Nikki demanded.

"Maybe you know something. Something you shouldn't know. And Andy knew it, too. Maybe you and Andy knew something that had to do with the guy at Madame D'Orso's."

"The dead guy?"

"Yes, except maybe he wasn't dead when you saw him the first time." He leaned closer still, a tone in his voice that sent tremors down her spine. "Maybe he said something, maybe there was something about him…and Andy died because of it. And that…well, that wouldn't be good news for you."

Nikki sat back, staring at Julian in horror. "What on earth are you saying?"

Julian, apparently realizing that he'd really frightened her, sat back himself. "Nothing…nothing! I don't know."

"Dammit, Julian.… You're scaring me big-time."

"I don't want to scare you. I want you to be careful. Beyond careful. Until the cops get…whoever. What I'm saying is that we need to understand what's going on around here. Oh, what the hell do I know? I'm just a storyteller."

"But still…"

"But still, we have to keep living, breathing—working. Making our lives normal, right? And look, here come the lovebirds, right on time. Right now we've got to get on with the meeting."

He stood. Nikki could see Patricia and Nathan coming their way, both carrying cups of coffee.

She forced a smile, still plagued with goose bumps.

So Julian thought that she knew something.

What?

All she had done was give a guy twenty bucks.

A guy who had wound up dead.

And she was really seeing ghosts.

8

Though he was feeling increasingly curious about Nikki DuMonde, Brent decided his best use of the early afternoon would be a few hours spent in the local library.

He wondered why he hadn't thought to come here before. Maybe he had just considered old Huey to be something of a whiner.

Growing up with a Lakota heritage had taught him a lot about bitterness and chips on the shoulder, but the past was just that—the past—and now people needed to focus on entering the twenty-first century, reaping the benefits of progress and technology, without losing sight of a heritage that was something precious, something to be preserved.

In Huey's case, though, he had lived in the past. His tormentor had a name. He should have looked into Huey's situation before this; he owed it to the old ghost.

Property records had been computerized by some wondrous soul, and once he had homed in on the right records using the family name, Brent had little difficulty finding Huey's sadistic master.

Archibald McManus.

Apparently old Archibald had inherited the plantation from his father, who had worked hard to bring the property along. He'd married three times, and his wives had not fared well, either, each of them dying within a few years of her marriage. Each marriage had produced a single child.

In 1861, soon after the outbreak of war but before New Orleans had been taken over by the Yankees, there had been a slave revolt. The plantation had caught fire. There was no mention of what had happened to the three McManus children, but Archibald's body had been found in the burned-out ruins of the grand foyer.

In pieces.

Not a happy ending. Not a death you would wish on anyone.

And yet…

God alone knew whether or not McManus had practiced a brutality that had not only robbed his slaves of their natural lifespan but of his young brides', as well.

McManus's remains had been interred on the property—public land now, having reverted to the parish of New Orleans. That was it. There was nothing more on any descendants. Wife one had borne a girl, Theresa, in 1848, wife two, a son, Alfred, in 1855, and wife three, another girl, Editha, in 1857. They must have left the area. There were no records regarding the family after the fire and the discovery of Archibald's body, and the ensuing reversion of the property to the parish.

Brent ran off the pages, folded them, paid the copy fee and thanked the very helpful librarian. He decided not to head to the cemetery then—it would be filled with tourists and tour groups that came by day, since visitations at night were fiercely discouraged by the local police.

Instead, he returned to the police station, wondering if he would even find Detectives Massey and Joulette in.

In fact they were both at their desks, entangled in paperwork.

"Hey, Blackhawk, what brings you back?" Massey asked him.

"I was wondering if you'd let me see what you've got on the Andrea Ciello case," Brent told them.

Joulette immediately stiffened.

"I think there might be a connection," Brent said.

Massey frowned. "That's what you said. But I don't see how."

"Could you humor me?" Brent asked.

He was certain that Joulette was about to tell him no, but instead, he went stiffer, looking past Brent, toward the entry.

Brent turned and saw that a man was coming toward the detectives' desks. He was tall and lean, with dark hair clipped close to his head, Ray-Bans and a black suit.

He seemed to reek of being a federal officer.

"Good afternoon, fellows," the man said, nodding curtly and looking a little curiously toward Brent. "I needed to see if you'd come up with anything new," he said to Massey and Joulette. "Who the hell are you?" he asked Brent.

Massey stood. "Vince Haggerty, this is Brent Blackhawk."

Haggerty had apparently heard Brent's name. He didn't look pleased.

"I didn't think you were going to be in the way, although I heard you'd be here," Haggerty said.

Brent looked around. "I don't think I'm actually in the way, though quarters *are* tight."

"We do life-and-death work," Haggerty told him, his tone dismissing Brent as if he were a candy-selling Boy Scout taking up space.

"Good to hear it," Brent murmured.

"We don't have anything new," Massey said, staring at Haggerty.

"If you hold back on me—"

"Hell, I wish I had something to hold back!" Massey said, his frustration evident.

"Are you actually doing anything?" Haggerty asked bluntly.

"Hell no, we're just sitting here with our thumbs up our asses," Joulette said, obviously furious.

"Our crime scene guys didn't give us a hell of a lot to go on, and gee—neither did yours," Massey reminded Haggerty, his expression bland. "So we've been hitting the streets. Bar after bar, looking for witnesses. Anyone who might have seen your guy. Eventually we'll catch a break. And we'll catch that break because we're doing things—like pounding the streets. You can feel free to do the same."

"I *am* doing the same," Haggerty said stiffly.

"Yeah, and I'm sure every low-down dirty drug dealer is going to be ready to talk his head off when you walk in, looking like a Hollywood G-man," Joulette said.

"You think I don't know my stuff?" Haggerty said, leaning on the desk.

"I think we all have squat so far," Joulette said, disgusted.

Haggerty was stiff as a board. He straightened again, then stared at Brent, eyes filled with suspicion.

"And you—if you get anything, anything at all, if you stumble on the smallest clue..." he said, pointing a warning finger at Brent. "I'd better hear it first thing. And if you're all so busy pounding the streets, what the hell are you doing in here?"

Joulette stood then, too. "Working something else—NOPD business, and nothing to do with your jurisdiction," he said. "Blackhawk, I'll get you those files you want."

Haggerty was frowning. "It was my understanding that Blackhawk was here on specific business," he said, his tone a warning one.

"Yeah?" Massey said. "Well, it's my understanding, straight from my lieutenant's lips to my ears, that Blackhawk is here under the highest authority, and that I'm to be as accommodating as I can be."

Haggerty leaned on Massey's desk, inhaled slowly, then exhaled. "Look, all of you. I know I'm coming on as a tight ass, but we lost one of our own. You're cops—surely you can understand how we feel about that."

"You know, Haggerty, we consider any law enforcement officer who's lost as one of our own," Massey said. "And we know our jobs. If we get anything, anything at all, we'll give it to you."

Haggerty straightened again. "All right, just as

long as you remember that." He managed a very stiff "Thanks." Then, "Blackhawk, glad to meet you."

He turned to leave.

"Well, looks as if he's trying not to be a complete ass," Brent said when Haggerty was out of earshot.

"Yeah, well," Joulette said, coming back in time to hear Brent's words, "he's a little too late. He thinks we're both a pair of country bumpkins who don't know our butts from a hole in the ground."

"Maybe he was friends with the murdered agent. That's hard to swallow. Pain can make people behave badly," Brent said.

"I don't think they ever met," Joulette said.

"Still..." Brent said with a shrug, trying to be diplomatic.

Massey laughed. "There's just something about the man...oh, well. You can take the Ciello files to the conference room over there."

"Thanks," Brent said, and added no more. He knew that he had been let into the inner circle not so much because these guys had begun to accept him or even like him, but because they really hated the fed who'd been thrust upon them.

It didn't really matter. He had gotten what he wanted.

As he sat in the dingy conference room and opened the first file, he knew he had also managed to get what he needed.

"So," Patricia said, sipping a café au lait and staring hard at Nikki, "Nathan and I are doing the St. Louis cemeteries tomorrow afternoon."

"Yes, just like you always do on a Friday afternoon," Nikki said, not understanding why her friend was staring at her. They were all staring at her, come to think of it.

"Okay, what is it?" she asked.

Patricia looked at Nathan, who looked at Mitch, who in turn looked at Julian.

"What?" Nikki demanded.

"We...well, if Nathan and I take the cemetery tour, that means you and either Mitch or Julian will get the Garden District."

"Right...so?" Nikki said.

Patricia looked at her with tremendous empathy. The two of them both knew the parish of New Orleans well. They had grown up in the same basic area, but were from such different backgrounds. Patricia had gone away to school in Virginia and learned to speak without any accent whatsoever.

When she wanted to, though, she could slip back into the Cajun patois. She had come from a family of shrimpers, honest, hardworking people who often had the whole group out to the bayou for some of the best meals ever.

Just as she had felt an immediate bond with Andy Ciello, Nikki had known from the minute she met Patricia that she really liked her. She had a wonderful sense of life and fun, and a passion for her heritage. They liked to shop together, and they were both bookstore fanatics who loved to find out-of-print volumes and triumphantly share their treasures with one another.

But now Patricia was looking at Nikki as if she were an elderly relative beginning to suffer from dementia.

"Nikki," Patricia said kindly, "we don't think you should be conducting tours of the Garden District."

Nikki groaned. "I have been doing tours of the Garden District since I began working for Max."

Mitch cleared his throat, running his fingers through his hair. "Um, you hadn't lost Andy when you began. We're thinking that now—it might be hard for you."

"I didn't *lose* Andy!" she said, angry. She groaned inwardly at the idea that she'd misplaced a friend. She shot an accusatory stare at Julian, who stared back blankly. "What the hell have you been saying to them?"

"Me? Nothing," he vowed, almost tipping his chair over. He must have known he looked guilty as hell. "Really."

"Madame mentioned that you were seeing ghosts," Nathan said softly.

"Well, I'm not. It's just nightmares. A natural response to trauma. And I'm just fine in the Garden District. Everybody got that? Any other order of business?"

"Just one thing," Patricia said, still sounding uncomfortable and looking at her cup of café au lait as if she wished it were strongly laced with liquor.

"What?" Nikki said, knowing she sounded terse and probably bitchy.

Patricia stared at her. "A replacement for Andy."

Nikki felt as if an icy fluid had been shot through her veins. She didn't allow her face so much as a ripple of emotion.

"Yeah, of course. I wish that Max was here, since he's supposed to approve his own employees."

"He makes you interview and hire, anyway," Julian reminded her.

She shrugged. "Still, I wish he was here."

"Why should he bother? You do everything for him," Patricia said.

"Don't worry. I'll compose a new ad and start interviewing ASAP. Does that work for everyone?"

They all looked at one another. Nathan was the first to offer a forced smile. The rest imitated it.

"Yeah, sure. Great," Patricia said. She set her cup down, giving up. "Well. I guess we're out of here, then."

"Now we come to a place where reality definitely outweighs the horrors of fiction," Nikki announced, turning to face her group as she reached Royal Street. She had a nice group tonight. No children under thirteen, a lot of couples and one girl, obviously a college student, with her glasses perched on her nose, notebook in hand. Since she was leading the tour, Julian had done the business bit, greeting the arrivals as they appeared, collecting their money and handing out tickets. She was pretty sure she had about forty people surrounding her. She preferred smaller groups of about thirty, but this size was manageable. Sometimes, in the height of tourist season, they wound up with huge crowds, and the simple logistics of speaking to that many people—getting them across streets and out of the way of traffic—were not easy. But she, along with every member of the business, had the ability to project her voice to a crowd, so she seldom had to repeat information, unless they had a wanderer who hadn't quite kept up. But that was the responsibility of the tail man—or woman—on the tour, making sure that the group was herded along like a little gaggle of geese.

"Cool house," a young man muttered, studying the building behind her and grinning.

"We've come to 1140 Royal Street, more commonly known as the Lalaurie House. It was in 1831 that Madame Delphine Lalaurie and her husband, Dr. Louis Lalaurie, bought the house from Edmond Soniat du Fossat. Reputedly, Madame Lalaurie was a great beauty, and a woman who was determined to rise high in the social spheres of New Orleans. She did so by dressing elegantly, attending party after ball after party, and gaining admiration for her grace and elegance as she moved among the elite."

People had scattered around a little on the sidewalk, looking up at the house as she spoke. The sound of a cool blue jazz tune came faintly from one of the clubs around the corner. Locals had a tendency to steer around the tour groups, and despite the occasional drunk who wandered past, the speeches usually went smoothly.

"By 1833, the admiration many felt for the beautiful Madame Lalaurie was turning to something else. Suspicion. There were rumors about screams and horrible happenings that first began to seep through the city, then rush like a current. Madame Lalaurie was married to a physician, a man fascinated by anatomy and the endurance of the human body. And then a terrible cruelty was actually witnessed. Madame Lalaurie was seen beating the child of one of her slaves. The tormented child ran away from her persecutor, headed for the balcony and was chased—until she fell. The girl died instantly."

"Was Madame Lalaurie arrested?" somebody asked.

"Well, those were different times," Nikki said softly, yet allowing her voice to carry. She loved questions. They added to the drama of any pregnant pause. "Madame Lalaurie was fined, and her slaves were taken away to be sold at auction."

"Thank heavens," a woman said.

Nikki smiled. "If only such measures had really been effective. You see, Madame Lalaurie wanted those slaves back. She led her relatives to believe that she had been poorly treated by the authorities, that the death of the girl had not been her fault. You've got to remember, slaves were property in those days. There were those who owned slaves and treated them well, but it was certainly not unheard of for slaves to be beaten for disobedience. At any rate, Madame Lalaurie convinced her relatives to buy her slaves and return them to her. So once again these poor people were in the clutches of a woman who appeared so beautiful and sweet in public, then returned to her home and...well, it was a fire that at last brought rescue workers into the house and into a den of horror that rivaled anything ever put down in fiction."

"What?" a woman called from the crowd.

"Her slaves were found, many chained to the walls in positions that would be impossible to achieve by the finest contortionists. Bones were broken, many were horribly crippled. Some were found in cages, smaller than dog kennels, and some were found strapped to crude operating tables, and only in the heinous mind of Dr. Lalaurie could the possible purpose of his torments be known. And in the attic, human body parts were found strewn about. It was said that many of the staunchest firefighters became ill—and a few actually passed out."

"So then did they get the Lalauries?" a woman asked.

Nikki started to answer, but her voice froze in her throat.

As she stared through the crowd, she saw Andy.

She was still wearing the suit in which she'd been buried. She looked beautiful, as always, but…

Gray. Pallid.

Dead.

Nikki just stared, and Andy gave her a rueful, apologetic smile.

"Well, did they get them?" a man persisted.

Nikki barely heard him. She just stared at Andy, still unable to speak. Then she managed to whisper, "You're not there."

A young man near her heard and asked, "Who's not there?" He looked around curiously.

"I've got chills," someone in the crowd said.

"Nikki!" Julian called.

She managed to rip her gaze from Andy's to stare across the crowd at Julian.

Someone else had joined their group, standing next to Julian. It was the man from the night before, and from the police station. The man who had shown her the picture of the bum from the coffee shop, the other ghost she had seen walking these streets. Brent Blackhawk.

For some reason, the sight of Brent Blackhawk

snapped her out of her frozen state. She refused to glance again toward the spot where Andy had been standing.

"The Lalauries..."

At first, her voice was nothing but a croak. She looked into the crowd again. Andy was still there, unnoticed by anyone else.

I *am* losing my mind, she thought.

No, she couldn't. She couldn't allow it to happen.

She turned away again, facing the house, afraid that she was suddenly going to see dozens of graying, decaying, tormented and tortured souls, streaming from the house. Ghosts. Ghosts no one but she could see...

"The entire neighborhood came bursting from their homes, sickened, horrified," she said, her voice strong and rising dramatically. "The citizens were so appalled that a dual lynching almost occurred. But somehow, just ahead of that furious crowd, Madame Lalaurie and her cruel doctor husband managed to escape. She got away in her carriage and managed to catch a schooner from St. John's Bayou to St. Tammany Parish."

"And then what?" a woman demanded indignantly. "They went after her, right?"

"Then, I'm afraid," Nikki said, "what is known begins to blend with legend. Some say that she went on to Paris, and whether she and her husband began their experiments anew on servants in Europe, no one knows. Others say they somehow remained on the North Shore for the rest of their lives. Some say that Madame Lalaurie died in 1842, and that her body lies in New Orleans somewhere."

"Ugh," said a girl of about eighteen, drawing a ripple of relieved and slightly uneasy laughter from the crowd.

"But the house is still standing," said a man. "So it didn't burn down?"

Nikki glanced back at the crowd. *Be gone, Andy. Please, be gone.*

Andy was no longer where she'd been standing.

Nikki took a deep breath.

"The house *did* burn down, but in 1837, it was rebuilt, and that's when the stories began about strange noises, about mysterious lights being seen. No one seemed able to stay in the house at first. One owner kept it for only three months. The voodoo queens of the city began to warn that there was a curse on the location. A barbershop on the premises lasted just a few months; a furniture store did little better. But then the Civil War divided the country, and attention was drawn from the house. For a while, during Reconstruction, the house was a school that was open to white and black girls alike. Then the school system was segregated, and it became a school for blacks only—that lasted one year. The house next became a conservatory, but its reputation had become such that no one would attend a concert, and the conservatory was a failure—and the night of the final performance was one on which locals swore they could hear Madame Lalaurie and her fiendish friends from beyond this world celebrating and partying loudly. This, of course, is all rumor, and hearsay. What is true..."

She turned back to face the crowd again and fell silent, swallowing hard.

Andy was back. She seemed to be trying to stay hidden within the crowd.

Far from Julian.

And Brent Blackhawk.

Blackhawk was staring at Nikki. Even in the shadows of the night, she swore that she saw the color of his eyes, that intense green, as he watched her closely, seeming to see all kinds of things within her that she wanted to keep hidden.

Andy, you're not really there. This is all in my mind.

"So what's true?" someone demanded.

Nikki gritted her teeth, staring hard at the image of Andy she was trying to convince herself existed only in her mind.

"What's true?" she repeated. "The house was divided into apartments, and in 1889, a man named Joseph Edouard Vigne began living in one of them. People believed that he was a drifter, a poor man, barely getting by. But when he was found dead in his apartment in the Lalaurie House in 1892, there was over ten thousand dollars found hidden away in various places among his belongings. How did he die? If he was murdered for his riches, the killer certainly hadn't discovered them. Did he die of natural causes? Or did the ghosts of the Lalaurie House catch up with him? That's for each individual to decide. But now, according to those who believe, Joseph roams the place looking for his wealth, along with the spirits of the tortured slaves, who are said to rattle their chains as they roam the halls seeking freedom and salvation."

"Yeah, right. Ghosts," said one big man, but he jumped when his wife touched his arm.

"What then?" Andy mouthed to her from her place in the crowd. Andy was smiling wistfully. This had been one of her favorite tales to tell.

"As you can see from the perfect condition of the house, the current owner is having no difficulties, or none that we know of. There are a number of apartments in the house now, all inhabited. In the early 1990s, there was a saloon here, and it did fairly well—it was called the Haunted Saloon. There was a furniture store here after that, and it didn't do so well. The owner assumed that he was being vandalized the first few times he found his wares wrecked, with a curious substance on the ruins, something that smelled quite bad and had an oily essence to it. After he felt he had been the victim of petty criminals one time too many, he took his shotgun with him and waited with his merchandise. The night came…and the night went. And in the morning, he'd seen nothing. But his merchandise was wrecked again, and the odor of decay permeated the place, along with the foul substance. Soon after, the owner determined that he would do much better setting up shop elsewhere."

"But…people live there now?" a woman asked, the wife of the big man who had jumped. She was hugging his arm tightly.

"Yes, and all seems to be fine," Nikki said cheerfully. *Okay, Andy, stay there. I've decided that I'm not sane, but I'm just going to live with the madness, and I am* not *telling anyone else about you.* "There's one final note. Around 1941, a grave marker was found in St. Louis Cemetery Number 1. It had the name of Madame Delphine Lalaurie on it. However, it wasn't attached to any specific tomb, grave or even wall vault, so...did she return to New Orleans? And, as some ask, is she still here? That answer is up to the mind of everyone who hears the story."

She turned and hurried onward toward the next stop on the tour. As she walked, she felt Andy at her side.

"You're not here," she said, not glancing around.

"Excuse me, dear, am I walking too close?"

She turned. The question had come from a pleasant woman of about sixty, with soft gray hair and powder-blue eyes, looking perplexed.

"No, no...I'm sorry," Nikki murmured, and tried to think of an explanation. "Practicing out loud," she apologized quickly.

"Ah," the woman said, and smiled.

Andy was there, of course, on her other side.

"Go away," Nikki murmured.

"Pardon?" the woman said.

"No, no, I'm sorry. I wasn't talking to you. Really."

The woman looked at her as if she was seriously deranged.

And that was the way she was behaving, she realized.

She had to ignore Andy.

So she did. Determinedly. Until she came to the next stop on the tour, a tavern where pirates had once met, now a bar that offered bluegrass but still advertised its past.

At some point, Andy faded from the crowd.

But Brent Blackhawk remained, always hovering at the rear of the group.

The tour turned out to be one of the best she had ever led. The customers were willing to suspend disbelief. They asked questions. They were fun. They shivered with pleasure at all the right places. They wanted to know what was fact, what was rumor and what was supposition.

When she finished, back at Madame's, most of them were planning on taking one of the cemetery tours the following day, and she had never received more tips in her entire life.

With the remnants of the tour still there, Madame's began a little nighttime business boom. Nikki talked with some of the attendees, while Julian, some distance from her, talked to another group about the other tours the company offered.

Andy stayed away.

But Brent Blackhawk was still there. He waited until the last of her customers had moved on to order café au lait or sweets from Madame's counter.

Then he approached her.

"Brent Blackhawk, Miss DuMonde. From the police station."

"Oh, yes, of course," she told him, and she knew there was a vein of ice in her words.

"We need to talk," he told her.

"I don't think so," she said, flushing slightly. He made her uncomfortable on so many levels. One, he scared the hell out of her. Two, he was terribly attractive, reeking of masculinity, of simple strength. Like a man who knew himself. Third, there was an electricity about him. Frightening, compelling. If she had met him under different circumstances… And last, there was the way he seemed to see right through her.

"No, I don't think we should talk," she repeated, looking away uncomfortably.

Where was Julian? Damn. Over there, flirting with a pretty twentysomething.

"I think I can help you."

Her eyes met Blackhawk's. She felt as if she had heard him say those words in a dream… In her sleep? Or in another vision created by a guilt-stricken mind?

"This is a very bad time for us," she murmured.

"Yes, I know. And I'm sorry."

"Thank you." Her voice remained stiff.

"But I…well, I think you need help, and I can help you."

"I'm blessed with very good friends," she told him.

He nodded, smiling. "Look…just have a drink with me?"

"I'm not drinking much these days."

"A coffee, then?"

She lifted a hand, indicating Madame's.

"Away from here," he said, grinning. Nice grin. Brought out the charm in his features.

So why was she afraid of him?

Because…

Because he might make ghosts real?

"I…um…"

"You saw her tonight," he said flatly. "You saw your friend, Andy, the one who was murdered."

Her jaw nearly dropped.

She shook her head. "No, no…of course not. She's dead. Ghosts aren't real."

He stared at her, smiling knowingly.

"What would make you say that?" she asked, feeling sick. "I mean…how could you know that?"

"Because I saw her, too," he said softly.

9

Brent's heart went out to the beautiful young woman. Torment, mistrust and, strangely enough, something like hope were at war with one another in the depths of her eyes. She stood stiffly, unyielding, and yet…

"You know," she said, "my friends are beginning to think I'm crazy."

"That happens," he told her.

"Great. So they'll wind up having me locked up. And you're not helping me at all, though I'm sure that's what you think you're doing."

"I can help you," he assured her. "If you'll let me."

She smiled then, ruefully. "Julian will never let me go off with you alone."

Brent studied the man who had been her defender in the fracas in the street and who had accompanied her to the police station. Was the man her lover? The thought disturbed him. Admittedly, he had felt an attraction to Nikki DuMonde, the sort of attraction he hadn't known in years. It was one thing to look on a woman and judge her as stunning. Youth itself was often beautiful, and Nikki was right at that age, in her mid to upper twenties somewhere, when the sophistication of maturity had combined with all the elements of face and form to give her an added elegance. He was alive after all. In the years since Tania's death he had lived and breathed, gone through all the stages of loss, met and been attracted to several women, made love, and…

Moved on. The world was filled with people. Those you met along the way. With whom you shared something…and moved on. A moment, an evening, a few weeks, even a few months.

But there hadn't been…this.

Back off, he warned himself.

He never mixed work with anything personal. He and the others involved with Adam's agency, were often the butts of jokes, due to their focus on the paranormal, but they were still professionals.

But there was something about Nikki DuMonde….

It wasn't just her appearance, it was her…

Soul.

The essence of her existence.

Her eyes, her passion, her movement, the sound of her voice…everything about her.

"Is Julian your fiancé? Your boyfriend?" he asked politely.

She smiled, lowering her eyes for a moment. "No, he's my best friend. My very best friend for years."

Brent smiled. "But he doesn't believe a word you're saying, does he? He thinks you've concocted ghosts in your head because you're traumatized by Andrea Ciello's death."

She looked uncomfortable, and he knew that he had judged the situation correctly.

"I told you, my friends think I'm crazy."

"So…what do *you* think?" he demanded.

Her eyes narrowed. "Just what are you? A cop?" Then she smiled self-mockingly. "A psychic cop or something?"

"I'm not a cop at all."

"FBI?"

"No."

"Then…?"

"I work for a civilian agency that does a lot of strange work for the government," he told her. "But we work privately, as well."

"I see."

"So will you have coffee with me?"

She hedged. "I don't see Andy anymore," she murmured.

"No, she isn't here."

Nikki hesitated again. "Did she…talk to you?"

He shook his head. "I didn't actually let on that I knew she was there."

"Oh, sure, of course not," she scoffed.

"She trusts you, not me," he said.

"Oh. So ghosts have to trust you to talk to you, huh?"

"Depends on the ghost," he said evenly, despite her combative tone.

She hesitated. For a moment he was certain she was going to blow him off.

"Give me a minute."

Brent watched as she walked over to Julian. The last of their tour group had said good-night and moved away.

Julian didn't trust him, Brent knew. Plus, he was very protective of Nikki. He'd been pleasant enough when Brent had joined the tour, but then, Brent had paid for the privilege of walking around and listening with the others.

Now Julian was clearly arguing with Nikki. But he didn't dissuade her. Apparently arguing with Nikki just made her determined to do the opposite. He would have to remember that.

When she turned to join him again, Brent saw Julian watch her walk toward him. The other man had a coffee cup in his hand and he lifted it in salute.

"'Night, then," he called. "Hey, where are you two going?"

Brent mentioned a hotel bar, one of the most frequented in the area, trying to assure Julian that he wasn't taking Nikki off anywhere alone or unsafe.

"Have a nice night."

Nikki joined Brent.

"He kind of sounds okay with this," Brent said, smiling, as they turned to walk down the street.

"No, he thinks I'm an idiot. Am I?"

"No."

"He'll probably be following us."

"Is that a warning?" Brent asked her softly. "Because I really have no evil intent."

"If you're going to play with my mind right now, I assure you, that *is* evil intent."

He sighed, silent. A group who had been on the tour passed by, calling out, "Great tour—thanks!"

"My pleasure. Come back for one of our other tours," Nikki called back.

"I swear, I could almost see ghosts," one of the women said, laughing, as the group disappeared.

The hotel was just up at the corner. Brent moved ahead and opened the door for Nikki. She murmured her thanks, and they made their way to the bar.

It was quieter than many of the local establishments. A pianist played softly, mainly performing show tunes. Businessmen were ranged in some of the oak booths. Women returning from dinners out were nicely dressed. Average tourists sat around in shorts, tank tops and halter dresses. Only two seats at the bar were empty, and only three booths were available. A hostess with copper skin, inky dark hair, a flashing smile and a pleasant cologne led them to a private little recess.

They sat, and Nikki opened her mouth to speak, then hesitated as a waiter approached them. She ordered a latte with shaved chocolate. Brent opted for the same.

The waiter moved on.

Nikki looked at him and smiled with no humor. She smoothed a cocktail napkin nervously with both hands. Her fingers were long and delicate; her nails a medium length, lacquered in a clear polish.

"So you're not a cop or an FBI agent, but you have access to the police, and you're walking around with the picture of a dead man, making once-sane people think they've gone over the edge. Or you're a shrink of some kind, making a study of the human mind," she said sharply.

"Nope."

"Okay, then...how long have you been seeing ghosts?" she asked.

"A while," he told her.

"You're Indian, right? Whoops, sorry, the term these days is Native American."

"Partly, yes."

"What kind?"

"Lakota. One grandfather."

"So..." She paused as the waiter arrived with their orders. He didn't seem distressed that they weren't drinking, since the lattes cost more than aged brandy in most establishments.

As soon as the waiter left, Nikki stared at Brent, aqua eyes hard and searching. "So, tell me, did you get into this whole ghost thing by peyote smoking or something?"

She was scared and angry, he knew, and therefore on the offensive. Still, he felt tension ripple through his muscles.

The little stirrer he'd been using snapped between his fingers.

Deep breath.

"No. It had nothing to do with peyote."

"Okay, sorry," she said, stirring her latte. "This is just...you can't imagine. *I* don't think *I'm* sane."

"But you are."

"All right, so you see ghosts," she said. "And, according to you, it's perfectly natural that I see them, too, and we should have a nice long chat about our spectral companions."

"I never said it was perfectly natural," he told her.

She played with the little stirrer, mixing the shreds of chocolate into the whipped cream atop her gourmet latte.

"So we're back to insanity?"

"No we're not. Some people are born with a musical ear. They can pick up an instrument and play a tune with no training while others can attend class after class, but never really learn how to play. Some people are born artists."

"So you were born seeing ghosts?" she demanded. "I guess that gave new meaning to the term *imaginary friend.*"

He shook his head. "What I'm trying to say is that there are gray regions in life. You're afraid right now. I don't blame you. Questioning your own mental health can be even more frightening than admitting you commune with ghosts. It's not perfectly natural, no. But it doesn't make you a lunatic. All scientists know that there are still things in the world that defy logic and explanation. We understand gravity, life, evolution, ages long gone. We're constantly questioning faith. Men live and die for their beliefs. But none of us has the definitive answer."

She offered a skeptical smile. "Not even you? Don't your ghosts fill you in on everything?"

He shook his head. "Ghosts are usually wandering around a little lost themselves."

"Right. It's that thing about a violent end, or a need

to finish something, find someone, even take revenge, right?"

It was half sincere question, half skepticism.

"There are different reasons."

She looked down, smoothed her napkin again. He had gone for his own. Their fingers brushed. She looked at him, startled, and he returned the intense stare, equally aware of the electricity between them. A tremor shook the length of him. She was appealing on so many levels, sensual in the most natural of ways, the opposite of intentionally provocative.

She didn't trust him, though. She wanted him at arm's length.

He drew his fingers away, afraid that he would lose her if he wasn't careful, that she would stand up and leave and demand that he stay away from her.

"Nikki, I believe with my whole heart that I can help you. And I also desperately need your help in return."

She didn't bolt, though her eyes remained downcast. Then she looked up at him again. "Who was the man in the picture you showed me today? And when did he die? Was he supposedly dead when I saw him at Madame's? Or was he killed after?"

He shook his head. "The ME could only give an approximate time of death. I think he might still have been alive the first time you saw him, but in serious trouble. I don't know. And who was he? An undercover FBI agent, a man above reproach. The kind of guy who couldn't be bought, not for any price. He'd been undercover in some of our worst slums, among the most heinous drug lords, in war zones. He was on to something here. He managed to keep his cover by keeping private until he really had something."

"You knew him?" Nikki asked.

Brent shook his head. "No. That's part of the problem."

"How do you know he was so lily white, then?" she asked softly. "And why is it a problem that you didn't know him?"

"I work for a man who travels in the highest government circles possible. But he never trusts anything without proof. Adam Harrison always goes to the people who knew someone best, those who were closest. When you don't hear anything but lily white all the way around, you can pretty much bet it's true."

"So I thought he was a bum, and he was really a great guy. There you go. I'm a great judge of character, huh?"

"You saw what you were intended to see," he told her.

"Why is it bad that you didn't actually know him yourself?"

"Because he didn't know me, either, so he has no reason to trust me now. But you saw him again. On the street the other night, and that's part of the problem, right?"

She licked her stir stick absently.

The tremors rocked through his body again.

Business. He was a professional. A professional ghost buster, some mocked, but still a professional.

Never mix business and pleasure. Never. Not in this. Not in matters of life and death. Not when there was the least chance it could weaken the perception or the wits...

"I saw him, yes," she murmured. Then she stared at him with her huge eyes pleading. "They must have made a mistake. He isn't dead. It's someone else—"

"No."

She exhaled.

"And you know," he added, "that Andy is dead, as well."

She looked at him, smiling sadly. "Yes, Andy is dead."

"But you keep seeing her."

"Yes," she murmured, looking down, then quickly back up. "She even changed clothes. From the T-shirt she was wearing when...to the suit I chose for her funeral."

"She's here to help you, you know," he said softly.

"Help me? So far, my friends think I'm nuts, and I nearly alienated a woman on the tour tonight."

He smiled ruefully. "It can be difficult, to say the least."

She twirled her swizzle stick in her now-empty mug. "Maybe I do need a drink," she said. "No, no, I'll start seeing polka-dotted elephants or something."

"Another latte?" he suggested.

She looked at him suddenly, aqua eyes assessing. "You're telling me that I have a special gift—something like an artist or a musician has. And it's been drawn out because Andy wants to help me. And you—whoever you are—have the same gift. And I'm not insane."

"Yes."

"And other people have this gift, as well?"

"Yes."

"Why haven't I ever heard of it?"

He shrugged, hands lifting. He was careful not to touch her. The scent of her perfume was so subtle. Like the whisper of her movement, the touch of her breath.

"Surely you've read stories about…well, hauntings. Usually written by people on the periphery. Those who have a touch of something on a different level than most people even experience. Those who have to become deeply involved…well, they're usually fairly circumspect about the whole thing."

"Um, sure," she murmured.

"I need your help," he repeated.

She sighed, staring at him intently again.

"And you need mine."

"Just…just exactly what do you want from me?"

"I need to get to know your ghosts," he said flatly.

"Can't you…just walk up and introduce yourself?" she asked, half laughing. Her laughter faded uneasily.

"They don't know me. They don't trust me."

"Andy would have loved you," she murmured. She shook her head. "Exactly how do I introduce you to my ghosts? I never actually had a conversation with your dead agent. I saw him at Madame's—either dead or alive—and again in the street when he was definitely… dead. And as to Andy…I never actually know when I'm going to see her."

"We can look for her. Together," he said. "If she knows that you trust me, maybe she'll trust me, as well."

"I don't know that I do trust you," she said.

"I think you do," he chanced.

That brought an uneasy flush to her cheeks.

She stood. He thought she intended to run.

"I don't need more coffee, and I don't need a drink. Walk me home," she said.

"Of course," he told her.

Julian was definitely nervous about Nikki going off with the stranger. Not that he controlled Nikki's social life, but something about the man bothered him.

And Nikki wasn't in her right mind. Not since Andy's death.

When they had walked away, he'd watched uneasily.

Paced in front of Madame's.

Then Madame herself had come out. "What's going on?" she asked.

"Um…Nikki…uh, kind of has a date," he told her.

"I see," she murmured, staring down the street. She was silent for a minute. "I don't think Nikki should have a date right now, do you?"

"I can't tell Nikki what to do," he said.

"You might have discouraged her."

"I tried."

"So…she's seeing ghosts, huh?"

"She's really upset about Andy."

"Of course." Madame studied him. "Do you know the guy?"

"Kind of. We met him the other night, then saw him at the police station."

"Cops have been known to be…"

"Be what?" Julian demanded.

"Dirty," Madame said softly.

"Think I should follow them?" Julian asked.

"Yeah."

Julian stared at Madame, then sped off after Nikki and Blackhawk.

He didn't like it. He didn't like any of it. The strange guy…the talk of ghosts. It was far too unnerving.

It wasn't healthy. Not for anyone.

Especially Nikki.

"This is a great apartment," Brent Blackhawk said, eyeing the place from the porch.

"I know. I love it," Nikki said. They stood awkwardly before the door for several seconds.

"I'll wait until you're in and the place is locked up," he told her.

She felt the breeze brush by her hair. The light scent of whatever cologne he wore drifted along with it. The solidity of his presence was ridiculously reassuring.

And frightening. She didn't really know him. He was definitely beyond the ordinary. She wondered idly what this moment would have been like if they'd been on a date. She'd always had her personal set of rules. A first date was a get to know you, and that was that. She was a big fan of *Sex and the City*, had all the episodes on tape, but that wasn't her lifestyle. In everything, personal and business, she had a tendency to be slow and careful.

But if it *had* been a date…

Her heart was racing as if this was the moment for a first kiss. The whisper of the breeze was perfect, seeming to urge her to step closer. Revel in the feel of his skin. The heat of his body. She was almost tempted to tilt her chin, close her eyes, smile, part her lips…wait.

Except, of course, it hadn't been a date.

Even so, her pulse was erratic, and she wondered how he would look without his shirt, how it would feel to just lie against him.

Her mind took things even further. She was sure he would be an aggressive lover, but a good one. Tender at times, but passionate. He would know his way around a woman's body. He would…

She took an instant step back, praying he couldn't really read minds.

"Um…we didn't really finish talking. You're…welcome to come in. I'm sorry, I just didn't want to sit in a bar anymore. My sanity is a little fragile at the moment, you know."

To her surprise, he hesitated.

"Nikki, I don't want to force anything on you."

Force? She was ready to…

"I need you to trust me, to believe in me. And if that means I should walk away now, that's what I intend to do."

This was all business, she reminded herself. He saw ghosts, she saw ghosts. They were like detectives, comparing notes. Not potential lovers.

"Well," she said, and managed an awkward half smile, "I can go inside and lock up, but that doesn't do much against ghosts, does it?"

"It will do a lot against real-live killers, who apparently got hold of both your friend and a government agent."

"Yes, I definitely have to be careful," she assured him. "Julian has been great, staying here with me a lot."

"Julian," he repeated.

"So are you coming in?"

He didn't reply.

She was both exasperated and a little offended. "You can check out the place for the undead as well as the living criminal element."

God, she loved his smile. Loved the way it softened the hard contours of his features. The light in his eyes, the slightly wicked curve of his lips…she loved it all. *Too fast.* She didn't know him.

She realized she was holding her breath. Because she was willing to take her chances. Right when the world was the most dangerous she'd ever known it to be. Right when she shouldn't.

"Please, I'd appreciate it if you would come in. I know there are living criminals in this city, but at this particular moment, it's those who aren't living who frighten me the most."

"Miss DuMonde, I would be delighted to come in," he informed her.

She turned away quickly, alarmed to realize that she was trembling.

She fitted the key in the lock, and he followed her in, surveying the downstairs.

"Living area downstairs, bedrooms up?" he inquired.

She arched a brow. "You didn't know that?" she asked.

He shook his head, smiling. "I'm not a psychic."

"No," she said. "You just talk to ghosts."

He didn't reply, as he made note of the art she had on the walls. Most of it was local. Scenes of the streets, the river, the people. She liked to buy from the local artists. A few pieces were of scenes from around the country, and she had a set of watercolors of Florence.

There was one oil of St. Louis Number 1 that he especially liked. It had captured both the beauty of the architecture and the decay. A young woman, head bent, was touching a tomb with a winged angel. The painting seemed to evoke the line between life and death, and it held a sense of mystery and possibility, as well.

"You know the artist?" he asked, coming closer to it.

"No," she said. "I think she was a grad student at Tulane. I bought it near Jackson Square."

"Nice," he said.

"Thanks. I love it. She captured something… It sounds strange to say it, but there's an aura about that picture. Maybe that's not so strange to say to you. I didn't mean that offensively," she added. Lord, this was strange. She couldn't speak normally or casually. When had things changed between them? There had been something about him from the beginning, but she had probably been smarter when she had been angry, and when she had wanted him to stay as far away from her as possible.

He laughed. "There *is* an aura to that painting," he assured her. "Whether you see ghosts or not. That's what creates art, don't you think? Not so much the perfect reproduction of a face or an object, but infusing the subject with emotion or warmth or something special."

"Yes…I guess you're right. But then again, we all see different things, don't we?"

"Absolutely. I have one friend who has a huge painting of dogs in a bar. He thinks it's one of the most underrated masterpieces in the world. So, yeah, we all see different things."

She felt flushed. "Yeah, like dead people walking around." She winced. "I'll, uh, make tea. Do you like tea?"

He arched a brow. "Is there a reason I shouldn't like tea?"

"No." She winced again. "I…I guess I never knew what India—Native Americans drank." Oh, God, she was sounding worse and worse.

"You mean, besides firewater?" he queried.

"I—" She broke off, realizing that he was teasing her.

"I think there's actually more Irish in me than Lakota," he told her dryly, "so on the ethnic side, tea is cool. But for future reference, some of the Lakota I know love tea, some hate it. Matter of taste."

She forced a smile and a nod. She lived in one of the most mixed-race cities in the world. Her friends were white and black and every shade in between, gay and straight, Catholic, Jewish, voodoo and Wiccan. She'd never fumbled around like this before.

He was staring at her, smiling. She was staring at him, feeling like an idiot who couldn't keep her foot out of her mouth.

She waved a hand toward the kitchen. "I'll go boil water."

"Thanks."

In the kitchen, she felt the first sense of unease. Everything was as she had left it. Counters neat, wiped down, coffeepot…

Just a little different. Out farther, closer to the edge of the counter than she usually left it.

Or was she just…searching for something to wonder about, to see differently?

She began opening cabinets and drawers. The silver set was exactly where and how it should be, in the farthest left drawer. Through the glass panes of the cabinets, she could see her good china, none of it moved in the least. She gave herself a shake. No one broke into an apartment to move a coffeepot out a few inches. The kettle was on the stove, just as she'd left it.

She set the water on to boil and kept looking around. Nothing was out of order.

When she returned to the living room, Brent was still looking around at the art, yet not really seeming to focus on anything.

"She's definitely not here right now, is she?" he asked.

Nikki had carried in a tray with cups, the teapot, milk, sugar and lemon, not knowing how he drank his tea.

It began to rattle in her hands.

"She?" she said, but she knew exactly who he was talking about.

"Andy."

He took the tray from her, setting it on the coffee table between the sofa and the love seat, and sitting down himself on the latter.

Nikki shook her head solemnly. "No."

She sat, as well, and reached for the teapot, ready to do the whole hostess thing, but he said simply, "I'll pour, okay?"

She nodded, too inexplicably nervous to speak.

"She doesn't come every night, does she?" he asked, his words casual as he poured. Nikki added milk and a scoop of sugar to her cup.

He drank his plain, she noted.

"Nikki?" he persisted. "She doesn't come every night, does she?"

"No, she doesn't come every night." She hesitated, taking a long sip of tea. "I'd probably be locked up by now if she did. Maybe she knows that."

"Maybe she does. I'm sure she's not trying to hurt you. In fact, I'm certain she's trying to help you."

Nikki shivered. His knee was brushing hers. Their faces were close. Here she was. She'd met the most attractive man she'd so much as seen in…forever. He was in her apartment. They were touching. Their faces were so close that she could see the flecks of darker emerald in his eyes. Almost feel the texture of his skin. His warmth seemed to reach out and embrace her.

And they were talking about ghosts. Matter-of-factly.

"If she's trying to help," she heard herself say too sharply, "why doesn't she just appear to Massey or Joulette and tell them who killed her?"

"She probably doesn't know."

"How could she not know?"

"She might have been attacked in the dark or when she was sleeping, so she never saw anything. But she knows, or senses, that you might be in danger, as well," he told her. "I need to speak with her. She isn't going to acknowledge me or let me get close to her unless she realizes that I'm trying to help, as well."

Goose bumps broke out on her arms. "Okay, so what about the FBI agent?" she asked. "I never knew him. Why am I seeing him?"

He shook his head. "I don't know. That's something else I need to find out."

Nikki cleared her throat. "Please tell me that..."

"That what?"

"That I'm not going to start seeing dead people wherever I go," she whispered.

"Trust in this, Nikki," he told her softly. "You're seeing them for a good reason, and they want to help you."

She sipped her tea again. "A good reason. My best friend is making me see a shrink. All my friends are tiptoeing around me as if I've got a disease. And it's going to get worse. Julian thought he could shock me out of it, so he announced to Madame that I'm seeing ghosts. So now she's worried, too. As for Massey and Joulette, they think I'm off-the-charts nuts."

"They think I'm pretty far gone, too," he assured her.

"Does that bother you?"

"Only if it hinders what I'm doing. Luckily, I don't seem to be as big a pain in the butt as their main FBI liaison. Quite frankly, he does seem to be a pompous ass. But that's working in my favor right now."

Nikki realized that she was still covered in goose bumps.

And she was afraid. Afraid as she had never been before.

She didn't know what she was up to herself when she then said, "Andy shows up in the middle of the night sometimes."

"Yeah?"

"I fall asleep with the TV on. She always liked television."

"She's watching over you."

The words tumbled out of her mouth then in a rush. "I have a guest room. If you really want a chance to meet Andy, you can stay in it, and if she appears…I can call you. I can tell her about you, and you can meet her right there and then." Oh, God! Her words sounded really and truly insane.

"I told you, I don't want to push things with you," he said very gently. "I want you to know me and trust me."

"Dammit," she said, standing. "You want me to know you and trust you. Well, so far, you've managed to scare me half out of my wits. What do you want, an engraved invitation? There's a guest room upstairs. Since I'm now afraid of my own shadow, I would deeply appreciate it if you would sleep there."

She watched his slow smile appear, that smile that changed his face from hard as rock to something that was entirely beguiling.

"Well, all right. If you put it that way…"

She turned away, shaking, afraid of saying even more. The next thing, she would be begging him to stay in her room, to sleep with her…to hold her.

"Are ghosts mischievous?" she asked him.

"How do you mean?"

"Do they play tricks? Move things?"

He shrugged, hesitating. Then he asked, "You mean…like poltergeists?"

"I guess."

"Why?"

"I'm just curious."

Again he hesitated, then said, "I don't have all the answers. Have I seen ghosts move things? Yes. There's one old guy in St. Louis Number 1 who likes to throw pebbles and things at vandals who sneak over the walls. He's very protective. But…okay, there are young ghosts and old ghosts. And moving things takes trial and error and experience. Even materializing when they want to can be difficult, especially at first. When they're frightened, it's almost impossible for them."

"How can a ghost be frightened?" she demanded.

"Okay, let's forget that most people think you're insane if you see ghosts. Now think of what a ghost would be. Made up of heart and soul and personality. If the person that they were could be frightened, so can their ghost. Especially a young ghost. Anything the person could feel, their ghost can feel."

She knew she was looking at him as if he were completely insane.

She lowered her head. "Could Andy have moved my coffeepot?" she asked him.

His brows shot up. Then he looked downward, playing with his teacup, a slight smile tugging at his lips. "Your coffeepot moved? You're certain?"

"Well, no. Not certain."

He looked straight at her then. "Perhaps you want to

look around your house. Find out if anything is missing. Is everything as it should be…here?"

She looked around the living room. "Seems to be."

"Want to check out the upstairs?"

She nodded.

He followed her.

He hovered in her bedroom doorway as she looked into her jewelry cases, drawers and closet.

"Anything?"

She shook her head. "I really am losing my mind," she said.

"No you're not," he promised gently.

"The guest room is next," she said.

But there seemed to be nothing out of the ordinary there, either. She let out a soft sigh. "I guess I just left the pot out farther than usual," she told him with a shrug.

"It's always safer to check things out," he told her simply.

"Well, then, I'll secure the balcony doors in my room, if you wouldn't mind checking out the rest of the place…?"

"Not at all."

Back in her room, she made sure that the balcony doors were locked and secure. They hadn't been left open, she noted.

"All locked up," Brent called to her from the hallway.

"Thanks."

"You're all right?"

"Absolutely. Um…you should be comfortable, I hope. Good night."

"Good night. And don't worry. I'm here. Just call out if anything frightens you in any way. Any way at all."

"Right. Thanks again. Good night."

She closed her own door but didn't lock it. Then she went through her bedtime ritual—brushing her teeth, washing her face, changing clothes—by rote.

In the bathroom, she hesitated again. In the cabinet above the sink, it seemed that one of the large bottles of her favorite perfume—a Christmas gift from Patricia—had been moved just slightly, too. It was a wee bit too close to the edge of the shelf.

It was ridiculous, she told herself. She could be too organized—she knew that. But, especially now, there was no reason to believe she was putting things back exactly as they had been. She had used the perfume that morning. Just as she had used the coffeepot that morning. She just hadn't been as precise as usual when she put them back.

Still…

It disturbed her.

Everything was disturbing her, she thought; she was undoubtedly making mountains out of molehills. She would start to see something evil in every face on the street soon if she didn't get a handle on her emotions.

With that she determined she was going to bed.

She lay down, certain she would never get to sleep.

Her things had been moved.

That was ridiculous. No one broke into an apartment to shift around a coffeepot and a perfume bottle.

Maybe it had been Andy. Whether she was a young ghost or not.

And maybe she was really nuts right now.

Sleep. She needed sleep.

No, she would never be able to sleep.

And yet…

Her eyes were closing, and she was definitely in a comfortable drowsy state. She'd invited a near stranger to stay in her house. But because he was there, she felt safe. Safe and secure as she hadn't since…

Since Andy.

She closed her eyes.

And the next thing she knew, it was morning.

10

Patricia woke early and was annoyed with herself. She hated it when she awoke before her alarm rang. Their nights could run late, and she treasured her sleep in the morning.

The room was still dark. There was nothing to have awakened her.

At her side, Nathan still slept soundly. She was glad of him being there.

Things had been perfect, in her job and her life, until…

Until Andy had died.

She felt a little shiver of fear, and a rush of empathy for Andy swept through her. She hadn't known her that well, but that didn't really matter—she *had* known her, and what had happened to her had been terrible. No, terrible wasn't nearly adequate to describe the fact that a gorgeous, vivacious young woman with everything in the world to live for was gone.

By her own hand? Or, as Nikki seemed to believe, with the help of another?

Had Andy fallen back into her old ways?

Or had she really been a victim?

Had she known her fate? Had she been terrified? Had she fought, then lost her fight?

Patricia swallowed, glancing to her side again. Nathan's dark hair was just discernible against the pillow in the pale light that filtered into the room. She heard his even breathing.

With Nikki being so insistent, the police had been forced to give Andy's case serious thought. But they had nothing. Detective Massey had been honest with them about that.

If Andy had been attacked, no one had heard anything. But then again, who had been around to hear? Just poor old deaf Mrs. Montobello?

Patricia wished suddenly and desperately that they'd never met Andy Ciello. Whatever happened to her must have happened because of her past.

Maybe not. Maybe she had been the random victim of a psychopath.

One who didn't leave behind a fingerprint, a fiber or a hair.

No, psychopaths didn't run around making it appear that someone had died from a drug overdose.

"Hey there."

She nearly hit the ceiling, the sound of Nathan's voice was so startling.

"Oh, jeez!" she gasped out.

"Patricia, what's the matter with you?" he demanded, slipping an arm around her. "You're cold as ice and shaking like a leaf."

"You startled me."

"How could I startle you? I've been here all night."

Been here all night.

Nathan. She had fallen into lust with him first—he'd walked her home after one of their tours, and somehow they'd looked at each other and started stripping themselves and each other—and only later had she discovered just how head over heels she was with him.

She was grateful that they'd discovered their passion for one another. She wasn't alone now.

Wasn't alone.

But that night…

The night Andy had died…

They'd all been out together, drinking. Too much. She and Nathan had gone home together. And in the middle of the night, she'd gotten up for aspirin. Staggered into the bathroom and back, falling down onto the sheets. And there had been something, something not quite right….

The bed had been…

Empty.

Or had it?

She didn't really know. She'd had too much to drink, and she'd been exhausted. She'd gone back to bed, thinking something was ever so slightly wrong, nothing warm touching her, but she'd crashed out again, and when she had awakened, he'd been next to her, just as if he had been there all night, and she figured she had just imagined in her silly drunken stupor that she had been alone.

"I was just…thinking about poor Andy," she whispered.

He drew her close. His arms felt warm and sure and strong.

"We can't spend our lives dwelling on what happened to her," he told her quietly.

"I know. But it isn't easy to forget."

"Of course not. And we'd be terrible human beings if it didn't cut to the core."

He was so serious, so caring.

"I feel so sorry for her."

"It's over now. No one can hurt her again. She's gone and in God's hands."

"Do you believe that? Really believe that?"

"Do I believe in God? Yes. And that after death, we can't be hurt anymore? Yes." She couldn't see his face clearly, but the rich tone of his voice was reassuring. He sighed softly, smoothing back her hair. "Patricia, you should think of Andy now as being in heaven, looking after us."

He pulled her close then, spooning himself around her. For a second, a fleeting second, she longed to break free.

"It's going to take all of us time to get over it," he murmured. Then he yawned. "Especially Nikki. She still doesn't look..."

"Good?" Patricia suggested.

He was quiet for a minute. "Sane," he said. He pulled her closer against his body. "We've all gotta keep an eye on her."

"Uh-huh," Patricia murmured.

"If she acts too strange around you, tell me, huh?"

Patricia inched away a bit. "What do you mean, too strange?"

"You know. Strange."

"Well, of course, I—"

"Shh…"

His hand crept from its gentle hold around her midriff so that his finger rested against her lips. "No more for now. We've got to move on now."

"I can't help but think—"

"I'll stop you thinking," he murmured.

He rolled her around so that she faced him. He didn't bring his lips against her mouth, but straight against her throat. He allowed his tongue a slow easy slide down to her rib cage.

"Nathan, I…"

"We're alive," he said, his voice muffled against her flesh. "And we're going to keep on living."

"Nathan…"

No slow teasing. Nathan slid his length down against her, lips going straight between her thighs, startling, forceful, sensuous.

She swallowed, felt instant arousal shooting through her. Her fingers tore into his hair; his hands lifted her higher still.

"Nathan…just do…"

"Just do what?"

"Me."

Another day.

Owen Massey lay in bed, staring at the dust motes that played in the air. He'd left the drapes an inch open;

the morning light showed the shabbiness of his little house out on I–10.

He might work the Quarter, but he couldn't afford to live in it.

"Yeah, another day," he muttered.

After a moment, he rolled over, crawled out of bed. He could hear the wheeze and whine of his old air-conditioning system. It could wheeze and whine as much as it wanted, just so long as it didn't break down. The summer heat was coming on. Killer heat. That was what they called it.

People snapped when it was too hot. But when someone just snapped, there were usually witnesses.

No cover-up.

Another day.

He walked into the kitchen, glad he'd invested in a good coffeemaker. Every day, at six forty-five, it automatically started brewing his coffee. Every day, when he came out at seven o'clock, it was ready for him.

He poured a cup, found his cigarettes—a no-no in the department, even in New Orleans, these days. But this was his house. Shabby it might be, but he owned it. He lit his cigarette. "So there," he said to no one and everyone.

Another day. Another stinking hot day.

No matter how someone had wanted it to appear, the death of Andrea Ciello had not been an accident. His gut agreed with Blackhawk. The man had made him feel like an idiot. Two people dead, the same way. Joulette would realize the truth of it soon enough.

Another day.

Massey rubbed his eyes. Another day of staring at what they had. Of trying desperately to find another angle. Not that the FBI were doing any better with the death of one of their own. Something had to break soon. A straight-as-an-arrow guy, suddenly dead of an overdose. No fingerprints found but his own. A girl—albeit a onetime junkie—dead the same way. Not a hair, not a fiber…no psychotic was that organized.

Everyone going in circles.

Except for the ghost guy.

The one person who'd seen clearly from the get-go that the two crimes were related.

Hell!

Massey crushed out his cigarette and rose, standing in front of the wheezing air conditioner and letting the cooling draft wash over him.

Just how much could the ghost guy see?

It seemed like a good morning.

Nikki didn't remember when she had slept so well, though when she awoke she had to wonder if she was really in her right mind, having asked a stranger to spend the night.

But sleeping so well had been wonderful. Now, aware of her physical attraction to the man, she showered, dressed and did her makeup before leaving her room, even to put the coffee on.

But she needn't have worried about the coffee. Her guest had started the pot.

She poured a cup and found him out in the courtyard.

"Good morning," she said.

"Good morning." Those eyes of his were instantly on her. She decided to get a firm grip on the physical-attraction thing, she thought. He studied her gravely, as if he were a zoologist and she were a rare species—but nothing else. And yet…

There was something going on. She liked the feeling of being with him, of having him near her.

"Sleep well?" he asked.

"Perfectly. You? Julian complains about the bed in there all the time."

He arched a brow. "It's not so bad." He sipped the coffee he had fixed himself. Then she wondered if there wasn't just the slightest change in his eyes as he frowned. "So Julian…is he gay?"

She shook her head, smiling. It was strange that people either made the assumption that there was something between them or else Julian had to be gay.

"No."

"Oh."

She laughed aloud then and realized that the sound was good. "Sleeping with Julian would be like sleeping with my brother. It's as simple as that. I've heard that it's impossible for a man and woman to be friends without one of them wanting more, but we really are just friends, and always have been."

"I see."

She wondered exactly how much he saw.

"Tell me about the people who work with you," he said. "And who the hell is Max, and where is he in all this?"

"Max has money and bankrolled the business. He's

also a genius when it comes to delegating work. He has me, so he can travel. I don't know where he is right now. Colorado or someplace. And the others…tell you what about them?"

"You know. Who they are, how you met them, what their relationships are with one another, how long you've known them…all that."

She wasn't sure why, but she was instantly on the defensive. "You're asking because of Andy?" she said.

"I'm asking because I'm trying to get a better picture of the situation."

"They're nice people, all of them," she said angrily.

"I'm not saying they're not," he told her, green eyes on her. "I'm just trying to get a sense of things."

"I thought you were supposed to be helping with the murder of the FBI agent," she said sharply.

"I am. But I'm convinced that Andrea Ciello was a murder victim, and that the murders are related. Otherwise, I can't begin to imagine why you keep seeing the both of them. Not to mention the obvious. Two overdoses. Heroin. Needle marks in the same place in the arm."

"But Andy used to be a junkie."

"Doesn't matter. You know she didn't do it to herself."

"Maybe I'm insane. Dealing with delusions because of misplaced guilt. And maybe you're in an even worse delusional state. Totally out of your mind," she informed him. He didn't rise to anger; he just kept looking at her with those eyes that seemed far too wise and compelling.

She looked away. He'd made her angry, but that only increased her urge to touch him, which made her angrier still.

"You want to know my tour guides? Let's head over to Madame's."

"Madame D'Orso's? That's where you first saw Garfield."

"I thought he was a bum."

He made a face. "I need to, uh, shower and change. I'll have to head back to my bed-and-breakfast first."

"Why don't you just shower and change here? Julian has some clothes in the closet, and you're about the same size."

"I hate to take his things."

"He won't mind. It's fine."

He hesitated. She was still feeling the tension of anger, but she didn't want him leaving, no matter how much he got to her.

"Really. He's a nice guy, and he dresses well. I'm sure you'll find something."

He lifted his hands, then let them fall to his sides. "All right."

Nikki decided not to go in with him; he could fend for himself. She had to keep some distance. She barely knew him, despite the fact she'd invited him to sleep at her house. She was sure that this pathetic urge to throw herself at the man had to be some strange psychosis seizing her because of what had happened.

And it wasn't as if he had attempted to knock down her door last night. As far as she knew, she thought dryly, he hadn't come near it.

"Go ahead, shower, take what you need. I'll be out here."

"All right," he said, still looking at her strangely.

"What?"

"Nothing, sorry. I'll get ready."

She nodded.

A few minutes later he came back down, smelling of soap and shampoo and faintly of aftershave, and appearing even more attractive in his slightly damp state.

"Lock up," he told her gravely.

"Of course."

The café was busy, but Madame greeted Nikki with her customary friendliness, despite the line that stretched along the counter.

"Nikki, good morning, you're the first to arrive. Just take your usual table." She smiled at Brent. "Hi, I don't think we've been properly introduced. I'm Madame D'Orso. Everyone just calls me Madame," she said, a slight smile curving her lips.

"She's really a Yankee," Nikki whispered in a teasing aside.

Madame rolled her eyes. "That's hush-hush," she said. "Are you going to be hiring this guy?" she asked Nikki.

Brent cocked his head slightly, studying Nikki. She realized that the idea had already occurred to him as a way of staying on the scene, though it hadn't crossed her mind.

"Oh…well," Nikki said, staring at Brent. "Max makes everyone pass a test first, you know."

"I'm willing to bet I can pass any test on New Orleans you throw my way," he told her.

"We'll see about that," she said.

Patricia and Nathan had come in, and were at the end of the line.

"You two just go sit," Madame called to them. "I'll see to it that one of the boys brings out coffee, beignets and some juice, how's that?" she asked Nikki.

"You're too good to us," Nikki said.

"Tourists," Patricia grumbled, shaking her head as she had to navigate a group of them on her way to the table just off the street. Despite the heat of the sun, Madame's sidewalk café area was cool and comfortable. She had artistic little fans going and a striped canvas overhang that kept out the most rays of the sun.

"May I remind you to be nice to tourists? We survive off them," Nikki said.

But Patricia wasn't listening. She was looking at Brent Blackhawk. "Hi," she said with a flirty smile.

"Yeah, hi," Nathan said, coming up behind her and studying Blackhawk. "I'm Nathan, and this is Patricia."

"Nice to meet you," Brent said, and introduced himself.

Patricia cast a curious glance Nikki's way as she asked him, "Are you coming on as a tour guide?" she asked.

"I'm applying for a position," he said.

"That was fast," Nathan told Nikki. He was doing his best to sound pleasant, but he, too, had a slight accusatory note in his tone.

Julian made an appearance then, coming up to the table on the terrace. "Brent. Joining us again?"

"You two know each other?" Patricia asked.

"We've met a couple of times," Brent explained. "And I think I'd make a good addition to your group here—at least as a temporary fill-in," he finished.

Patricia looked at Julian, who was frowning as he looked at Brent.

"I have a shirt just like that," he said.

"This *is* your shirt," Brent said. "Nikki convinced me you wouldn't mind if I borrowed it."

They all stared at her then. She felt herself blush, because she knew exactly what they were thinking.

"Julian, I really didn't think that you'd mind."

"Hey…" Julian said, lifting his hands.

A little smile curved Patricia's lips. "Oh," she murmured knowingly. "I see."

"Brent is a friend," Nikki said.

"A *new* friend," Julian said.

"Oh?" Nathan murmured.

"Hey, there's Mitch," Nikki said. She waved to attract his attention.

Mitch walked over to them, staring curiously at Brent as he came. "Hi."

"Brent is Nikki's new friend," Patricia said after more introductions had been made.

"Julian's met him before, too," Nathan said, frowning at Julian.

"There was a little fracas the other night," Nikki said, "and Brent stepped in on our side." She glared at Julian, the look in her eyes warning him not to open his mouth about her visions of ghosts, or the fact that they had officially met Brent at the police station.

"How nice," Patricia said. "I mean, not that there was a fracas."

Julian waved a hand dismissively. "A bunch of drunk college kids." He added, a bit grudgingly, Nikki thought, "It was a good thing Brent happened on us."

Nikki smiled, slipping her hand around Julian's arm. "Julian stuck his neck out, defending my honor."

"Bravo," Patricia said. "Drunk teenagers on the streets of New Orleans. Imagine," she added jokingly.

"Yeah," Julian muttered. He offered Nikki a perfunctory smile. "And now Brent's one of us. Wearing my shirt."

Just then Madame herself appeared, carrying a massive tray with a dexterity few people possessed. She set the tray down on their table.

"Madame, I'm sorry you had to come out here yourself with this. We could have stood in line," Nikki said apologetically.

Madame laughed, her eyes twinkling. "You're my steadiest group. If I can't take care of you, I shouldn't be in business." She plopped herself into one of the chairs and picked up a napkin to fan herself for a moment. "I declare, autumns are getting hotter and hotter."

"Brent is applying to be a guide," Nathan said to Madame, though his eyes remained on Brent, his look slightly suspicious. "He claims to know the area. And we do need a fill-in."

Madame nodded, still fanning herself, looking at Brent.

Nikki noted that everyone—including Madame—seemed wary of Brent. Fascinated by, but definitely wary of, him. Of course, he was a newcomer. Maybe he just didn't look like the kind of guy who'd be applying for something as simple as a job as a tour guide.

There was something about him that warned people that he was a no-nonsense man with steel in his backbone, no matter how pleasant his manner. Yeah, he would make a good cop. Or a spy, or an FBI agent. But he claimed to be none of the above.

No, he was a ghost hunter.

"So, young man, you know New Orleans?" Madame asked.

"Like the back of my hand," he said lightly.

"Right off the top of your head?" Julian persisted. "All about the city? Garden District? French Quarter? Pirates, French, British, Spanish…the Louisiana Purchase…'Beast' Butler, the Civil War? And, most importantly, our haunts?"

Brent laughed softly. "I can definitely deal with your haunts," he assured them, looking straight at Nikki.

"Impressive," Madame said, pouring coffee from the urn and passing it around. Finally she took a sip from the cup she had poured herself. "Have a beignet, young man. They're the best in the entire parish, if I do say so myself."

"You really think you have all that stuff down pat?" Mitch asked.

"Really," Brent said, nodding, sipping coffee, accepting a beignet.

"What did you two have planned for the afternoon?" Mitch asked Patricia and Nathan.

"Nothing important," Nathan said. "Not until it's time for our St. Louis No. 1 tour."

"And you?" Patricia asked Mitch

"What are you all getting at?" Nikki demanded.

"The Garden District tour this afternoon. It's scheduled to be you and Julian, but I think we can all hang around and give Brent here a chance to prove his stuff."

"Oh, no. You all did that on paper, remember?" Nikki said.

"But I don't think any one of us were as sure of ourselves as Brent," Patricia said, smiling.

Nikki suddenly realized that thc other men all wanted Brent to fall flat on his face. There was a little bit of a testosterone thing going around the table. Patricia seemed to be a bit in awe. Brent Blackhawk was definitely an imposing presence.

"That's not how we do this, putting someone on the spot," Nikki said uneasily.

"There, see?" Julian stated.

Apparently no one needed her approval anymore.

Brent was staring hard at Julian. "No problem," he said, taking another sip of coffee, his green eyes hard. "You're on."

11

"In New Orleans, you'll often see references to 'cities of the dead.' And I'm sure, as you walked through the gates to Lafayette Cemetery Number 1, you felt like you were entering a city, a city filled with structures representing an amazing range of architectural styles. The word *cemetery* actually comes from a Greek word meaning 'to put to sleep, or to lay to rest, a resting place.' We often see the words *Rest in Peace* etched on headstones, and that is what we pray for for those we lose, that they will rest in peace. In New Orleans, for many reasons, we let our dead rest in peace in magnificent structures that rival those we plan for the living."

Hanging at the rear of the group as Brent conducted the tour, Nikki glanced at Julian, who shrugged, lifting his hands with a we'll-have-to-see-how-he-finishes gesture.

"He looks good up there," Patricia whispered to her.

And he did.

As Nikki had known, Brent didn't disappear in any crowd. It wasn't just his height but his carriage that made him such an imposing figure.

"Let me say," Brent continued, "that a great deal of the history that makes New Orleans unique can be seen and felt as we wander here. Some call it the most northern of the Caribbean cities. Others consider it the most European of all American cities. This cemetery was established in 1833, created from plantation land that had been owned by the Livaudais family. By that time the city was already rich in French, Spanish and English culture, and others were pouring in, German, Irish and plain old mixed-American immigrants from the North. They all brought a sense of their pasts along with them, and combined that with the need to build aboveground here in this land where floods come all too often. Remember, we're not in the oldest cemetery—that's another tour. But besides the flooding, there were other factors to consider in building the many different kinds of tombs you'll see here. The concept of 'a year and a day' wasn't born because of water levels and heat—it goes all the way back to Judeo-Christian mourning rituals and the sense of what is proper. You'll often see many names on a tomb, and that is because, after a year and a day—if in so short a time burial space is needed again—the earthly remains of a loved one are separated from the coffin, which is discarded, and interred in the rear of the tomb or in a cache below. In death, many families are thus joined as one."

"Ugh," a pretty girl in the crowd said. "You mean… they pull the bodies out? Get rid of the coffin and mix them all up?"

"Ashes to ashes, dust to dust," another woman commented.

"Hey, you'd save big on people expecting you to buy a really expensive coffin," a heavyset man offered, obviously considering that a major plus.

"True," Brent told him. "But death is never cheap—we all know that."

"There's a fact," the big man said, and they moved on.

Brent pointed out the many different surnames etched on the tombs, then went into a speech about the epidemic that had gripped the city soon after the cemetery's establishment. After that he talked about the Civil War, pointing out a number of tombs where good Confederates had found their final resting places, and also those tombs where soldiers who had remained loyal to the Union had come home to rest.

At one point he talked about the fact that Lafayette Number 1 still served as a final resting place for many who passed away.

His eyes met Nikki's across the crowd, and she felt a warmth despite the sudden breeze that rose, ruffling her hair.

As if they had somehow forged a special bond, something beyond the fact that she still felt, far too frequently, the urge to throw herself into his arms.

For comfort, security…

For much, much more.

She turned away. His voice became a drone as she found herself hanging back.

Cities of the dead.

This particular city…

Rows and rows of mausoleums, some decayed, fantastic angels, sad as they lowered their heads in prayer.

Her own family's tomb.

A woman standing before it, head lowered.

She found herself slowly walking away from the group, toward the beautiful Grecian-style mausoleum where so many of her ancestors lay.

Mingled together now in death. Ashes to ashes. Dust to dust.

And a woman standing there, her back to Nikki.

Fear rose in Nikki's throat. She looked at the dark hair, the slump of the woman's shoulders.

She swallowed hard. "Andy?" she whispered.

The woman turned.

It wasn't Andy.

She smiled at Nikki. "Sorry, I'm Susan Marshall."

Nikki felt like a fool. "No, *I'm* sorry. I thought you were someone else. Excuse me."

"This is a gorgeous tomb."

"Thank you."

"It's yours?"

"It's my family's tomb."

"Wow. To know that you're a part of something so historic, it must be wonderful," Susan Marshall said. She shivered then. "I mean…a little creepy, but still cool," she said, smiling.

Nikki almost screamed when hands fell on her shoulders. She gulped back the sound and turned to see Julian standing behind her.

"You scared me to death," she said accusingly.

"I was worried about you—you suddenly disappeared," he said, scowling.

"This is Susan Marshall," she said quickly, to distract him.

"Hi," Julian said, offering a hand and introducing himself. Nikki suddenly realized that Susan was very attractive.

"You're here by yourself?" he asked Susan.

"I understand it's safe here in the Garden District," Susan said.

"It's safer in a group. Why don't you join the tour?" he suggested.

"Oh, well, I couldn't do that, I didn't pay—"

"We're more than halfway through. Please, just join us," Nikki said. She glanced at Julian. He hardly seemed to notice she was there. All his attention was on Susan.

"Please, join us?" he said.

"If you're sure…"

"Absolutely," Julian said.

Nikki trailed slightly behind them. She was startled when she heard a rumbling in the sky. Looking up, she saw that the storm clouds were gathering.

"Good thing we're more than halfway through," she murmured.

Neither one of them even seemed to hear her.

They caught up to the rear of the tour. Mitch flashed Nikki a questioning smile, and she flashed a reassuring smile back.

The rain hadn't begun, but the sky was darkening. Nikki didn't think that it made scientific sense, but a mist was beginning to rise from the ground, which shouldn't have happened until rain actually fell and the heat of the ground turned water to vapor.

"What a day for this tour, huh?" Nathan, an arm around Patricia, whispered to Nikki. "Even the weather complies to make him look good. He really is good, Nikki. The guy has come up with bits of history I didn't know myself!"

"I think he's terrific," Patricia said.

Nathan gave her a little shake. "Quit looking at the guy's butt, huh?"

"I am not looking at his butt," Patricia protested, giggling. "Honestly, though, he really knows this place."

"Snap him up for Max before he applies to one of the other companies," Mitch suggested.

The mist seemed to sweep around Nikki. She found herself suddenly tempted to look back, but like Lot's wife, she was afraid that she would turn to salt if she did.

Yet...something beckoned.

She stood stiffly, refusing to give in to the inclination.

The others moved ahead, but she remained where she was, afraid to so much as breathe.

At last she gritted her teeth and turned.

The mist seemed to whirl along the path back toward her family mausoleum. Ghostlike in every way, haunting, mysterious, beckoning her to that place between light and darkness, life and death...

But there was nothing there.

No sign of Andy.

She turned back.

And jumped, a scream rising in her throat.

Andy was there. Just in front of her. Hovering away

from the rest of the crowd, surrounded by the whirling gray mist…

She turned back, looked at Nikki.

Nikki shook her head. "No, no, no…please don't be there," she whispered. She needed to get Brent's attention.

He was far ahead, listening gravely to a young brunette's question as they stood next to one of the society tombs.

"Andy, go away," she pleaded, closing her eyes.

She felt something, someone, coming closer.

Felt breath against her cheek.

She opened her eyes.

Julian. He had left Susan's side and was staring at her, frowning in concern. "Who are you talking to?" he demanded.

Nikki looked past him.

Andy was gone, as if she'd disappeared into the mist.

"I'm not talking to anyone," she lied.

"Nikki, you were just—"

"I stubbed my toe," she muttered, and, brushing past him, hurried to stand at the front of the crowd.

Brent's eyes met hers, and he frowned.

She forced a smile. Andy was gone. There was no sense in interrupting now to tell him that she had seen her friend.

Not now, in a cemetery, with a strange mist rising when it wasn't even two o'clock in the afternoon.

"Wow," Mitch said, congratulating Brent.

"I will have to admit, you've pretty much shown us up," Julian had the grace to agree.

"How do you know so much?" Nathan demanded.

Brent gazed at Nikki as he replied, "I was born here."

"But you're an Indian," Patricia interjected, then reddened, realizing how politically incorrect she had been. "I'm sorry…Native American."

He laughed. "Partly. Part Irish. And my grandfather's wife was actually of Nordic extraction. My father and mother happened to meet and marry in New Orleans, so even though we traveled a lot, I basically grew up here."

"You feel like conducting the St. Louis Number 1?" Mitch asked.

Nikki was being silent, and her silence disturbed Brent. He held still for a minute, letting the breeze whisper around him. It was getting late for whoever was going to meet the group at the other cemetery.

He didn't mind doing the St. Louis tour—though Huey might be a bit disconcerted to see him—but Nikki's continuing silence disturbed him. She was smiling, but it was a forced smile.

She had seen Andy, he thought.

A flare not so much of anger but futility swept through him. She hadn't told him.

He should have felt Andy's presence. He had known that at least a dozen other haunts had been following the tour that day, intrigued. None that he knew, though, and none that could have been Andrea Ciello. She had no intention of making herself known to strangers.

He wanted to shake Nikki and tell her that she had to help him. He took a deep breath.

"Hey, where'd your new girlfriend go?" Patricia suddenly teased Julian.

"She had an appointment to meet her sister," Julian explained.

"That's what they all tell me, too," Mitch said with a sigh.

"I have her phone number," Julian told him, shaking his head.

"Hey, love and games later," Patricia said, glancing at her watch. "Time for St. Louis Number 1, guys."

"So will you lead that one?" Mitch asked.

"If it's all right with Nikki."

She shrugged. "Sure. The rest of you can follow Brent around."

He was thinking of a way to protest, when Patricia beat him to it. "Oh no. You're the one who talks to the boss. You know damn well that if you say to hire him, that's exactly what Max will do."

Nikki shrugged. "Max isn't here, and we need to fill the slot. So Brent gets the job," she said simply.

"Then let's head out," Mitch said. "I've got the van. I'll drop you in front of Madame's to greet the hordes."

"All right," Brent said.

"We'd better hurry before our group thinks they're not going to have a guide," Patricia said.

"I'm sure Madame is watching out for our interests," Julian said. "But yeah, let's get going."

Brent had no chance to talk to Nikki in the van; they were pretty much packed in like sardines. But when they piled out at Madame's, Nikki seemed to have regained her composure. "Nice job," she said to Brent, her aquamarine eyes guileless. She even offered him a smile.

"Thanks."

Julian moved ahead, announcing that they were ready for anyone interested in the St. Louis Number 1 tour.

Nikki started to follow the others, but Brent caught her arm. "You saw her, didn't you?"

She looked at his hand on her arm, then into his eyes. "No."

"Why are you lying to me?"

"I'm not."

"You are."

She let out a sigh. "Okay…I might have seen her. But so briefly, I'm not even sure."

"You've got to tell me when she's there."

"Look, I just told you, I wasn't sure. And you were giving the tour, you were busy. And you're hurting my arm."

He instantly released her. "Nikki, please—" he began.

"And this," Julian was announcing, "is Brent, your guide through the streets down to the cemetery, and to the fascinating history and lore of the oldest of the cities of the dead."

Brent stepped forward to lead the crowd of tourists: couples, families, a few loners, teens, one pair of silver-haired octogenarians, both with sparkling powder-blue eyes.

"Good afternoon, and welcome to the Crescent City, the Big Easy, N'Awlins. I'll talk about the city's history while we head on over to the cemetery, and please, stay with the group at all times, because as wonderful a city as this is, we have our share of pickpockets."

Though the distance to the cemetery was only a matter of a few blocks, given the size of the group, progress was slow. Brent talked about the French, Spanish and English, and the Louisiana Purchase, the power and might of the Mississippi, and stopped in front of one of the old taverns, where it was said that pirates met and Jackson had assignations with men of ill repute before recruiting them to his cause. At a house at the edge of the canal, he told the story of a twentieth-century murder in which the perpetrator had been convinced he was a vampire and had drained his victim of blood. When the police convinced him that he was deranged, he shot himself. There were those, he said, who believed that his victim now stalked the streets in ghostly form, convinced that he was an afterlife vampire and seeking to drain people of their very breath.

Other groups were in the cemetery when they arrived, but Brent had no trouble holding the full attention of his audience. He started out with the tomb of the famous voodoo queen Marie Laveau, then led the group to view the tomb of Homer Plessy, involved in the 1896 landmark case of *Plessy vs. Ferguson*, which established the concept of separate but equal. Certain that Huey was somewhere around, he decided to tell the haunt's story. "In cases of epidemic or need, vaults could be used by those who didn't own them. There's no actual data on precisely where, but near here was interred a hardworking elderly slave, Huey, slain by his master, some say through cruelty, some say through forethought and murder. It's said that Huey haunts St. Louis Number 1, looking for justice. He can be playful or tough—he was bitter about his own death, but a fine old fellow, and he has it in for anyone who intends to vandalize this place."

He raised his voice. "Huey should know, however, that his wretched old master, Archibald McManus, died in horrible agony. Perhaps there is such a thing as retribution, and though we often wonder why it doesn't seem to occur often enough in this life, in some cases, it does."

He gazed around, letting his words settle with his audience and looking for Nikki. She was standing with Julian, whispering. She seemed at ease now, even entertained. Huey's story was one they probably hadn't heard before.

"Archibald McManus?" exclaimed an attractive young woman somewhere in her early twenties. She was on the tour with two other women.

"She's a McManus," one of her friends said.

"It's a common enough name," Brent said.

"No," the girl in question said. She laughed. "I'm here because my roots supposedly go back to this area. My dad said that my great-great-grandfather was a plantation owner here, that something terrible happened, and his children moved away and all lost touch with one another. Do you know any more about this guy?"

Brent nodded. "Public library, though you may not like what you find out."

"Every family probably has one inhuman wretch, huh? Ouch!" she cried suddenly, turning to the redheaded friend at her side. "What did you do that for?"

"What?" the redhead demanded.

"You pulled my hair."

"I did not."

Brent winced, wishing he hadn't told the story. Now he could see Huey. Instead of being relieved and at peace with the satisfaction of knowing that old Archibald had gotten his comeuppance, he was angry with the girl who was a descendant of the man's.

"Let's move on," he said quickly.

He started walking, leading the crowd through the maze of tombs in the city of the dead. He felt Huey at his side.

"You leave that girl alone," he ordered softly.

"She comes from his blood. Bad blood."

"The sins of the fathers are not visited upon the children," he said.

"What?"

Brent glanced to his right. Huey was gone. Julian was there, frowning at him.

Brent turned, teeth grating. He had to be careful. Nikki was next to Julian, looking at him curiously.

He jumped up on a broken tombstone. "The sins of the fathers are not visited upon the children," he repeated. And he told them about a beautiful young Creole woman who had run away with the son of a wealthy English family. "When the man died in an epidemic, his mother saw to it that her daughter-in-law was cast from the house and the marriage annulled. In a few years' time, the Creole beauty died of illness brought on by her struggle to survive. However, years later, when the Englishwoman was sick and alone, she fell in the streets of the Vieux Carré one day. She was helped up by a beautiful young woman who might have been the reincarnation of her late daughter-in-law. It was her granddaughter. The girl might have thrown her grandmother back into the street, but she brought her instead to the nuns, who nursed her unto death. The girl then saw to it that the old woman received a decent burial here in St. Louis Number 1. Now they all rest together. The granddaughter, by the way, sought nothing from the estate, but the lawyers found her, and she inherited a home near Jackson Square. She, in turn, married a dashing young American soldier, and they had five children, many of whom are also buried in the vault there. The stone is wearing away, but the motto above the elaborate iron gate says, 'God is my witness, Christ is my judge, life is to live, and in living, love.'"

Huey was staring at him from the center of the group. At least he wasn't pulling hair anymore.

It was getting late. The gates would be closed and locked soon, and Brent knew it was time to get everyone out, himself included.

He thanked everyone for coming, suggested the other tours the group gave, and assured everyone that he would get them back to Madame D'Orso's, so they could proceed with whatever they had planned for the evening.

As he led the way out, Huey was at his side. "You comin' back, Injun boy? You going to tell me exactly what happened?"

He hung back and let the others lead the tour out of earshot before he responded.

"Works two ways, Huey. I need your help."

"Yeah, yeah."

"And quit pulling hair."

"She's the spittin' image of old Archibald."

"Oh, bull, Huey."

"Who's Huey?"

Patricia had hung back to meet him, and was smiling warily.

"Pardon?" he said.

"Who's Huey—and what's bull?" she demanded.

He flashed her a quick smile. "Sorry, I'm talking to myself."

"What a relief," she said with a smile. "I thought I was the only one who did that."

They came out on the main street, and Brent paused to see that their group was all together.

Nikki came over then. "Good job," she said softly. She wasn't touching him. She was just up on her toes, whispering in his ear. A simple thing. So simple. The moisture of her breath was warm, the air cool, and he was almost staggered by the instant sense of heat and electricity that shot through him, tightening every muscle in his body, creating a hunger that was almost painful.

But not evident, he prayed.

He couldn't speak. He simply had to move ahead and get a firm grip on his libido.

Nikki didn't want to return to Madame's, and she'd pretty much had it with tours for the day. Brent had proven himself as far as she was concerned, but if the others wanted to force him into taking the night tour, as well, that was their concern.

She trailed somewhat behind as they left St. Louis Number 1. Julian walked by her side. "He certainly knows New Orleans," he said.

"Yeah, apparently he does," she agreed.

"You still didn't have to give him my shirt," he said.

She glanced at him, surprised. "Julian, you've never been like that. You're really mad that I let him borrow your shirt."

"I'm really worried that you let him stay at your house," he said.

"Oh. That."

"We don't really know anything about him."

"The cops seem to trust him. He's with some agency that they all bow down to, as far as I can tell. Anyway, he only stayed at my house. I didn't sleep with him."

She hadn't realized that Patricia had joined them until she said, "You didn't? I would have. Well, if I weren't head over heels in love with Nathan, of course." She tossed aside a length of her hair. "Seriously, I'm kind of glad he walked into our lives. He'll protect Nikki. I really believe that."

"Nikki has me," Julian said.

"Right. And what happens when you go out on a date?" Patricia demanded.

"I really don't think I need protection," Nikki insisted.

"Yes you do," Patricia said simply, and she looked at Nikki in a way that very briefly showed her that Patricia was scared herself.

"You," Julian said, pointing at Patricia, "just trust him because he's good looking. I think there's something weird about the guy. Nikki needs to be careful."

Unease filled Nikki again. *You don't know the half of it,* she longed to say.

They were back at Madame's. Nikki had hardly been

aware of moving through the streets. Mitch moved over to join them. Nikki could see the McManus girl talking to Brent. He was writing something down for her. Marie was speaking earnestly. She handed Brent something that appeared to be a card from her hotel. She saw him nod, and she thought that he might be agreeing to give her any information about her family she might find.

"We should have dinner somewhere," Mitch suggested.

Nikki shook her head. "I'm going to beg off. That is, if—"

"Nathan and I have the night tour," Patricia assured her. "But you must want dinner."

"Actually, I don't. I just want to get home."

The McManus girl walked into Madame's. Brent came over to where they were standing on the sidewalk. "So, what now?" he queried.

"Dinner. My stomach is growling," Mitch said.

"Nikki is all in," Patricia told him. "She's not coming with us, but you're welcome to come along."

He looked at Nikki. "Maybe. I'm walking Nikki home first."

"I'm okay. It's still light out, and the storm never came," Nikki said.

He shook his head. "I'm walking you home."

Nathan said they were going to a place on Royal Street and told Brent to come by later, and they parted company, Brent telling them not to wait for him, Patricia assuring him that they wouldn't.

"Honestly, you're welcome to go with them," Nikki said.

"No way."

She glanced at him. There had been an edge to his voice.

"You're still angry."

"No, of course not."

"Yes, you are."

"All right. You have to tell me the minute you see Andrea. And it doesn't matter what's happening."

"Right. In the middle of dozens of people, I'll just wave a hand in the air and say, 'Oh, Brent, here she is, Andy Ciello, the ghost you're so eager to meet.'"

He glared at her.

She shook her head and walked past him. "Seriously," she called over her shoulder, "I'm fine. You don't need to escort me."

But she couldn't shake him.

And the truth was, she was glad.

He followed her through the gate and on to the porch, then through her private entrance.

It hit her the minute she stepped inside.

A feeling that, once again, something was subtly different.

She looked around. Nothing was out of place.

"What is it?" Brent asked tensely.

She shook her head. "Nothing."

"It's something."

"Okay, it's a feeling."

"Of what?"

"Of something different. Of something having been moved. But nothing has been. So it's just another psychotic episode, I guess."

"Let's check the place out. You can make sure everything's okay."

They walked through the downstairs, then the upstairs. Nikki couldn't find anything out of order, though the feeling wouldn't go away. They wound up back in the kitchen; Nikki took two Cokes from the refrigerator.

"Hot as hell out there today," she murmured, handing him his and feeling suddenly awkward.

"Yep, N'Awlins in the heat," he said, putting on a perfect accent, causing her to smile at last.

She stepped back, though. There was a little too much charm in that smile, in that husky tone.

She was still feeling the slight rush of anger through her blood, mingled with gratitude that he was there and a feeling that there was a burning deep in the very erotic center of her body.

"You really can go to dinner."

"We can order in, too. Or cook."

She took another step back. "Listen, I'm hot, cranky and miserable. I'm going to shower. I'm feeling like a salt lick." She didn't know why, but she was suddenly sure that the last words had sounded entirely wrong. Salt…lick…

"You're welcome to do the same."

Pop in with me...

No, no…

Was that what he was hearing? Or merely what her mind really meant?

"I'd have to borrow more of Julian's clothing," he

said, apparently not taking any of her words at anything but face value.

"Feel free."

"I'll tell you what, let's both shower. Then we can wander over to my B & B, I can get some clothing, and we'll pick up food on the way back here," he suggested.

"All right," she said. She hesitated. "You're staying here again?"

"That's up to you."

Her shower felt really good. She hadn't been lying about the heat. And she had felt like a salt lick.

Hot, sweaty, on fire…

She turned the water on harder, pouring shampoo into her hair, sudsing, closing her eyes as she stood under the spray, letting it thunder down. Then she opened her eyes.

And screamed.

12

It was evident that when Julian stayed, he stayed in the guest room. Pieces of his clothing hung in the closet, and a top drawer was filled with clean socks, T-shirts and Calvin Klein briefs. The soap in the shower was something brisk smelling as well, an Irish brand that left a man smelling like a "cool spring wood," according to the commercials.

The day had been a scorcher, and it was good to strip down and step beneath the spray. Brent had wondered at first if he should have waited; some of the old places didn't have the water pressure for two showers going at the same time, but the spray came on hot and hard. Standing beneath it, he clenched his jaw, reminding himself that work and raging desire did not mix. He needed to keep his distance, keep a cool head. She was in serious danger, and he didn't dare let down his guard, not with the dead, and certainly not with the living.

A scream.

For a split second he thought he'd imagined it, but then heard it again and knew it was all too real.

He jumped from the shower, dripping wet, naked,

and tore through to the main bedroom, sprinting to the bathroom. He went for the shower curtain and ripped it from the steel rod.

Nikki screamed again as she turned, stunned at the sound of the ripping curtain.

"What?" he cried, seeing nothing at all terrifying.

"What are you doing?" she cried, reaching for the torn curtain. Her eyes slid up and down the length of his wet naked body, then rose to his eyes and locked on them. She flushed a brilliant shade of crimson.

"You screamed!" he accused her. "What the hell happened?"

She moistened her lips. Wet, sensual lips. Her lashes fell over her eyes. Rich, long lashes, ridiculously dark, considering she was a blonde.

A true honey blonde.

Top to bottom.

She made a croaking sound, uttering a word he didn't understand.

"What, Nikki?" he asked, trying to modulate his voice, moving a step closer.

Her eyes met his. "Roach," she said more clearly.

"Roach?" he repeated.

"Roach," she said, sounding angry. "A big one! The kind with wings, a Palmetto bug. It was on the showerhead, and it flew right at me."

"Roach?" It was an exhalation of relief, disbelief, even anger. Good God, the fear he had felt for her, the panic, the way his heart was rushing…

"Damn you, don't you dare be angry with me," she cried. "It startled the hell out of me."

"It startled *you?* You just cost me a decade of life," he told her.

She stared at him, ready to argue back. They were both tense.

And both naked.

And suddenly she wasn't angry anymore. She smiled.

"You look pretty alive to me right now," she said softly.

He knew that he did. He felt as if he were made of steel. Molten, hot and strong.

His eyes didn't fall from hers. Where her anger had paled, his suddenly soared. Maybe it was the feeling of burning with fire, constricted, conflicted.

He started to turn away, but her fingers, damp and gentle as the breeze that seemed to come with her touch, fell on his shoulder.

"Brent."

The way she whispered his name…

Nothing had ever made him ache with such subtle allure. He turned back.

The curtain was down. The water was still rushing. Steam rose, billowing around her. The sound was a rush in his ears, like the pounding of his heart.

"Is there…is there something wrong with me?" she asked, her eyes as brilliant and deep as a Caribbean sea.

"No," he said curtly.

"Then…?"

"Then what?" he asked, tone curt, feeling as if he was about to shatter into a million pieces.

"Two adults…night, the distant sound of music. A man and woman. Naked. The one, tall, dark, obviously aroused. The other…longing for him to take her into his arms, so fascinated by him she could just die or…or totally humiliate herself for all eternity," she finished.

He wanted to explain that she was the most erotic, compelling woman he had met since…it seemed like forever, but…

But she was in danger. Mortal danger. And if he gave in to his feelings, he could well endanger her to an even greater degree. He was ready to tell her, explain…

But…

The words simply wouldn't come.

He reached out and clasped her waist, then lifted her over the tile step into the shower, drawing her against his body as he eased her back to the floor, his arousal imprinting itself on every inch of her flesh with which it came into contact. Sound escaped him at last. A groan. He buried his face against her throat, lips against the delicate skin of her neck and shoulder. His fingers slid into the thick wet mass of her hair as his mouth found hers.

Dear God, she was sweet.

Her arms wound around him, slid down the slick wet length of his back, hands shaping his buttocks, pulling him more closely to her. Flesh rubbed against flesh, hot and wet, the steam rising all around them, the beat of the water like a pulsing crescendo. His mouth tore from hers, found her shoulder again, then slid insanely over the rise of her breasts. His lips found her nipple, curved around it, teeth teased, and he heard her gasp, felt the heavy thud of her heart, then her erratic pulse. Her hand was somehow between them, sliding down the length of his chest, finding his sex, curling around it. And her eyes were on his, aqua and huge, as misty as the water, taunting and alluring.

He lifted her again, carried her back into the shower, then hiked her higher and pressed her back against the tile, cool against the heat. He lifted her higher and higher, gazing at her all the while, as the water streamed down on them in a steady cascade, like a honeyed oil, adding to the friction, the insanity, the desperation.

When she was high enough, he lowered her, bringing her down on his erection, slowly at first, his eyes never leaving hers, until she cried out with a soft sound, tearing her own gaze away, burying her face low against his shoulder as he began to move. The searing, driving pulse of the spray seemed to echo the thunder in his veins, resound in the knotted wire of his every muscle. He was completely unaware of her weight, barely aware of her limbs wrapped around his waist. She sheathed him, rode the thrust and fire of his desperate arousal, the soft sounds escaping her lips driving him into a frenzy. Her fingers dug into him. Her lips found his in a deep and jagged kiss, tongue driving hard into the depths of his mouth. There was a moment when he lost recognition of anything other than the steam, the heat, the rising pulse and the need centered in that one portion of his body. Then he was wrenched from the spiral of his own satisfaction by the cry that tore from her lips. Her back arched against the tile, and he felt the eruption of his own climax, ripping through him like a tidal wave.

She was draped around him now, lax and trembling slightly, almost as if she had passed out against him.

Then she moved, eyes meeting his, fingers trailing through the wet length of his hair. She smiled and, to his amazement, whispered, "Thanks."

He eased her slowly down, turning the water off at last, his eyes never leaving hers. He inched back, feeling lost when his penis slipped from her body, loath to set her slowly on her own feet.

"Thanks?" he asked, leaning against her again, gently finding her cheek with the pad of his thumb.

"I was beginning to think there was something wrong with me."

She was trying to be light, he realized. Not denying anything, just leaving him plenty of room to take an emotional step back.

He shook his head gravely. "There's nothing wrong with you. Quite the contrary, there's far too much right with you."

Her smile deepened, then faded as she looked into his eyes. "Then…what took you so long?"

"I came rushing in here the second you screamed."

"I didn't mean just now."

"Actually, we haven't known each other that long."

"I knew the second I saw you that I wanted you," she whispered, her voice serious and ever so slightly wistful.

"Because…?"

"Because you touched me," she said simply.

He pulled her close against him. With the water off and the fever of the moment released, the air-conditioning was kicking in, and he was growing chill, standing damp and naked. Brent reached for a towel, wrapping it around her shoulders.

He touched her chin, lifting her eyes to his.

"Because I touched you?" he whispered. "I didn't think you even liked me at first."

"I didn't."

"That's honest."

"I didn't want to like you," she said quietly, and walked out of the bathroom.

Brent followed. She was standing in the growing darkness at the foot of the bed. It was fall but the balcony doors were closed, the drapes drawn, and the room was cast in soft shadow.

She threaded her fingers through her drying hair, waiting. She had dropped the towel. In the soft light, she was ethereal, yet far too real, a piece of mystical art, Venus rising, something perfect caught by the imagination of an artist.

He walked toward her, not touching her at first, then reaching for her chin. His lips met hers with a slow, infinite tenderness, and then he drew her to him. "Confession…I did little but think about you the night after I came upon you in the street. I've been so fascinated by you that I've had to walk away at times. The way I feel…scares me."

She smiled, head tilted close to his. "I don't usually behave this way. I'm usually reserved. I guess you couldn't tell tonight, huh? But there's such a thing as chemistry. And…I'm…I don't know what I'm saying."

"But I do," he told her, and he folded her into his arms again.

There were some things in life that simply…were.

And once they began…

This time he wanted everything, and he meant to give everything in return. He felt as if they had a lifetime to catch up on, a lifetime to get to know each other, and at the same time, he wanted no words, no sense of before and no thought of after. This was a time for breathing, scent and feel, flesh and heartbeat, and all that came between. And so he was slow, deliberate, moving her hair, kissing her nape, his lips exploring the length of her spine, inhaling the sweet scent of her skin, learning the essence beneath, shape and form and feel. For long moments she was still, allowing his exploration, savoring. Then she turned in his arms, and when she met his lips, her own were hungry. The kiss was long and deep, wet, hot and intimate, promising all that was to follow.

Their hands were all over one another then, and he wasn't even aware of when they fell upon the cool length of the bed. He was aware only of her fingertips sliding over him, the feel of her lips against his flesh, the erotic graze of her teeth against his shoulders, his ribs, down his chest, teasing, touching…

Hands, lips.

His.

Hers…

Brushing, searing. The most intimate of hot, wet caresses.

Dusk became dark. They remained entwined, drifting….

He felt her start, and his eyes flew open. His arms tensed around her.

"Nikki?" he said gently.

She was taut. "I thought I..."

"Andy?"

"No...just something silly. I thought I heard someone turning the knob on the front door. I probably couldn't hear that from up here, could I?" she asked very softly.

He slid from bed, stooping down for the towel she had discarded. Wrapping it around his waist, he started silently from the bedroom.

"Wait," she entreated.

"Nikki, you should—"

"Come with you," she said firmly.

She slipped into the bathroom for a second towel, then followed him in the darkness through the house. A small light burned in the kitchen, enough to guide them quickly to the door.

He didn't touch it at first. He waited, listening. There was no sound, and the knob didn't move. After a moment, he silently slid the bolt, then opened the door.

Outside, the streetlights of New Orleans burned through the night, casting a glow over the brick wall, creating shadows by the tree, the porch and the swing. A breeze stirred, bringing a touch of relief from the day's heat. If anyone had been on the porch before, they were gone now.

"Silly, huh?" she murmured.

He stepped back in, locking and bolting the door. He cupped her chin. "Nothing is silly. Anytime you think something's wrong, tell me."

She smiled. "I'm feeling something right now."

"Wow. I'm flattered."

She laughed, and the sound was good.

"Hunger," she told him.

"Consider me an all-you-can-eat buffet," he teased.

She laughed softly. "I meant for dinner."

"It's almost 2:00 a.m."

"I know an all-night diner where they make fantastic po'boys."

He considered her suggestion. "We can get something to eat, then go to my B & B for some of my own clothes."

She smiled. "I'll get dressed. You should, too."

She headed for the stairs, but he hesitated, listening.

There was nothing to hear. Whether Nikki had imagined the earlier sound or not, he didn't know, but it troubled him.

Andrea Ciello had returned to her apartment at about 2:00 a.m.

Soon after that, she had died.

At just about the same time.

And Brent was certain, just as Nikki was, that Andrea hadn't brought on her own death.

Someone had entered her apartment without any sign of force. From what he had gleaned from Nikki, Andy didn't know herself who had come through her door. So either she had forgotten to lock it, or someone had access to her apartment.

Nikki's door had been locked and bolted tonight. Had someone been trying to enter with a key?

"Brent?" Nikki called curiously from upstairs.

"I'm on my way," he called back.

He checked the lock on the door once again. It was secure.

He followed her up the stairs.

Patricia awoke with a start, wondering why. Then she realized that she was lying alone in bed. She got up, found a robe, slipped into it. She could hear the old air conditioner thumping and whining as she made her way out to the kitchen.

Nathan was there, pouring a glass of juice. He was barefoot and shirtless, but wearing jeans.

"Hey," she said. As she walked around the counter, she nearly tripped over a pair of shoes, edged them out of the way and made her way to him.

"Did I wake you? Sorry," he said. His dark hair was mussed. Very sexy, she thought.

She smiled, coming up behind him, slipping her arms around his waist and laying her cheek against his back. "You didn't actually wake me. I just woke up, and you weren't there, and I missed you. That's a little scary, huh?"

He eased around to face her. There was a soft sheen of sweat on his body, as if he'd had a nightmare, or been engaged in some kind of physical activity.

"I've had trouble sleeping lately," he told her.

"Is it me? Are you doubting that we should be together?" she asked seriously, her heart thundering painfully.

"No, of course not."

"I'm a big girl. You can tell me if it's true."

He touched her cheek with tender affection. "You're

the best thing in the world. The best thing ever to happen to me," he said quietly.

She took the juice from his grip, caught his hand and started to lead him back to the bedroom. "I'm going to make you sleep," she promised him.

"Oh, yeah?"

"Well, not right away. But trust me. I'm going to wear you out. Then you'll sleep."

Only when he fell asleep and lay deeply, peacefully breathing beside her did she think about the fact that he'd been wearing his jeans.

And he'd left his shoes, with bits of damp dirt clinging to the soles, in the kitchen.

Had he been out?

The city was always alive somewhere.

But if he'd been out, why hadn't he mentioned it?

Nikki couldn't remember a time when she'd been out on the streets quite this late—or early. Though there was activity—music pulsing faintly from the strip joints—the relative quiet was actually kind of nice. Building facades were ever so slightly ghostly; lights created color as well as shadow. A few people were about—mostly drunks—but there was still something oddly enchanting about the darkened city.

She brought Brent to a place called Maxie's. It was near the casino, which provided a twenty-four-hour clientele.

It offered little other than sandwiches, but those were excellent. Nikki was ravenous, and still feeling a sense of exhilaration. She wondered if she looked flushed, her eyes as brilliant as diamonds. There was probably a lot of truth in the belief that sex made the entire world better.

Brent seemed pleased by the place, and at least as hungry as she was.

"You've never been here?" she asked him when they had both been served iced tea and po'boys.

He shook his head. "And see—I thought I knew the city backward and forward."

"Actually, you do. You came up with all kinds of tidbits today that I knew nothing about. Like the slave, Huey. That was certainly extraordinary, that a descendant of his old master was in the group."

Brent shrugged, looking down at his food. "Maybe not so extraordinary. McManus left three children all those years ago. By now there could be lots of descendants. And people have a tendency to want to explore their roots."

"Still, that she was in the crowd yesterday—that was pretty amazing."

He shrugged. "Interesting, certainly."

He wasn't looking at her, he realized. He was staring past her. He was seated with his back against the wall, facing the door, while she had her back to it.

"What?" she said, turning to look. "Mitch," she said in surprise.

Mitch was at the entrance, waiting to be shown to a table. He heard her and turned quickly. Seeing her and Brent, he appeared startled at first; then he smiled, and walked over to join them.

"What on earth are you doing out at this hour?" she asked him.

He brushed back a strand of tawny hair that had fallen over his forehead and pulled out the chair next to Nikki's. "I'm hungry. What are you doing here?"

"Same," Brent said.

Mitch grinned at Nikki. "But you—awake? That's amazing."

She shook her head and glanced at Brent. "I'm known as the deadbeat in the crowd. I'm not a late-night person."

"And I'm from a place in Pennsylvania where everything shuts down at ten, and I love it that any time of the day or night, there's something going on here," he said to Brent.

"Are you always such a night owl?" Brent asked him. His tone was casual, his smile open, but Nikki was certain that his interest wasn't casual at all.

"Actually, no. But that's my point. You may not want to be out at three or four in the morning all the time, but when you *are* awake, there's always something to do."

He twisted around, searching the restaurant as if he was looking for someone, Nikki thought.

Whether that had been the case or not, he found someone.

"Hey," he said softly. "Over there…in that back booth…isn't that the cop working Andy's case?"

Both Nikki and Brent twisted to look in the direction Mitch was indicating.

Indeed, it *was* Owen Massey. Head down, he looked haggard and worn as he leafed through a stack of pages.

"That's Massey all right," Nikki said.

"Well," Mitch said, glancing at his watch, "it's really late. Or early. I should get going."

"Get going?" Brent said to him, those steely green eyes sharp. "You just got here. Thought you were hungry."

"Oh, hell, yeah. I forgot to order and eat," Mitch said. He raised a hand, and their waitress came over. "I'll just have tea and that same chicken po'boy the lady is having," he said, indicating Nikki's plate.

The woman nodded and left them.

"So…how did you like your first day?" Mitch asked Brent.

"It was fun."

"It *is* fun, working with people," Mitch agreed. "Hey, should we go say hello to the detective, see if he's got anything new?"

"Actually, we should," Nikki agreed, looking at Brent for confirmation.

Brent lifted his hands. "Sure."

As they approached his table, Massey looked up. He quickly closed the manila file that contained whatever papers he'd been reading.

"Hi, Detective," Nikki said, smiling. "We saw you and just thought we should say hello."

Massey nodded gravely, looking at the three of them. "I saw you all come in," he said. "Didn't know if you wanted to be bothered or not. Especially by me."

Nikki was quick to speak. "Hey, you've been nothing but great to me. I know how hard you're trying. I appreciate your effort."

"Nothing new, is there?" Mitch asked.

"I'm afraid not," Massey said. "It could be a long haul," he said gently. He looked at Brent oddly, Nikki thought. Maybe, whether he believed in ghosts or not, Massey was hoping that Brent would come up with something for him.

"It's late for you to be out, isn't it?" Brent asked Massey casually.

"Couldn't sleep. I'm not due in for hours, but..."

"I couldn't sleep, either," Mitch said. "Strange night, huh?"

"Maybe there's something in the air. Saw a few more of your group in here not too long ago," Massey said.

Nikki was both startled and curious. "Who?"

"The handsome young fellow who's always hanging around with you, for one," Massey said.

"Julian?"

"Yep. He was over in that corner." Massey pointed across the room. The opposite corner was very private. "He was with a woman so I didn't intrude."

"Who else was here?" Brent asked.

"That pseudo French woman."

He said it with the slightest indication of distaste.

"Pseudo French woman?" Mitch said, puzzled.

"Madame?" Nikki said. "She's nice, even if she's not really French," she said, laughing. "Her place is wonderful. Haven't you ever gotten anything there?"

"Her prices are a bit high, if you ask me." He pointed. "Looks like they just served more food over at your table."

"My sandwich," Mitch said.

"Well, we'll see you, Detective," Nikki said.

"Yep. You know, call me—"

"If I think of anything at all. Thanks," Nikki said.

She realized only after she followed Mitch back to their table that Brent had lingered and slid into the booth opposite Massey. The two were talking intently.

"What's that all about?" Mitch asked Nikki.

"Don't know."

"Hey, you think Julian got lucky with that girl from the cemetery today?" Mitch asked.

"Well, I guess he got lucky with someone," Nikki said.

Mitch frowned suddenly. "And you…who is this guy? You need to be careful right now, too. I mean, I'm not saying he doesn't seem decent enough, but…he looks pretty cozy over there right now, talking to Detective Massey."

"He's fine, don't worry. He's got an in with the police," Nikki assured Mitch.

"Oh yeah?" Mitch queried.

She nodded. "He does work for an agency that does some work for the police. I don't know the whole story, but he's definitely all right," she said.

"I thought he was working for us now."

"As long as he shows up for his tours, I don't care what else he does with his time."

"Hmm." Mitch chewed and studied the two men in the back booth.

"I think you guys are just worried about having another male in the mix."

"Maybe. But I think I'll just keep my eye on him

anyway," Mitch said, sounding very much like an older brother.

She grinned. "Okay. You do that."

A few minutes later Brent returned to their table, offering no explanation. They lingered for a few more minutes, Mitch raising the idea that they should write a book of ghostly legends. "Everyone is doing it," he assured them.

"That's the problem, isn't it? Everyone is already doing it," Nikki told him.

He shook his head. "We would use our stories—"

"Most of the people working in New Orleans have the same stories. They're part of history, remember?" Nikki reminded him.

But Mitch shook his head. "Hey, Brent had great stories I hadn't heard before today. And besides, ours will be more dramatic and wonderful, like we are."

"Get started on it, then," Nikki told him.

"We'll have a truly unique book. We can put in our own ghosts, right?"

Put in their own ghosts. *Like Andy.*

Nikki stood abruptly. "It's really late," she said. "We have to get some sleep."

"We have to pay the check," Brent reminded her.

"I've got it," Mitch assured them. "Go ahead—I'll turn it in with my expenses," he told Nikki with a grin.

As Brent rose to join her, Massey was hurrying from his booth at the back. He shook his head. "Fool kids. There's been an attack over by St. Louis Number 1. Take care. Call me," he reminded them distractedly.

Outside, Nikki linked arms with Brent. "So what was that all about?"

"What?" He looked at her, green eyes like gems, giving away nothing.

She sighed. "You and Massey."

"Just a rehash," he said briefly. "Strange, though, huh? Everybody out tonight."

"Well, *we're* out," she reminded him.

"And Mitch. And Julian. And that woman who runs the café."

"And Detective Massey," she said impatiently. "What are you getting at?"

"Nothing," he said. His eyes were on the street. More people were beginning to stir, but it was still dark and fairly quiet. "It's just a strange night. So many of the living about, and other than that…"

She frowned, looking at him. A little shiver stirred in her. "Do you see ghosts all the time?" The question seemed absurd. But it was real. And unnerving.

"No. Not all the time." He hesitated. She knew that he didn't like to sound absurd himself. "New Orleans… it's one of those places," he said simply. Then he said flatly. "The dead are quiet tonight. The living seem to be in an uproar."

"Hardly an uproar," she murmured.

"We need to take a left. To get to my bed-and-breakfast. And my clothes," he said.

She knew the house off Conte where he had chosen to stay. It dated back to the mid-Victorian period. He fitted his key quietly in the front door, and they made their way even more quietly to his bedroom. He packed a small leather duffel bag, while she sat on the bed, waiting. Then they slipped back out, Brent testing the door to make sure it was locked when they left.

The very first streaks of dawn were beginning to appear in the sky as they headed for her apartment.

"Curious," Brent said, almost to himself.

"What?"

"Your friends all being up and about."

A knot of tension formed in her midriff. "Why is that curious?"

He looked straight ahead. Instead of answering her, he said, "There was no sign of forced entry at Andrea Ciello's apartment," he said.

"Oh, I get it. So she was murdered by someone she knew."

He didn't reply.

"Don't go getting suspicious of any of my group," she warned him.

"Don't go getting angry," he said. "Whenever you're looking for anything, you get rid of the impossible. Then you look at what you're left with. No matter how improbable, your answers have to be there."

She pulled away from him, staring at him. "Ghosts are supposedly impossible," she said angrily, then walked on quickly.

She suddenly had a feeling, like a premonition.

Her world was about to split wide open.

Treacherous times loomed ahead. Fear, anger… mistrust.

She suddenly, desperately, wanted the future never to come.

When they entered her apartment, she turned to him, pulling the duffel from his shoulder, casting it to the floor. "We can fight later." She realized that her voice grew thin as she spoke. "But this morning...let's pretend that we don't see ghosts. Let's not think or talk about anything that's terrible or frightening or...deadly. Please."

She touched his cheek with the palm of her hand, gentle, entreating.

He caught her fingers, keeping them there, against his face.

A split second later, she was in his arms.

Clothing was strewn even as they moved up the stairs. She felt his touch on the naked flesh of her back, and then they were in her room, in her bed.

The sun rose over New Orleans, and the new day began in earnest.

In the draped shadows of her bedroom, Nikki chose not to notice.

13

Nikki and Brent made it to Madame's at about nine-thirty. Mitch was already at their regular table, Patricia and Nathan arrived a few minutes later, and then Julian.

"So you had a wild night, huh?" Mitch teased Julian.

"What?" Julian said, startled as he took a seat.

"We heard you had a tête-à-tête last night at Maxie's," Mitch informed him.

Julian stared at Mitch, then the others. "Wow. I didn't think the city was that small," he said.

"Brent and I went out to Maxie's, too," Nikki said.

"And Mitch…?" Julian asked, puzzled.

"Showed up separately," Brent offered.

"Give," Patricia teased. "Who were you with?"

Julian grinned. He didn't seem disturbed that everyone knew he'd had a date. Brent wondered if Nikki really had heard someone at her door, trying to connect that to the others, given that everyone he had recently met in New Orleans seemed to be running around at all hours of the night.

"Was it that girl you met in Lafayette Number 1 yesterday?" Nikki asked, smiling.

"Yes, and I guess I owe you my thanks," Julian said. "Wouldn't have met her without you, Nikki." He looked pleadingly at her. "Nikki, can you and Brent take the Lafayette tour first this afternoon? Patricia and Nathan can do the St. Louis, and I'll pick up on the Vieux Carré tour tonight with Mitch—if that works for everyone. Please?" he entreated.

"Another hot date—in the afternoon?" Mitch queried.

Nikki was smiling at Julian. She seemed to be having a good time, Brent thought.

It was almost as if, since they had returned to her place last night, she had allowed herself to forget, for a few hours, what had happened.

Madame made an appearance just then with her coffee urn. "Any refills here, *mes petites?*" she queried.

"I'd love more coffee, Madame," Nikki said.

"Thanks," Brent agreed. "So you were out late last night, huh, Madame?"

She arched a brow at him. "Goodness, how do you know that?"

"Our friendly local police detective was out dining on po'boys, too," Nikki replied.

Madame laughed. "Well, he sure keeps his eye on us. Then again, it's hard not to notice when people you know are around. Let's hope he also keeps his eye on things that matter a bit more, eh?" She smiled. "Strange night, though. I simply couldn't sleep."

"You shouldn't be walking around alone at night, Madame," Julian said firmly.

"Oh, good heavens, child, I know this city. I'm careful. I know where to be—and where not to be."

The fact that Andy Ciello had considered her apartment a safe place suddenly seemed to hover unspoken on the air between them. Brent was dismayed to see Nikki suddenly turn ashen.

"Just be careful," Julian said.

"I will. And thank you for being concerned," Madame said. "But I also travel with my trusty pepper spray at all times." She smiled, then looked past them. "Goodness, that's Harold Grant coming into my place for coffee!" She seemed pleased. "He must think he's about to lose his seat to that young whippersnapper Billy Banks. He's looking positively haggard."

Brent turned to look. Harold Grant had to be somewhere around sixty years old. He was sturdy looking, tall, broad shouldered, with a thick crop of iron-gray hair. He had a reputation for grave care in his decisions, but not a lot of humor or charm.

"He and Billy Banks are having a debate in Jackson Square this afternoon," Madame said. "There will be cops all over today, that's for sure. That means a brisk business for me. Our boys in blue do love my café au lait and beignets." She gave them a wave and left the table.

Brent's cell phone started to ring, startling them all. With an apologetic look, he answered it. "Blackhawk."

"It's Massey. Can you come down to the station for a minute?"

He looked at the others. They were all staring at him. "Sure. What's up?" he asked tensely.

"Just get down here as soon as you can." There was no accusation in the words, just weariness.

"I'll be right there."

He snapped his phone shut. "We start at Lafayette at twelve, right?" he said to Nikki.

"Twelve," she agreed, studying him with a curious frown.

"Will you two stay with her…go with her over to Lafayette?" he asked Patricia and Nathan.

"It's broad daylight—there are tourists everywhere," Nikki said. "And there are cops all over the city, too—didn't you hear what Madame just said?"

"We'll be happy to hang around with Nikki and get her over to Lafayette," Patricia said.

"Sure…we can even hang around and help with the tour, if you want," Nathan said.

"Please," Nikki protested. "I repeat—it's broad daylight, there are cops roaming the city as thick as flies."

"Sure, that's great. You all stick together," Brent said as if she hadn't spoken, rising.

"I don't need anyone," Nikki insisted.

"We all need someone," Brent said wryly. "Nikki, please, your friends want to hang with you. Let them," he said.

She threw up her hands.

"Hey, let's wander over to Contessa Moodoo's Hoodoo Voodoo shop, huh?" Patricia suggested.

"For what?" Nikki demanded. She didn't want to say, certainly not when they were all behaving this way to begin with, that she was uneasy, that she had been there with Andrea not long before she had been murdered.

"Oh, I don't know. Maybe you should buy some

chicken feet, dance around, raise a little ruckus," Julian told her. "I thought you liked the place."

"Go with her," Brent said firmly to Nikki. Something was bothering her. Being with her friends? He doubted that. Going to a voodoo shop?

She offered him a smile, aware that he wouldn't go if he wasn't feeling secure about her. "If you've never been there, I'll have to take you some time," she told Brent.

He smiled and nodded. He knew the place. The woman had been around a long time.

Certain that Nikki wouldn't be alone, Brent turned and left them on the terrace, hurrying toward Royal Street, anxious by then about what Massey wanted.

When he arrived, Massey was waiting for him alone in his cruiser.

"Where's your partner?" Brent asked when Massey indicated he should get in the car.

"Busy questioning people for the hundredth time, armed with pictures of our victims," Massey said wearily.

"So what are we doing?" Brent asked him.

"Heading to the hospital."

"For...?"

"Remember I was called to St. Louis Number 1?"

"Right."

"The girl who was attacked is a Marie McManus. She gave us your name."

He groaned.

"You know her, right?" Massey said.

"Yes. She was on the tour yesterday. But the cemetery was closed and locked. Surely she and her friends knew to stay out of the area."

"Apparently not. One of her friends had some book on conjuring up the spirits of the deceased. She wanted to do some ritual and apologize to the slaves on behalf of her ancestors."

Brent shook his head, both sorry and angry. When the hell would people learn?

"How badly is she hurt?"

"Conk on the head, a few bruises and scratches. When rocks started flying, her friends crawled back over the gate. They screamed, got the cops on patrol. This girl, Marie McManus, didn't see or hear anyone. She just got it from behind. But she wanted to talk to you. And who the hell knows, you might be able to find something out."

"Sure. I'm happy to see her," Brent said.

Marie McManus looked frightened and bruised. She was anxious to leave the hospital, but was being kept twenty-four hours for observation. She had brushed her hair, but she wasn't wearing makeup, and she looked young and really scared.

"Hi. Thanks for coming," she said.

She was in a small private room, barely allowing enough room for both him and McManus.

"What on earth were you doing?" Brent asked her. "I told you last night that it was dangerous to go anywhere near the cemeteries at night."

She flushed, looking downward. "Honestly, we weren't going to vandalize the place or anything. I'd gotten some candles at one of the voodoo shops...a little silver cross, some herbs. We were just going to sneak in and say a little prayer. But then someone started throwing rocks, and someone bashed me in the head. The next thing I knew, I was here, at the hospital."

Brent glanced at Massey and discreetly shrugged. "Marie, you're lucky you weren't killed."

"I know that now," she murmured. She flashed a glance at Massey. "The detective told me that it's going to be almost impossible for them to find who did this."

"I'm not sure what makes you think I can help you, then," Brent said.

She shook her head. "I...know. I didn't really want you to help me, I guess...I guess I felt that I needed to apologize."

He shook his head and spoke gently. "Marie, you were the victim. Some hood needs to apologize to you. But if you want to help in the future, help the cops. Stay out of areas where they warn you that it's dangerous to be, okay?"

She nodded. "You said you had information on my ancestor, Archibald McManus. May I have it?"

"You can probably find out more than I did at the library, but I'll be happy to give you what I've got. I'll try to get back out here sometime soon."

"No, no... We're staying in the French Quarter—Josie, Sarah and me. If you wouldn't mind just dropping it at my hotel, I'd really appreciate it."

"All right. And you swear you won't go near that cemetery again without lots of people in tow?"

"I swear," she told him.

He wished her well, Massey did the same, and they left. "What do you make of it?" Massey asked him.

Brent shrugged. "I think she's lucky that all she came out with were a few bruises."

"Yeah, my take exactly. She didn't see anything." He sighed with disgust. "They never see anything. Well, if you can think of anything...let me know. Where shall I drop you?"

Brent glanced at his watch. Not a lot of time before he needed to be in the Garden District, but all he had to do was run up the street from St. Louis Number 1 to the trolley, and he wouldn't need more than a few minutes to reach Lafayette Number 1.

"The cemetery. I'll take a look around myself this morning."

"We've already pulled the crime tape, and tourists are moving around in there."

He nodded. "I'll take a quick look anyway."

"Think one of your ghostly buddies can help?" Massey asked.

Brent looked at him. He wasn't sure if Massey was mocking him, or if he was just beginning to feel desperate.

"I just wouldn't mind taking a look around," he said. "I hear there's a political debate in Jackson Square today. You boys will be busy."

"The uniforms will have a tough time, yeah," Massey agreed.

A few minutes later he dropped Brent off right at the gates. Brent promised to keep him advised regarding anything he learned.

There were several tour groups going through, but they seemed to be massing at the tomb of Marie Laveau. Brent chose the back wall, by the oven vaults.

He waited a second, watched the last of a group walk around a tomb, and said in a low but heated voice, "Huey, you get your sorry ass out here right now."

A moment later, pale and gray, barely substantial at all, Huey appeared. "My sorry ass? Who the hell are you to talk about *my* sorry ass?"

"Huey, you hurt that girl."

"You're puffed full of cotton, son, and that's putting it nicely. What the hell do you want, Injun boy?" he demanded. There was a guilty tone in his voice. Guilty and defiant.

"Huey, you've gotten real powerful in here. You can pretty much do things I've never seen another ghost manage."

"Spirit or essence, that's what we liked to be called these days," Huey cackled. "Well, that's what one o' dem wise-talking rangers said."

"Great. Now you're going to start being politically correct? The 'essence' who calls me Injun boy all the time?"

"It offend you?" Huey asked.

"No. What offends me is violence. There was no reason for you to hurt that girl."

Huey hung his head, then looked up, his eyes flashing. "Actually, I didn't mean to go hurting her. Honest Injun," he said, and laughed at his own pun. "And I wasn't the one who did hurt her, not unless it was by accident or she got hurt running out of here."

"You threw something at her by accident?"

"Nah…these fellas were in here again last night. Bad seeds, real bad seeds, I just know it."

"What fellas?"

Huey waved a hand in the air. "Junkies. And not junkies. Folks giving stuff to other folks to make some money. They don't care about the cemetery. They got no respect for the dead. Hell, they ain't got no respect for the living, either. Them girls…" He shook his head with sad but tolerant impatience. "They're just silly. Don't know what folks think…don't know what gets into 'em. They shouldn't be in this place after dark, and that's a known fact. They just got in the way. Bad folks are in the cemetery after dark. Them girls were lucky they weren't kilt, and that's a plain fact."

"I need to know who those bad seeds are, Huey. If I can get them, catch them in the act, the cops can put them away, and you won't have to worry about them anymore."

Huey shrugged. "Don't know if I could rightly point them out to you—not if they walked in on a tour this minute. Don't it just beat all? Eighteen million degrees in the shade, and them guys wear knit masks."

"Do they come every night?"

Huey looked around, shaking his head. "Not every night. I never know exactly when they'll come. But…they've been coming."

"A while now?"

"Hell, yeah. Weeks…maybe even a month or more. Every few nights…I never know."

"Thanks. I'll be back around. You still haven't seen the FBI guy, huh? Tom Garfield."

Huey shook his head. "Now how the hell would I know? We dead folk don't just go around introducing ourselves to one another, you know. We've got our own things to do. I mean, you don't go saying who you are to everyone on the street now, do you?"

"Try to help me, Huey, please. And by the way, that McManus girl was trying to say prayers for you."

"All right, all right...if'n I can help, I will. And hey, I'm telling you God's truth. I didn't hurt that girl." He hesitated. "I think I helped her. I did do some rock throwing, but I was aiming at the bad guys."

"Good man, Huey."

"She's still a McManus." Huey sniffed.

"Not her fault, Huey. I'm going to get the cops watching the cemetery, looking out for your junkies, Huey."

Huey cocked his head, looking at Brent. "I'd be careful on that. I mean, if you really want to catch these fellows. They see cops...they'll just move on over somewhere else. There's plenty of dark corners in N'Awlins for them folks to find. You want to catch 'em, better not spook 'em out of here."

"Good point, Huey, thanks."

A tour director was coming around the corner of one of the majestic society vaults. Huey faded away.

Brent slipped past the group and exited the cemetery. As he came out onto the sidewalk, he was startled when a man almost collided with him.

He looked up.

It was the FBI man, Haggerty. Today he was in a

baseball cap, sunglasses, jeans and a tailored shirt. Seeing Brent in his way, he swore. "What the hell are you doing here?" he growled.

"Visiting the cemetery."

Haggerty swore again. Brent assessed his appearance. The man was good. He no longer looked like a stereotypical agent.

Haggerty came closer to him. "Look, you idiot, don't screw me up. I work alone, I keep away from others, you got it? I don't like talking to other cops—even other feds—when I'm working. A man can get killed that way. So I sure as hell don't want to see you. Now get the hell out of my way, and never, ever act like you know me."

Haggerty hurried by him. The cops were right, Brent thought with disgust, the man was a jerk.

Shaking his head and feeling irritation sweep over him, he hurried on. Haggerty was apparently trying to follow in Tom Garfield's footsteps. A loner.

And yet, maybe he was right. Staying alive wasn't always an easy thing to do. Especially for an FBI man. Still…

Grimly, he decided he wanted to know more about the guy. Adam would be able to help him. And they would be forewarned in the future, should Harrison Investigations come across the man working any future projects.

Shaking off the unpleasant encounter with Haggerty, Brent jogged to catch a trolley and make it over to Lafayette Number 1. Glancing at his watch, he was amazed to see that it was only eleven-thirty.

He hesitated, winced and decided it was time to make a painful visit of his own.

* * *

"Who are you voting for, Mitch? Can you vote? Did we give the vote to Yankees yet?" Patricia said teasingly.

Mitch made a face. "Of course I can vote! I'm a resident."

"So who are you voting for?" Nathan pressed.

"Hell, I don't know. On the one hand, we've got an old liar. On the other hand, we've got a young liar," Mitch said.

"That's pretty cynical," Nikki said as they walked idly down the street. The area was, beyond a doubt, even busier than usual. And there were cops on every corner as crowds headed toward Jackson Square.

"How many times have you seen a politician carry through with a promise after he's been elected?" Mitch asked.

"Maybe it's harder to carry out a promise than it is to make one," Nikki suggested.

"But that's the thing—someone out there should be an honest politician. Tell the truth. No, I can't change the world, but I can take a few little steps," Mitch said.

Nikki laughed. "Well, if you acted as if you couldn't change much, no one would vote for you at all, probably."

She stopped to look at a flyer that had been pasted to a light pole. It was for Billy Banks. Nice looking, good smile, lots of charisma.

Mitch slipped an arm around her shoulders. "He's a cutie, huh? That'll make you vote for him, right?"

"Mitch, that's insulting. I'm voting for the best man."

"So which one is the best man?"

She shrugged. "I don't know yet."

"I don't, either. And I'm not here to listen to the debate. There's Contessa Moodoo's Hoodoo Voodoo. I'm going in," Patricia said, having had it with politics for the moment.

Nikki hesitated on the street, frowning.

Something in the crowd had distracted her. Something that she'd seen with her peripheral vision that had caused a little jump somewhere in the back of her mind.

But she didn't know what it was. She watched as people streamed down the street. She saw tourists in shorts, young women in halter tops, others in T-shirts. Men in business attire.

What could have bothered her about the group that had just passed?

Something had been oddly familiar.

But what?

She gave her head a shake, grateful that at least it hadn't been Andy, and followed the others into the shop.

While her friends chatted, looking over Contessa's wares, Nikki realized that she was uneasy.

And that Contessa was watching her.

While the others were checking out the potions, Nikki wandered into the part of the shop dedicated to the history of voodoo and those who currently practiced the art. She felt someone near her and tensed, always afraid now that she was going to see someone who couldn't possibly be there, and that sooner or later she would simply scream, fall down and be committed to an asylum.

But it was Contessa, her marbled eyes deeply concerned. "She died, yes? Your friend, she is no longer with us."

"Yes, she died. And you knew she was going to die," Nikki said. It was an accusation.

Contessa shook her head. "There was a color around her, and it was dark. It boded great danger. I didn't know she was going to die. She did not die by her own hand."

"Most believe that she did."

"That was not a question. I was telling you what is so."

Nikki nodded. "Well, I agree with you on that. I think she was murdered." She grimaced. "You don't happen to know by who or why, do you?" she queried.

Contessa shook her head. "But—"

"Nikki," Patricia called. "We've got to get going."

Nikki nodded. "But what?"

Contessa hesitated, just briefly. The others were heading for the door, calling out their thanks and waving for Nikki to follow.

"But what?" Nikki persisted.

The marbled eyes, deep and grave, touched hers. "You are in danger, too. The same danger. The same color, a deep, angry purple…it is around you, as well."

14

Walking into the cemetery, Brent hesitated. He opened his eyes.

There were so many.

So many ghosts.

Those who acknowledged him and those who did not. Those who sat around, looking morose, lost, and those who seemed angry, purposeful.

She was not among them.

She had moved on long ago. Years ago now.

He made his way to the grave, aware that several tours were gathering and that there were a number of people about who had come specifically to join the Myths and Legends of New Orleans group.

He didn't know who exactly, and it didn't matter.

He had time.

Her tomb was a single sarcophagus, always maintained—he saw to it. She had loved her church, and there were still nuns who kept the grave up while Brent was away. A statue of a weeping angel rose above the head of the concrete and brick bed where she now lay for eternity. Her name was written across the tomb, along with the dates of her birth and death, and the simple words "Daughter, wife, forever beloved."

He lowered his head, and he tried for the sense of peace he should feel. There had been justice at least. Her killer had gone to jail for life. Brent's bitterness had been so great that he had longed for Louisiana to make use of its capital punishment law, but that had not been the case. She had been killed by a stray bullet, in the wrong place at the wrong time.

Her killer had been murdered by a fellow inmate. Stabbed in the throat, his dying had been long and hard.

But Brent had discovered that vengeance, however decreed from above, didn't end the pain of loss. He should have possessed a greater ability to heal than most people, but the simple effect of death, no matter what a man's beliefs, was to leave human beings missing those they had loved. There were those without any extra abilities who dealt with the injustices of life better than he did because they were blessed with such deep and abiding faith. No matter. Nothing could change the fact that life here must be lived without the loved one.

And he had loved Tania. Her brilliant smile, her laughter, the sound of her voice, the very essence of her. She could laugh and tease, and then, when the moment called for it, say the most profound words. She could look at the world without judgment.

He placed his hand on the tomb and wished that her spirit was still present. Here he was; a man who could see and speak with ghosts, but his own wife had moved on. What remained of her was in his heart, his mind, his memories. He was grateful she had moved on, for if ever there had been a deserving soul, it had been hers, and yet…

So many lingered. So many stayed, some not even knowing why, what they needed, what they searched for, what could bring them peace.

Not Tania.

And for her sake, he was glad.

For his own…

For ten years he had been the one to wander the earth like a wraith, lost and alone, a pale shadow of himself. But there had also been moments when he could feel that he had a purpose. That his life counted. And it was true that time was the greatest healer of all.

I wish I could feel you, he thought.

But he couldn't. Nor had he reached either of his parents, ever again, after the night they had died.

What he felt, standing there, was the sadness that would always remain. But he had moved on now, and he knew it. And that made him feel a twinge of guilt, something he hadn't experienced before. He had known, laughed with and enjoyed other women since he had lost Tania.

But he'd never cared again, nor felt so alive, as he had when he'd been with Nikki. He'd never—even with Tania—felt such an instant bond, such an electricity.

He was deeply caught in his inner thoughts; it was as if he were surrounded by nothing but air and shadow. The world receded until there was darkness around him and the grave he stood before.

Then the world came back. And he knew that Nikki was there even before she cleared her throat.

He turned to her. She looked pale, distraught, sympathetic and a little uncomfortable.

"Your...wife?" she said softly.

He nodded.

"I'm so sorry."

"It's been a very long time."

"You...um...you might have told me that you'd been married and that your wife was buried here," she murmured.

"You never noticed this grave?" he asked.

She winced. "It's new. We usually tell tales about older grave sites."

He nodded and saw that Nikki gave a little involuntary shudder. She stared at him, eyes wide. "Is she... does she...do you...?"

"Does she walk the cemetery? Like Andy?" he suggested.

Nikki nodded.

He shook his head. "She's not here. She never has been. I mean, she's buried here. But...she's gone on. Long ago."

"What happened?" she asked gently. She had moved a short distance from him, on the other side of the sarcophagus, as if she felt that respect for the dead demanded that she do so.

"Stray bullet," he told her briefly. "She happened to be on the wrong street at the wrong time."

Nikki winced, lowering her head. "I would think... I would think that..." She looked up at him. "I would think that would make her stay. It's so horrible. So traumatic."

"The man was caught, sent to prison. He died there," he said simply. He heard a bird chirping and felt the breeze. "You would have liked her. She would have liked you. But she's gone. She wasn't the type who could hold a grudge. She was full of life and faith and...serenity. Whatever lies beyond, she's chosen it."

Nikki nodded uncomfortably, swallowed and looked away. Her arms were crossed over her chest. "When she died...is that when you began to...see ghosts?"

He shook his head. "No. I've seen them from the time I was a child. When my parents died."

Her eyes widened. "When your parents died?" she repeated.

He knew, of course. Nikki hadn't realized all these years that she'd had the same sense. She'd recognized only shadows, only the feel of what had been. But for her, it had been the same. The extra ability had been hers for many years.

It had only been since Andy died that Nikki had come to realize just what she was capable of seeing, hearing, feeling.

He smiled, tilting his head to the side. "Hey, I think we're supposed to be doing a tour."

"Um, yeah. You're all right?" she asked him.

"I am. You can read the stone. Tania died a long time ago. How about you?"

"Of course," she told him.

Still, he thought there was something a little strange about the way she said it. "You saw Andy again?" he asked.

"No."

"Really?"

"I really haven't seen her. But maybe she'll show up again this afternoon." Nikki shrugged. "I guess this is kind of…her place."

But Andy didn't show up that afternoon.

The tour went off like clockwork, which felt strange to Nikki, since she had been so unnerved ever since leaving the voodoo shop.

She had been determined that she wasn't going to say a word to anyone about the strange comments Contessa had made to her. After all, Julian already had her going to a shrink. And there were voodoo queens throughout the city. There was no reason to take Contessa seriously.

Except that Contessa had also seen something strange surrounding Andy. And it had been evident that day.

Still, she had been determined not to say anything to anyone. Including Brent. And she had made that decision before she found him so deep in thought before his wife's tomb that he hadn't even noticed her at first.

As the tour ended uneventfully, they decided that Brent would give the night tour with Mitch as his backup, giving Julian the night off.

"I can do the tour tonight, but I might not always be available," Brent warned them.

Nathan stared at him suspiciously. "Pressing business?" he demanded.

"Sometimes." Brent cast Nathan a cool stare, and Nathan looked uneasily away.

"Fine. Just fill in tonight. Patricia and I need a night off. And Julian does, too."

"Yeah, time for the new love in his life," Patricia teased.

Back in the Vieux Carré, Mitch asked Brent and Nikki if they minded him tagging along for dinner, and Brent assured him that he didn't. Nikki was glad of the company, feeling suddenly shy around Brent, though she wasn't certain why. He hadn't lied to her; he'd never said he hadn't been married. She'd just never thought he might be a widower. And having come upon him at the grave site, she felt slightly like an interloper.

They chose an Italian restaurant. The food was good, the service even better, and it was a pleasant, casual evening.

At one point Brent set a hand on Nikki's knee. She barely managed not to jump. When she looked at him, he smiled, and she realized that he had known she felt awkward and didn't want her to.

She smiled back and curled her fingers around his hand, where it lay on her knee.

As they sipped coffee, a shiver ripped through her; Contessa's words seemed to come back to haunt her. The same color that had surrounded Andy was now surrounding her. A deep purple. A warning, though Contessa hadn't exactly said so, of death.

She told herself that she didn't believe in omens.

But maybe she did. Andy was certainly dead.

She glanced at Brent. He was watching her strangely, as if he was aware that something was going on in her mind. She forced a brighter smile. She wasn't going to tell him about Contessa's words at the voodoo shop. She wasn't going to be such a mouse.

In fact, she was suddenly determined that she wasn't going to be afraid to see Andy anymore. She *wanted* to see Andy. She was going to find out what had happened, to make sure it didn't happen to her.

Mitch yawned, stretched and sighed. "I think I should have been rich. I like being a tour guide, but I think I could be happy just being rich. I'd just sit on my porch and sip mint juleps all day."

Nikki laughed. "You told me once that you didn't care for mint juleps."

"I'd get used to them," Mitch assured her.

"But none of us is filthy rich," Nikki said. She frowned, looking at Brent. "You're not filthy rich, are you?"

"Sorry," he told her.

"Well, I'm definitely not, so let's head for Madame's and pick up our tour, huh?" Nikki suggested.

There was a huge crowd around Madame's when they arrived.

"Is this all for us?" Mitch murmured.

"No," Brent said, his gaze directed through the glass panes in the front of the café. "There's a politician inside."

Nikki craned her neck and saw Billy Banks. Handsome and charming, seated at one of the inside tables, he appeared to be speaking with his public and signing autographs as he greeted voters.

Madame was behind the counter, looking flushed and pleased.

"He's young and passionate and energetic," Nikki mused. "He may just make it."

"What are his issues?" Brent asked her.

"Crime is his main issue. But then, it's Harold Grant's main issue, too. I don't know. I don't think Harold Grant has done such a bad job." She wrinkled her nose. "I just think Billy Banks is kind of a funny name for a politician. Do you think I'm holding that against him?"

"I think you're conservative by nature," Mitch said.

She shook her head. "I don't ever vote by party—I vote by what I believe. And I'm not all that conservative. Madame must be in seventh heaven, though. Harold Grant was in here a while ago, and now Billy Banks. This is really becoming the in place."

"Excuse me," a voice said quietly.

Nikki turned. A pretty woman with three teenage children and a skinny-legged man in shorts were at her side. "This is where the tour meets, right?"

"Absolutely," Nikki said. "We leave in—" she glanced at her watch "—ten minutes." She pointed to Mitch. "There's your moneyman, Mitch. The other gentleman is Brent Blackhawk. He'll be leading the tour. Go ahead and ask him questions now, if you like." She arched a brow and offered a wry grin to the men, indicating that she was only along for the ride. It was their tour.

While the tour-takers began to surround Brent and Mitch, Nikki found herself looking into the coffee shop. Madame had come out from behind the counter. Wiping her hands on her apron, she was standing in front of

Billy Banks, flushing, smiling, pleased, as she got him to sign one of her menus.

"Hey!"

Nikki turned. Mitch gave her a "we're going thataway" sign with his forefinger. She nodded and waited for the last of the group—a sizable one that night—as they moved forward.

From a distance, she watched Brent and felt a sweet warmth inside. He was damn good.

He seemed to honestly like people, and he enjoyed answering questions. His voice was deep and rich, his smile quick. She liked everything about him.

Maybe too much.

They stopped on a corner of Royal Street where there was an antique shop. He told a story about a Civil War soldier that she'd never heard before.

She wondered if he'd learned the story from the soldier himself.

A block later she was leaning against the wall, idly listening to a story about Andrew Jackson, when she stiffened.

What had caught her attention earlier was the bum. The bum who was really a government agent. Tom Garfield.

She hadn't recognized him because he was dressed in a handsome suit. Shaven. Hair trimmed. Clean and handsome.

And she was seeing him again.

He wasn't next to her. He wasn't even looking at her. He was in the midst of the crowd, apparently deeply intent on the story as he listened to Brent. Nikki moved away from the wall.

For some reason this man apparently trusted her. And Brent was desperate to get to him.

But they were in the middle of the tour. She could hardly just shout out, "Ghost! Ghost of the FBI guy, right in the crowd."

She had to reach the man herself, actually talk to him.

As she hesitated, still half-frozen, the story ended and the crowd began to move.

Nikki walked as quickly as she could, threading her way toward him.

But just as she neared the ghost, he looked to the right and frowned.

Then, instead of following the crowd, he ducked into a little alleyway in the middle of the block, which was partly residential, filled with courtyard homes, B & Bs and a few businesses.

Nikki almost ran, but by the time she reached the dark walkway, the man had disappeared.

"Damn," she swore.

She jogged about twenty feet down the shadowed trail.

"Sir? Mr. Garfield? Oh, please. Where are you? Help me now, please. I can help you, too. Please, I know you're here, I saw you. Please, don't take off on me."

Where to go?

There was a brick wall to her left, the backside of someone's courtyard. There were garbage cans, a gravel parking area and the sounds of jazz coming from her right. A few steps farther and she reached a low red brick property divider. There was the slight scent of restaurant refuse from the opposite side.

"Mr. Garfield?"

She felt the rush of wind before she heard the footsteps pounding up behind her. She spun around in a split second, in time to see the figure rushing at her, but not much more.

He was wearing a ski mask and gloves. In the heat of New Orleans.

She screamed, loud and shrill. In an instant she realized that he intended to silence her with a black sheet or sack of some kind.

Before he could reach her, she kicked out for all she was worth. Her purse tended to be heavy, and she swung it at the same time.

The man swore. A grunt of pain escaped him, and he doubled over.

Her heart racing, she turned to run down the alley.

He caught her ankle, and she went down.

But she did so screaming. Screaming, shrieking, her heart pounding like thunder.

The man started to crawl over to her.

"Nikki!"

She wasn't sure if she heard her name at first or not. But then she heard it again, along with pounding footsteps.

Her attacker froze, then began to scramble up. A sense of fury swept through her, and she found herself furiously fighting to hold on to him.

Help was coming. *Brent.*

But her assailant was powerful. He disentangled

himself, trying all the while to wrench her purse from her arm.

It was just a purse. Filled with material things, not even that much money. She'd always thought it was idiotic to hang on to anything material when under attack. *Let it go,* she told herself.

But she didn't.

She didn't know why she held on to it, but she did, still fighting, kicking and lashing out from the ground, even as the gravel and grit in the alley bit into her back.

The figure wasn't going to fight for it, she realized. He, too, had heard her name shouted, heard Brent pounding down the alley, closer and closer....

The figure released her purse and ran, a black form disappearing into the shadowed alley.

Brent reached her side, fell to his knees next to her, eyes sharp and anxious, features taut. "Nikki, are you all right? What the hell happened? Nikki, dammit, talk. Are you all right?"

She nodded, swallowed. "Fine. I'm fine."

"What the hell—oh, we'll talk about it later."

Apparently assured that she really was all right, he was instantly back on his feet, racing in pursuit of her attacker.

She heard his footfalls as he disappeared down the alley.

Then the blaze of a police siren blasted away any other sound. She elbowed herself up to a sitting position. By then Mitch had reached her, falling down on a knee by her side. "Nikki, my God, Nikki! Are you all right?"

She went through telling him that she was fine, then reassuring the several dozen tourists who crowded around, and then she had to tell the same thing to the first police officer on the scene.

Suddenly it seemed that officers were everywhere, crawling through the alleyway. One was begging the crowd to disperse.

People had come out from the rear doors of the jazz club and the restaurant, too.

It seemed forever before she could get her well-wishers to move back far enough that she could get to her feet, even with the help of one of the policemen.

She answered questions. The officer who had helped her gave sharp orders to the other men to get busy searching high and low.

Mitch kept worrying.

At last he spoke to their tour group, offering refunds.

Though they were still far from the tour's end, no one would take a refund. They all hovered, though.

In the middle of the bedlam, Brent returned, looking haggard and disgusted. He hadn't been able to catch her attacker.

The next thing she knew, she and Brent and Mitch were down at the station, and the first officer, a man named O'Malley, was telling her that there had been a number of purse snatchings, and the offender had matched the same description.

She was left alone in one of the conference rooms with Brent. He stared at her with impatience, and she saw that he was barely controlling his anger. A vein ticked hard in the side of his neck.

"Brent, I heard you coming. That's why I fought with the guy."

"All right, that was idiotic, too," he said, rising, pacing.

She was startled. "He attacked me! I had to fight back."

"He could have had a knife…he could have…" He threw up his hands, ending with an oath. He spun on her. "Why were you in the alley to begin with?" he demanded.

Startled, she opened her mouth. She knew the explanation was going to make him even angrier.

He set his hands on the table between them and leaned toward her, eyes sharp. "You followed someone into the alley, right?"

She hesitated, wondering how he knew it for a fact, how he could read her so easily.

"Andy?" he demanded.

She shook her head, glancing toward the door, hoping that the officers weren't about to walk back in. She hadn't entirely convinced herself that she wasn't crazy yet.

"The bum," she said. "Except that he's not a bum anymore. I'd actually seen him earlier in the day, but I hadn't realized it. He's…clean shaven. And in a suit. I saw him walk by earlier, but…"

"When?" Brent demanded.

"On our way to the voodoo shop." Now there was no way in hell she was going to tell him that Contessa had seen a purple aura around her.

She cleared her throat. "Look, I definitely wasn't

attacked by the ghost of an FBI agent. The man who attacked me was solid. There's no connection between the two of them. And I should never walk into an alley, no matter what. I've got that. I understand it now."

"You saw Tom Garfield, and you didn't tell me?" he asked quietly.

"I couldn't—"

"I asked you to tell me the minute anything happened."

"Dammit, Brent, you were giving a tour, and he didn't even come up to me. He was ahead of me. I followed him, hoping to…I don't know. Make contact, I guess. I mean, this whole thing is like I know this ghost, and I'm supposed to introduce you to him. Well, I don't know him. My God, this is the most insane conversation we've had yet," Nikki finished.

The door to the room opened. Brent stepped away, and Nikki straightened in her chair.

Neither of them was going to have this conversation in front of the cops, whether they knew about Brent's connection with the next world or not.

"Detective Massey," Nikki said, surprised that he was there.

"You like to keep us hopping around here, huh?" Massey said, smiling and trying to be light.

She shrugged. "I'm sorry. Did you just drop in to say hi, or do you think this purse snatcher is in on drugs and murder, too?"

Massey shook his head. He was staring at her strangely, and Nikki noticed that Brent seemed concerned by Massey's attitude.

Massey himself looked a little perplexed.

"Okay…what?" Brent said.

"This is nuts," Massey said.

"What?" Brent pursued.

"There was a young cop named Robinson who was one of the first on the scene," he said.

Nikki frowned, then nodded. "Robinson. Yes, he was with the officer who took the report. They're partners, I take it."

"Tall, slim guy?" Brent said to Massey.

Massey nodded.

"Well?" Nikki said.

Massey sighed and pulled out a chair at the table. "Okay…the guy who tried to take your purse…you didn't see him, right?"

"Oh, I saw him. Do I know what he looked like?" Nikki asked. "No. He was wearing a ski mask. He wasn't small, just medium height, medium build. He was strong, though."

"And…uh…real?" Massey asked. He flushed as they both stared at him. "I mean, you didn't think you were being attacked by a ghost, right?"

Furious, jaw clenched, she sat back. "Detective Massey, I am not ready to be committed. The man was real," she said tightly.

"And very much alive. I saw him running, and I chased him," Brent added, now at her side, tightly under control, but ready to lash out in her defense if need be.

"Is there a reason why you're asking this?" Brent demanded.

Massey sighed, shaking his head. "Please, don't take

offense, either of you. It's just that Robinson was on duty when another woman had her bag snatched. She didn't see the man who took her purse, but she was certain she knew who had stolen it. Robinson used to be a sketch artist, then went back on the street. He wants to apply for detective."

"I hope he makes detective, if that's what he wants," she said politely. "But what does all this have to do with anything? I told you, I can't describe the guy."

Massey glanced over his shoulder, at the closed door. "Don't either of you repeat what I'm about to say," he warned them, his tone a growl that couldn't mask his unease.

"What is going on?" Brent demanded, tense and impatient.

"The woman gave Robinson a description of the man she saw hanging around before her purse was stolen. The thing is...she gave him a description of Tom Garfield. An exact description. You...uh, didn't happen to see the man you identified hanging around in the alley, too, did you, Nikki? I mean, hell, I know Tom Garfield is dead. But either he has a double running around this parish, or else..."

"Or else what?" Brent asked sharply.

Massey glanced his way wearily. "Or else his ghost *is* stalking the town, and I'll be damned if I can figure out what that has to do with a purse snatcher."

15

Brent was silent most of the way as they walked back to Nikki's place. He still seemed tense, so she kept silent herself until they were back in her apartment.

She didn't know why, but the minute she opened the door, she felt uneasy. Once again, she had the bizarre feeling someone had been in her home.

"What?" Brent said.

She shook her head, taking her key from the lock. "I don't know."

"Is it Andy?"

"No."

"Then…?"

"I honestly don't know. I just keep having the feeling that someone has been in here." She hesitated, thinking the questions she was about to ask didn't bode well for her mental health. "Would I get this strange feeling if… if a ghost had been walking around in my place when I wasn't here?"

He shrugged. "Maybe. I don't know. Let's check the place out."

They did, but there was nothing missing, nothing moved.

But she still had a sense of something being just slightly out of focus.

She was walking toward the kitchen, telling herself that she was simply on edge, when Brent took her by the shoulders, fiercely turning her around to face him.

"Listen to me, you *can't* keep walking yourself straight into danger the way you did tonight."

"I don't go walking into danger," she protested.

"I told you to tell me the second you saw a ghost."

"I would have—"

"Forget *would have.* You can't let this happen again. You might have been killed. If I'd known..."

"If you'd known...what? Tom Garfield probably would have disappeared a whole lot faster," she responded. She pulled away from him. "Excuse me, will you? I'm still wearing half an alley."

He let her go instantly. His head was lowered, and she couldn't see his eyes, couldn't ascertain what he was thinking. But his body language was still tense.

She walked up the stairs and felt the distance escalating between them with each step she took. She hesitated, looking back. She could go downstairs, of course, and ask him what he thought about the fact that the victim of another purse snatching had been certain she had seen Tom Garfield just before the crime.

But that would just be an excuse. She didn't want to play games.

She held on to the railing at the top of the stairs and called down to him.

"Hey!"

"Hey what?" Startled, he looked up at her.

"Um…I don't have to see a bug again, do I?"

"Pardon?"

She let out a soft sigh of aggravation.

"I don't have to scream to get you to come up here, do I?" she asked softly.

His smile was instantaneous, and he threaded his fingers through his hair, pushing a dark lock back from his forehead.

"I'm on my way," he told her.

"I really do need a shower."

"Nothing wrong with cleanliness," he agreed, taking the stairs two at a time. She waited for him. And when he reached her, she forgot everything that had haunted her during the day.

Contessa saying she was surrounded by a dangerous purple aura.

The cemetery…his wife's tomb.

The ghost of Tom Garfield, now clean shaven, still walking the streets…

A very real man in black in the alleyway, attacking her…

In his arms, she was alive and life was good. The hold he had on her was powerful, the touch of his lips electric and combustible, eliciting a flow of heat that sped through her veins.

There on the stairway…just his kiss…the feel of his arms around her…

Tangled together, they moved toward her room, toward the bathroom, casting away the clothing they stripped from each other as they went.

His lips were still locked with hers as she fumbled for the shower spray.

Their tongues were entwined as they stepped beneath the cascading water.

Then there was the feel of his lips and tongue sliding down her naked flesh, along with the fall of the steaming water. There was the mist of heat that rose around them, creating a sheer physical eroticism that gripped her, the excruciating carnal feel of his hands, fingers, tongue…delving.

Here a brush, a touch, an invasion…

She very nearly collapsed atop him, but the urge to cling was great, the urge to respond greater, and her hands were suddenly wild as they played against the flesh and muscle of his body, teased with ever greater abandon, tormented him.

She had never imaged that simple soap could become such a stimulant, that bubbles could become so wickedly erotic. She was trembling and limp, yet ready to be aroused anew, when they stepped out, groping to turn the water off.

They left a double trail of damp footprints from the bathroom to the bed, where they began all over again. In those blissful moments the world receded, and nothing was real but the blatant sexuality that rippled and pulsed with the strength of his every movement, the power of his muscles, the depth of her hunger. They twisted, they moved, and in the end he fell to her side, heart still racing, breath rasping.

And then he pulled her close, and she felt as if all was right with the world when she lay there with him.

Soft light fell from the bathroom, but the bedroom itself was in darkness. Nikki basked in the sense of safety that came with lovemaking, and despite everything that had happened, she found herself drifting to sleep.

It meant something.

But what?

Brent lay awake in the night, glad of the feel and warmth of Nikki's body cradled against his own, relieved that she had drifted off.

He couldn't sleep himself. His thoughts kept racing. Why the hell would the ghost of Tom Garfield keep showing up at the sites of purse snatchings?

It made no sense. None at all. Maybe the woman who had given Officer Robinson the description had merely been agreeing with what the officer had drawn, and maybe it was just coincidence that the resemblance was so great.

He adjusted his position, loath to get up and leave Nikki, aware that he was restless and afraid that he would wake her.

He needed to lie still, to rest, to find the sense of serenity he could usually summon. There was nothing he could do now. Tomorrow he could go back to the police station, find out more about the woman who had worked with Robinson on the drawing, somehow finagle a name and address from Massey so he could talk to her himself. If he spoke with her, he might find out what the connection was, or decide there wasn't really a connection at all.

He slammed his pillow and tried to sleep.

Purple...

It was surrounding her, just as it had surrounded Andy.

No, she didn't believe that colors could surround people. She didn't believe in palm readings. Ouija boards.

But she believed in ghosts.

No, she merely believed in a sense of the past, of history, of lives gone by...

Nikki twisted, aware that she was half-asleep, and yet she was half-awake, as well. She knew she was in bed, that Brent was next to her. She was in her own home, a place she loved.

A place that seemed oddly invaded, even though nothing was out of place. Yet she had a sense that someone had been here tonight.

A sense.

A color.

Purple.

Brent sat up with a sudden jerk. *The cemetery.* He'd forgotten that he had told Huey he would be at the cemetery. He'd also forgotten all about dropping off information about McManus for the man's descendant.

"Brent?"

He nearly jumped a mile at the sound of Nikki's voice.

"What's the matter?"

He hesitated. He should have said nothing, gone to sleep and headed for the cemetery the following night. Instead he looked at her in the shadows. "Are you all right here alone?"

"I'm not alone."

"I know. But I have to go out…just for an hour or so. Will you be all right?"

"Brent, do you know what time it is?"

"I'll be all right. Trust me. But I'm worried about you."

"I'm worried about *you,*" she said.

He grinned in the darkness. "You don't need to be. And I won't be gone long. I just made a promise, and I need to keep it."

"A promise to who?"

"A ghost. And I won't go if you don't want me to."

"I'll be all right."

He hesitated.

"Brent, go. I'm all right. I'll double-bolt the door. No one will be able to get in."

"Nikki, what if…"

"I'm not afraid of ghosts," she said.

"But—"

"I used to be afraid of ghosts," she told him quietly. "I'm not anymore. I'll be fine. Honestly."

Brent rose quickly then. The sooner he went, the sooner he'd be back. "I'll hurry," he promised her.

"It might be nice if you explained this a bit further," she said.

"I'll tell you later. Promise."

He dressed quickly and headed for the door. She was

out of bed, slipping into a robe. "Right—you need to lock the door after I've gone."

"Take my keys," she said. "I'll probably be sound asleep before you get back."

"You need to bolt the door," he said.

She grinned suddenly, looking sleepy, mussed, beautiful. "I don't think a real human being has been here. I mean, I don't think a living human being has been in here. I think it's just been Andy, hanging out."

"You still need to bolt the door," he repeated firmly.

"All right," she said. "You go ahead. But be forewarned. From now on, you'd better have explanations as to where you're going. And be careful. Do you think you're invincible? I don't see you wearing a gun belt."

"I don't have a gun on me, that's true."

"Then you're just as vulnerable as I am."

He decided not to correct her. Nikki was certainly no coward, but he was a lot tougher than she could ever dream of being.

But she was right. He should go back to the B & B for his gun. No. No time, he decided.

"I stand chastised," he said, and gave her the breath of a kiss on the forehead.

He waited outside until he heard the bolt slide home. As soon as he heard the click, he began to hurry.

As ever, the streets remained alive. Jazz drifting on the air. A few drunks calling out to one another, weaving down the street.

A man stepped out of a strip club and lit a cigar.

On a street corner near one of the major historic hotels, a young woman played a flute. She had a hat set out in front of her for tips. He dropped in a few dollars, even in his haste.

Reaching the cemetery, he hopped the wall.

The place seemed quiet.

Far too quiet.

Brent found a seat next to one of the larger mausoleums and waited, still and silent. In a few minutes, he began to notice the mist.

Not the kind that lay on the ground but startling pools of fog and light, flitting quickly from monument to tomb, around corners, out of sight.

He realized that the ghosts were keeping their own vigil.

The longer Brent sat, the more he began to see. The young woman who had offered to help Huey was on duty, moving like a sylph, eyes wide as she watched.

He saw an old pirate on a peg leg dissolve around a corner. Then a couple in Victorian garb.

But he didn't hear a voice. Or see a living soul.

He leaned his head back against the wall of the tomb, closing his eyes. He needn't have come. Huey wasn't here, and the junkies working the cemetery weren't coming tonight. He'd had such high hopes. Catch one person involved, and they might begin to unravel the whole mystery.

He tried to get himself to think logically. Fact: An undercover FBI agent was dead. The cops knew he'd been onto something, but no one knew what. He'd been working the clubs. He'd met Nikki and Andy in Madame D'Orso's, and then Andy had died.

The exact way. But Andy had once been a junkie,

so her death could have been an accident, even though Nikki was certain it had been murder.

Fact: Andy was appearing to Nikki.

Fact: Tom Garfield was doing the same.

Fact: There was a purse snatcher at work in New Orleans. Tom Garfield's ghost had been witnessed before at least two of the attackers.

So where was the key?

Back at Madame D'Orso's? With one of the tour guides?

For that matter, where was the elusive Max Dupuis, who owned the tour company?

Tomorrow he had to talk to the other woman who had seen the dead FBI agent.

Suddenly his introspection was interrupted as something slammed against his thigh. His eyes flew open, and he looked up.

"I'm not afraid of ghosts. I'm not afraid of ghosts. I'm not afraid of ghosts," Nikki chanted.

She had thought she was fine with the idea of seeing ghosts. That she had become accustomed to it.

That it was much better to believe in ghosts and her own ability to communicate with them than to believe she was out of her mind and involved with someone who was just as nuts.

And she *was* involved. Deeply. He'd barely come into her life, and suddenly…

He *was* her life.

Good God, it wasn't that serious.

Yes, it was. She'd never felt anything like being with him.

Every light in the apartment was on, so there was nothing to fear from the shadows, because there weren't any shadows.

She had actually considered going back to bed when Brent had first left. But the mind played tricks. It teased and tormented.

So she wasn't going back to bed. She had no intention of waking from a deep sleep to find Andy was staring at her again.

She stayed downstairs, turned on the flat-screen television in the living room, making sure she was tuned to a sitcom, and nothing about forensics, cold cases, haunted America, haunted Europe or even historical tragedy. With the television blaring, she put the water on for tea.

Brent wouldn't be gone that long. He had said so.

The teakettle began to whistle. She forced herself to hum loudly as she made the tea.

Cup in hand, she returned to the living room.

There was an old episode of *Cheers* on, and she quickly found herself laughing. She just had to keep her mind off…

Don't think. Don't allow fear to slip in.

She was fine. She would be just fine until Brent got back.

Then…

She felt a prickling sense of unease wash over her, as if it had crept in slowly at first, taking her unaware. The teacup began to rattle in her hands. A deluge of dread began to sweep through her, and with her peripheral vision, she could see…

She turned, and her scream lodged in her throat.

"Huey," Brent said, shaking his head. The old ghost had given him one good fright.

"Injun boy, you're late," Huey told him.

"I know. Sorry. It was a really busy day."

Huey shook his head, grinning. "Don't matter none. It wasn't one of those nights. Told ya, I don't rightly know when they is and when they isn't gonna be here. But we're watching the place, the lot of us."

"I noticed."

Huey grinned broadly. "You noticed nothin'. I crept up on you like as if you was one of them usual fools." Huey's grin deepened then faded. "Hey, Injun boy, it's one thing if I creep up on you, but don't you be so easy when you're in here again late at night."

Brent rose, dusting his hands on his pants. "I promise. You taught me a good lesson."

"Go home, boy," Huey said. "They ain't coming tonight."

"All right. But I'll be back. And I won't be so late," Brent promised.

As he headed for the easiest place to jump out, he hesitated, turning back. "Hey, Huey, have you had any purse snatchers in here lately?"

"Purse snatchers?" Huey said. "Boy, them are drug runners in here now."

"Right. But that doesn't mean a purse snatcher couldn't come in here, too."

Huey shook his head. "Haven't seen any such thing lately. Maybe out on the streets, but in here…no. There's always suspicious folks around, some of 'em I could swear I see walking around the streets, just like you and me, and them thinking they're all different, masquerading when they pull off their shit in the cemetery."

"Who?" Brent demanded. "You have a description for me?"

"Some cops are good and some ain't!"

"Massey? Joulette?"

"When I know something, I'll be telling you."

"Huey—"

"When I got something, I'll tell you. Right now… just a feeling in my bones. Or…well, hell, where I used to have bones."

"All right. Thanks, Huey."

"You be back here, you hear?"

"You bet, Huey."

Brent started back the way that he had come along the streets, where people still wandered, just not as thickly as they did during the day.

A saxophone played a sad lament.

A drum beat out the rhythm of a rock tune.

On the corner, the girl still played her flute, the tune plaintive and beautiful.

He started down Nikki's street. And stopped.

He was suddenly certain that he had been followed. He turned around slowly.

There were discarded flyers for the contenders in the day's political debate strewn on the ground. Cleanup crews hadn't gotten around to picking them up yet. The wind picked up a piece of paper, and cast it back down again. A group of giggling young women went by, talking about the next club they were heading to.

No one seemed to be following him.

But New Orleans was full of shadows.

He started walking again, senses heightened. Had he heard footsteps? Real footsteps, set down by the living?

Or…

He heard the sound again. The footsteps had been real. He spun around. No one there.

The girls had moved on. He was well past the flute player. A middle-aged couple, arm in arm, was coming toward him. They smiled and wished him a pleasant evening.

He wished them the same.

He had been followed. He was sure of it.

He walked back in the same direction he'd come from, cut over a block and kept walking. He listened, waited.

But no one was behind him now.

Unease filled him. He had been almost back to Nikki's. Now she was there alone. He quickly turned and headed back toward her place.

He began to run.

When he reached the old house, he saw that all her lights were on. He quickly opened the gate and hurried to her door. Without bothering with the key, he slammed on the door, hard.

"Nikki! Nikki, it's me. Brent. I'm back. Let me in!"

For a moment there was nothing. He felt fear cloud his heart. Then the door opened.

He let out a sigh of relief when Nikki opened the door. She was in the long flannel robe she had donned before he had left. She stared at him in silence. She was pale, and her eyes seemed far too wide.

"Nikki?" he said, worried, and he grabbed her shoulders, ready to push past her, determined to meet whatever might have threatened her from within.

She touched his face then, quickly. "I'm all right," she told him.

"Then, what…?"

She caught his hand, clasping it warmly in her own, then taking the time to close and lock the door behind him before she started for the living room.

She wasn't alone.

There was a beautiful young woman, or the essence of a young woman, seated on the couch.

Dark and lovely, she stared at him like a frightened doe.

Her hand flew to her throat.

She started to rise, started to fade.

"No, no, Andy, don't go. Please don't go," Nikki said. "I want to introduce the two of you properly. Brent, this is Andy, Andrea Ciello. Andy, this is Brent, and there's no reason to be afraid of him. I've been telling you all about him."

Brent's heart thundered. He stepped forward, offering his hand. He felt the touch of mist. The slightest sensation as Andy offered her hand.

She stopped fading and managed a grin for Brent.

"How do you do—wow, Nikki. He's something," she said.

"You don't have to be afraid of me," he said softly.

"Well..." Nikki said, "We could all sit down, I guess."

"I should leave," Andy said quickly, giving them a subtly knowing look.

"Don't you dare leave," Nikki said.

"Please...you have to tell us what happened," Brent said.

Andy let out a sigh. "No, you have to tell *me* what happened," she said firmly.

But she sat.

And it was evident that she intended to stay.

16

"You have to believe me," Andy told Brent. "I *was* a junkie, but I'm not a junkie now. I was a junkie. Well, I'm not anything now, am I?" she murmured bitterly. "But I was clean when I was killed."

Nikki couldn't believe that she was sitting in her living room, in the dead of night—no pun intended, she told herself—listening to Andy's ghost try to explain herself to Brent.

It was cold, she realized. Ice cold with Andy here. Had she noticed that before?

Walking the streets, feeling ghosts, getting a sense of the past...no, she had never realized before that it got icy cold in a room with a ghost.

She felt as if she were dreaming, playing a part in some kind of theater of the absurd.

At the same time, she was proud of herself.

Andy had appeared again.

She hadn't had a heart attack. She hadn't even screamed. She had talked to Andy, and convinced her to wait for Brent to return.

She had learned some things about ghosts, as well.

Sometimes Andy could concentrate and be where she wanted to be.

It was easiest to be in the cemetery, and it was fairly easy to be in Nikki's apartment, except that unexpected noises made her evaporate. She was still afraid, very afraid, and not at all sure how she could be a ghost and still be afraid.

After all, she was already dead.

"Andy, you don't have to convince me," Brent told her seriously. "Nikki has told me about you. I believe that you were murdered."

"Oh, God," Andy said with a little sob. "Murdered."

"But you've known that," Brent reminded her gently.

"Yes, I just don't like hearing it. It makes it so… real."

"Nikki tells me that you're here because of the man, the bum. And he's dead, too," Andy said.

Brent nodded, never taking his eyes off Andy.

"I saw him, you know. I saw him wandering the streets. I tried to get here, you see. I knew Nikki believed in me. I knew she would help me."

Pain seared into Nikki's heart.

She hadn't been able to help her friend at all.

"Andy," Brent said, "we both want to help you now. And *we* need *your* help. Desperately."

Andy's beautiful eyes widened, appearing deeply troubled. "I don't know how I can help you. I don't know what happened. And there are times now…it's like learning to walk again. Sometimes Nikki's able to see me, hear me…and now you can see me, too. Sometimes I want to be with her, but I can't. Sometimes I can talk. I try to lift things, move things…but I'm not real, am I? Sometimes," she said wistfully, "I wonder just where I'm supposed to be. I need to leave, but I don't know where I'm going, and I need to be here because… what happened to me was wrong."

"We need your help, Andy," Brent repeated. "You're here now, so tell me, please, do you remember leaving the bar, leaving your friends, that night?" Brent asked her.

"Yes."

"What else do you remember?"

She shook her head. "I made it home."

"Okay. So you made it home. Did anyone follow you?" Brent asked.

Andy rolled her eyes. "A herd of rhinos could have followed me home and I wouldn't have known it," she said with a sigh.

"Okay, but you didn't notice anyone."

"Like I said…"

"Okay, how about at the bar. Did you see anyone watching you there?"

Andy shook her head.

Nikki sighed. "Everyone was watching her. She's very attractive."

"I was kind of cute, huh?" Andy asked Nikki wistfully.

"Gorgeous, actually," Nikki assured her.

"Stunning," Brent agreed. "Did you notice anyone weird at all that day?" he asked. "Do anything weird?"

She laughed. "Well, we went to a voodoo shop. But

this is New Orleans. I guess that makes Contessa normal."

"I know the shop," Brent murmured.

Nikki felt a twinge of guilt. She still hadn't mentioned her own strange visit to the shop or what Contessa had said. And she wasn't going to say anything. Not right now.

"The bum," Andy said. "The way he ran into the two of us at Madame's…that was weird. And that was it."

"Do you remember if you locked your apartment door?" Brent asked.

She lifted her shoulders. "I'm not sure."

"Andy," Brent said tensely, "this could be important. Really important. Think back for me. *Did you lock your apartment door?*"

"I don't know…I…yes. Yes, I think I did."

Brent sat back thoughtfully.

"What are you looking for?" Nikki demanded.

"You're just going to get mad when I tell you."

"Tell me anyway."

"All right. Andy locked her door. There was no sign of breaking and entering when she was found. That means someone else had a key. Who else had your key, Andy?"

Andy gave him a grim smile. "Only Nikki."

"And I didn't give it to anyone," Nikki told him firmly.

"No, of course not, I don't believe you did," he agreed.

"Then…?" Nikki asked.

"It's obvious. Someone borrowed it from you without your knowing it."

"Don't start on that again," Nikki snapped. She instantly regretted her words.

Andy began to fade.

"Wait, Andy, please," she said softly.

"Oh, Nikki, I'm sorry.... I'm not a very good ghost. Yet..."

As the sound of Andy's "yet" faded away, so did she.

Nikki hopped to her feet. "There, you've done it. She's gone."

He didn't even respond to her anger. He was deep in thought once again. "She'll be back," he said. He looked up at her. "Don't get angry. There's a connection somewhere. You know there has to be."

Nikki shook her head. "It wasn't one of my friends."

"Nikki, don't get mad," he said.

"I *am* mad."

But he ignored her. She wanted to fight it out. He wasn't going to be baited. He was deep in thought again, not looking at her.

Nikki shook her head, exasperated, and started for the stairs. She really needed some sleep. Maybe that was it....

She was sleep deprived, living in a world she had created in her own mind.

Nikki dropped her robe and slipped into bed. She closed her eyes and thought how remarkable it was that she really wasn't afraid now.

She began drifting to sleep, exhausted.

She didn't even start when she felt the hand on her

hip, the soft whisper of his words as they drifted against her ear.

"How mad are you?" Brent asked.

She turned to him. Saw his face in the shadows, felt his warmth, the vitality and life that radiated from his body, so near her own.

"Pretty mad," she murmured.

"How mad?"

He touched her, sliding in beside her.

"Maybe not *that* mad," she said, and seconds later she whispered, "Never *that* mad."

She remembered vaguely that she had heard couples should never spend a night in anger. And she wondered even more vaguely if it was still night.

It didn't matter.

Later, just before she drifted to sleep, she wondered if she dared believe that they were a couple.

And she knew that she didn't care if she spent the rest of her life seeing ghosts. She wanted the rest of her life to be with him.

Massey stared at Brent Blackhawk with disbelief. "You're not even a cop, but you want me to let you talk to a victim of a purse snatching."

"Yes."

"You have a lot of nerve, buddy."

He did. The guy always managed to appear relaxed and in control—except when he was with Nikki DuMonde. When he thought that she was threatened. Then he was as wired as a pit bull.

That was important. Massey made a mental note of it.

"Look, we both want to catch the perp who killed a federal agent and an innocent woman."

"We still don't know the two are related. In fact, a lot of the guys don't think they can possibly have anything to do with each other."

"They're wrong, and we both know it," Brent said.

Massey felt a little chill. Could this guy read minds, as well?

"Look, it's not legal for me to give you names and addresses. You know that."

"We're talking public record," Brent reminded him. "There was a police report, right?"

"Public record and contacting a victim are two different things."

"It would be perfectly legal for you to leave a slip of paper on your desk, and then I could read it," Brent pointed out.

Massey shook his head. "Look, I'm supposed to be helping you out. But you haven't given me anything. Nothing at all."

Blackhawk actually hesitated, dead-black lashes falling over those green eyes that seemed to cut like a laser. "Give me a few hours. I may have something for you."

"What's wrong with now?"

"I just need a little time."

"Blackhawk—"

"Leave that slip of paper on your desk. I swear, I'll have something in a few hours."

Massey shook his head in exasperation.

"You're becoming a bigger pain in the ass than that FBI guy."

"Really?"

"Well, maybe not quite. Hell, now I've got some of his partners in here looking for him. The guy wants to be the Lone Ranger, without even letting Tonto in. Sorry, no offense meant, no ethnic slur intended."

"No offense taken," Brent said.

"At least he thinks the rest of his own office is as inept as we are. Hold on," he muttered.

He dug in his desk, then shoved a file toward Brent.

"I've been playing straight with you, Blackhawk. So help me, you'd better be playing straight with me."

"I'll be back with info. Honest Injun," Brent said wryly.

Nikki realized, as she went to meet the morning cemetery tour, that she had forgotten to ask Brent about his late-night excursion. She had even forgotten to ask what he was doing that morning.

She was scheduled to work with Julian. She arrived at Madame's first, and as she nursed a café au lait, she wondered how his romance was going, and then began to hope that he would show up. She realized that she was feeling good—better than she had felt in what seemed like forever.

And all because she'd had a good conversation with a ghost.

She had no intention of telling Julian about the previous evening, and she knew now why you rarely heard about people who had conversations with ghosts—they kept quiet because the rest of the world would think they were crazy.

Julian arrived in sunglasses, looking sharp in a polo shirt and chinos. He sat across from her, sipping coffee as if it were a lifesaver.

"Hey," she said.

"Hey, yourself."

"You look tired."

"She's a barracuda," he said.

"Susan?" she asked, smiling.

"You don't think I've started acquiring a harem by going to *Girls! Girls! Girls!* do you?"

"You do look a little worn." She laughed.

He groaned. "She never sleeps."

"I'll do the talking. You just trail behind, how's that?" she asked him.

He frowned. "You're looking chipper. How is it that you're so happy when I seriously doubt you're getting any more sleep than I am?"

She grinned in return. "It's just that I'm getting quality sleep," she assured him. "Hey, look. That's Harold Grant inside again, isn't it?"

As Julian turned, she studied the man inside Madame's, buying coffee at the counter. She was surprised to feel a pang of pity for him, and she wondered why. He was a stalwart politician. To the best of her knowledge, he tried to keep his promises. And he hadn't lost the election. Not yet, anyway.

"He looks tired, too, huh?" she said to Julian.

"Why not? Billy Banks is yapping right at his heels."

The man walked out of the coffee shop, two of his

aides in tow. Passing their table, he smiled at them absently and hurried on.

"He didn't even tell us to vote for him," Julian said.

"You think it makes all that much difference, who's in and who's out?"

Julian shrugged. "I don't know that much about politics and local government," he said, "but the guy looks tired. I wouldn't want the job. I can't imagine where in the world it would be harder to create a climate of honesty and ethics than here, in the land of *Girls! Girls! Girls!* People love New Orleans because there's a sense you can do what you want to do here—short of the obviously illegal, of course. If someone could come in and maintain that, and still wipe out the stuff that comes with it—you know, murder, hard-core drugs, child porn, all that stuff—I'd vote for him in a minute. Maybe that is Harold Grant. And maybe we need Billy Banks, although he seems to me like a Bible-thumper who doesn't show up in church come Sunday." Julian shrugged. "I'll probably be voting for old Harold. He looks worn but tough. You know, like a good old bulldog."

Nikki rose. "Our customers are starting to arrive."

"Where's lover boy this morning?" Julian asked.

"Off somewhere."

"Good heavens, the romance can't be over already?"

She smiled. "We didn't turn into one person," she told him.

He inched his sunglasses up. "No? Just about. It seems as if you don't need me anymore."

She kissed his cheek. "I'll always need you. You're

my best friend. But…well, looks like you've got your barracuda."

He groaned. "You're not going to believe this—and if you repeat it, I'll call you a liar and wash your mouth out with soap—but I can't keep up with her."

Nikki laughed. "So where is she now?"

"Back at my place." He shook his head. "Nikki, I may have to move. Hey…maybe I could have to work late tonight, huh? We could have a planning meeting or something."

"Hey, I'm not the boss."

"Oh, convenient. Push us all around in his absence, then, when I need help, pretend that Max cares."

"I think he does care."

"Not enough to be here," Julian said.

"He knows what's going on," Nikki said. "He can be generous when he wants. And I'm willing to bet he knows everything that's happening."

"So call him. Tell him we need a planning meeting."

"Julian, be a big boy. Tell her that you have a life. Now come on. Those people over there are looking for a tour guide."

Julian nodded and followed her over to the group that was forming.

The most striking thing about Nancy Griffin was her resemblance to Nikki, at least from the back.

She was the same height, and she had very similar hair. Her eyes were different, a deep brown, but she was attractive, about the same weight, and she moved in the same easy, naturally sensual way.

She met Brent at Café du Monde. He knew who she was the second he saw her coming.

"Mr. Blackhawk?" she asked, coming over to the table.

He had risen. "Yes, and thanks for meeting me."

She shrugged. "The police have basically said that they can't do anything about it. I've already canceled my cards." She sighed. "What I'm really sorry about are the pictures, some of nieces and nephews that I probably can't replace. One of my sister and me as little kids… well, you know. I lost some cash, but hey, that can be replaced."

"They may still find your discarded purse somewhere," Brent told her.

"I hope so. Are you some kind of special agent?" she asked. She flushed slightly. "The only reason I'm meeting you is that you called me from the police station."

"Smart girl. You checked that out?"

"Caller ID." She laughed. "Luckily, my cell was in my pocket. Anyway—"

She broke off as their impatient waiter came to the table. "Miss?"

"Café au lait, please," she said.

"No beignets?" Brent asked.

She smiled again. "I'm on a diet. Eternally. You can gain some mean weight in New Orleans. So…what can I tell you? It was night, and I was pretty much so an idiot. I saw the bum—that police officer did a perfect sketch of him—and a minute later, my purse was gone."

"From what I understand, you didn't actually see the person who lifted your bag."

She shook her head and thanked the waiter as he delivered her coffee. "No, I was standing by an alley."

"Off Royal?"

"Yes. I felt a tug, and it was gone. That's all there is to it. What else can I tell you?" she asked.

"I'm curious about the rest of your day," he told her. "Before your purse was stolen."

She frowned. "Why?"

"You might have been followed."

"Why would anyone follow me?"

Because you look just like someone else, he thought.

"You never know," he told her. "I may not be able to get your pictures or anything else back for you, but…" He shrugged. "I can try."

"Let's see…I came here for breakfast. I went to the Civil War museum, and then the new museum on World War II."

"Go on. Did you take any tours…go into the cemeteries, anything like that?"

"Not that day. I came here, went to the museums…and we—my girlfriends and I—were shopping in the French Quarter. It was night by then. Oh, we ate hamburgers that night at a place on the fringe of the old area…lunch was at the hotel. That's about it."

"You weren't in any of the cemeteries, you're certain?"

"I'm certain."

Brent was disappointed; he had been sure he would find a connection to Nikki, especially once he had seen Nancy.

He didn't show his disappointment. "I'll do anything I can to help find your pictures," he assured her.

"Thanks," she said, and asked, sounding puzzled, "Are you a cop?"

"No, I'm with a private agency, and what happened to you may be connected to a few other things going on," he told her.

"Ah." She lingered with her coffee cup, looking down at it for a minute, then back at him. "You're nicer than the cops. They just seemed tired. I guess they get too much of this kind of thing."

"Maybe."

"Well, feel free to call me if you need anything more."

"Thank you."

He set a bill on the table and rose. She did the same. "Seriously, feel free to call me any time," she told him.

He smiled. Not long ago, he might have been happy to pick up on the obvious invitation. "I will."

"You're not from here, I take it?" she said.

"Actually, I am."

"Are you married?" she asked bluntly.

"No. But…"

"Involved," she said with a sigh, and smiled, a dimple showing. "All the good ones are. Ignore me. And thanks. And if you can get those pictures back, great."

She started to walk away, hesitated, then turned back. "Actually," she said with a frown, "now that I think about it, we didn't come here for breakfast that morning. It was another little place. I can't think of the name of it. But you'd asked me about tours. Tour groups meet there. It was called…"

"Madame D'Orso's?" he suggested.

She snapped her fingers. "That's it! That's where we ate. Anyway, good luck."

With a wave, she was gone.

"Marie Laveau," Nikki said, "has the reputation of being *the* voodoo queen of New Orleans, though there were those in power before her and those who came after her. Actually, at the end of her life, she returned to being a devout Catholic, and throughout her practice, Marie combined gris-gris with statues of saints. There were those who said she was in league with the devil—Papa Las Bas, as he was known—and there were those who thought that she had divine connections. What she definitely had was an uncanny ability to listen. As she did the hair of the rich, she eavesdropped. She was careful to learn everything she could about everybody. She was definitely a woman who wanted power and knew how to achieve it.

"She died in 1881. We're here now at her grave. Many people come here now, some with their own beliefs—and others because it's the thing to do," Nikki said, smiling. "As you can see, there are exes and crosses marked on her grave…and someone left an offering of a po'boy! Interesting. The cemetery insects are going to be very happy. As to Marie's spirit, many believe that it rises every June 23, St. John's Eve. They believe that she reigns over a magnificent ritual carried out on that night."

Nikki's audience appeared to be entranced. No matter what other stories she and the others told in the cemetery, Marie Laveau's legend was the one people wanted to hear.

She saw Julian at the back of the crowd, leaning against one of the tombs. His head was lowered. He really was exhausted, she thought.

"So her fortune-telling was just repeating what she'd overheard, right?" a man asked.

Nikki was surprised that the question suddenly made her uncomfortable. She smiled and kept her eyes on Julian as she replied. "Well, if a fortune-teller foretells a hundred incidents and a few come true, is it something uncanny, is it coincidence—or is it simply being aware of people, their thoughts, desires and secrets? Maybe it's a bit of all those things combined."

The man said something else, but she didn't hear him.

A chill had washed over her.

Tom Garfield was here.

In his suit, looking handsome and sad. He walked right past Julian, who looked up suddenly in confusion, glanced around, frowned and closed his eyes again.

Garfield came through the crowd.

As he did, people stepped aside. One girl shivered, looked up at the sun, then shook her head in confusion.

Garfield stopped then, just a few feet in front of Nikki. His mouth was working, but she couldn't hear what he was saying.

"Miss?" She was barely aware of the word.

Then he stopped talking and his image faded into the sunlight.

"Miss? Are you all right?"

She started and looked at the man who was talking

to her. She glanced toward the rear of the crowd. Julian had straightened. He was staring at her, looking worried.

As if he was about to haul her back to the psychiatrist's office.

She smiled at Julian, and turned to the man at her side.

"I'm sorry, what?"

He laughed. "You gave me a start there. Looked as if you were going into some kind of trance or something. So, I said, do you think her ghost prowls this cemetery?" he asked.

"I…I imagine she's a very busy ghost," Nikki managed to say lightly. "*If* one believes in that kind of thing, she might wander here, or all around New Orleans and the bayou country."

She lowered her head, inhaled deeply, looked up and around.

There was no sign of Tom Garfield.

But he had been there. And he'd been trying to reach her. He had something to tell her.

And she was almost certain she had figured out one of the words he had said.

Brent decided he wasn't going to have to worry about staying awake that night.

In the time he spent seated at Madame's, watching those who came and went, he was certain that he consumed several gallons of coffee.

He waited until the lunch crowd had dwindled.

As usual, Madame came out with her coffeepot, refilling cups.

She came to his table. "Well, hello there. All alone today?" she asked cheerfully.

"At the moment," he replied.

"So you're working with the tour group now?" she said, offering him a big smile.

"Yes. It's a good group."

"Yes. Terrible thing about Andy," she said, sighing.

"Very sad. Did you know she was a junkie?"

Madame glanced around, sighed and joined him at the table. "It does appear that she…well, she must have just slipped."

"Some people don't believe that," Brent said.

Madame shook her head. "Nikki. Well, that's Nikki for you. She sees the best in everyone."

"So you think Andy fell back into her old ways?" Brent asked.

"Honey, I don't know what else to think."

"You must have seen the newspapers, the television," Brent said. "An FBI agent was killed with a massive dose of heroin. In fact, the girls saw him in here that day."

Madame looked distressed. "I know. And I so badly wanted to help the police. But I never saw the man! It must have been busy…mornings can be crazy, you know." She knocked on the table. "Thank the good Lord or the voodoo gods or whoever. Everyone in New Orleans passes through here, honey. Everyone! Politicians, doctors—even movie stars and jazz messiahs."

"Right. The French Quarter really isn't all that big, is it?" Brent murmured.

"Not at all, honey, not at all."

"Hey, what do you know about Max?" he asked.

"Max?"

He offered her his best engaging grin. "Yeah, the boss. I haven't met him yet."

Madame sniffed and waved a hand in the air. "He's a user. He's got Nikki doing all his work, and that's the way it's been from the beginning."

"Well, it may just mean that he knows how to delegate."

She sniffed. "Andy died, and he didn't even make it back into town."

"What about the others?"

"The other guides?" Madame sounded surprised. She apparently liked to gossip, however, because she seemed happy enough to linger with him at the table. "Well, they're all right. Let's see, Patricia, she's a little doll. I don't know if she should trust Nathan or not, though. Seems he's a little…I don't know, out of it sometimes. There's Mitch. Nice guy. Trying too hard, maybe."

"And Julian?"

Madame waved a hand in the air, shaking her head. "He's good. If he had a little more energy, he could make it in Hollywood. The boy is one good actor."

"And what about you, Madame?" he said teasingly.

"Me?"

"How would you be as a tour guide? You must know

all about this town. Think of all you get to hear on a daily basis."

"Honey, most goes in one ear and out the other, I'm such a busy woman." With a sigh, she rose. "I need to be getting back to work."

"Madame, you're absolutely sure you didn't see that FBI agent, Tom Garfield?"

She shook her head. "Honey, if I had seen that bum, I'd have had the cops in here. You know, you're pretty nosy. Thinking about being a cop yourself?"

He shook his head.

"See you later then, Brent. Hang in there. You'll do well enough."

Brent studied her as she served coffee to the next table. She was the perfect hostess. Was she too perfect?

Though she hadn't been scheduled for it, Nikki volunteered to take the afternoon tour through the Garden District and cemetery, trading with Patricia and Nathan, who agreed to take on the tour of the French Quarter that night. It was easy enough to convince Julian to trail along behind her.

The tour was uneventful.

She was a little sorry that Andy didn't make an appearance. Now that she had found the inner strength to deal with what couldn't possibly be but was, it seemed she was going to be left in peace.

But Tom Garfield had been in the cemetery on Basin Street. And she could have sworn she knew what he had tried to say.

Tonight.

Something was going to happen in the cemetery that night.

There was a flower vendor outside the gates, and once Nikki had finished with her group, she went and bought several bouquets.

She took one to her family mausoleum and lingered there. If Andy was going to make an appearance, it should have been there.

But though she waited, wondering vaguely where Julian had disappeared to, no one came by. At last she walked to the tomb of Brent's wife.

There she laid down her second bouquet of flowers.

That was when she realized she was being watched.

17

From Madame's, Brent headed back to the police department.

When he left the café, he knew that he was being followed.

And by whom.

That was fine. Interesting, even.

But first he had to talk to Massey, and he knew it was going to be a difficult conversation.

"It has to be you, and you alone," Brent explained for the hundredth time.

Massey glowered at him. "But if this is a major operation—"

"I don't know what it is," Brent said.

Massey shook his head. "And you know about this because...?"

"If I told you, you wouldn't be happy."

Massey shook his head again. "What's going to happen?"

"Maybe nothing."

"Great. Like I have lots of free time. Like I want to crawl around a cemetery with you at night."

"Have you got anything else?" Brent asked him.

Massey sighed. "No," he admitted with a scowl.

Marc Joulette, bearing a cup of coffee, walked over to Massey's desk, staring curiously at the two men.

"I'm asking Massey for help on what may be a wild-goose chase."

"You sure as hell better invite me in on it," Joulette warned. "Where are we going, and why?"

"I have reason to believe that a drug ring is using the cemetery," Brent said, explaining as much as he felt Joulette would be willing to buy and using the attack on Marie McManus as further evidence. He left out the ghost, since neither cop would be willing to believe that an old slave haunting the cemetery had been his source of information.

"You weren't going to tell me?" Joulette said, frowning at Massey.

Massey shook his head, but looked guilty. "I wonder if we should try to locate Haggerty and tell him."

They were all silent.

"We have to keep this quiet," Brent finally said.

Joulette scowled. "You think we don't know how to run a stakeout?"

"I didn't say that. Look, I could be an alarmist," Brent said politely. "But the way I see it, you're just staking out a possible drug connection. You wouldn't want to notify the feds, because it could turn out to be nothing, a wild-good chase."

He rose. "I'll be in there, waiting. See you tonight."

Brent left the station.

He knew Patricia was going to be out on the street, but he didn't expect her to panic and start to run away.

He caught up with her quickly. He didn't touch her, just said her name softly.

"Patricia."

She went still and slowly turned to look at him. He smiled. "You followed me. Why?"

"I…I don't know. Because I was near Madame's and I saw you there, talking to her…and I was curious. And then you came here."

He nodded. "You know that Nikki was mugged."

"I don't think that's why you were here," she said. "You're not a real tour guide, either. I don't know what you are…." She flashed him a quick glance. "And I'm not sure I want to know."

"So you followed me."

She looked upset. "I shouldn't have."

"Patricia, I can tell something's bothering you. I don't know how to convince you of this, but anything you tell, I'll consider a total confidence."

She still looked upset. "Want some coffee?" she asked.

"I'll have an iced tea. Let's grab something and find a quiet corner."

He was afraid she was going to back off, refuse to talk to him. But she was obviously miserable, and at last, it seemed, she decided that talking had to be better than what she was feeling.

"All right."

A few minutes later, she had a large coffee and he had iced tea, and they were seated in a shady corner of a small brasserie, far from the few other afternoon stragglers.

Patricia played with her stirrer, and then her napkin, looking down at it as she folded it and refolded it.

"I shouldn't be here," she said.

"But you're worried about Nathan."

Her eyes shot to his with wide surprise; then she flushed. "Well, I guess it didn't take a palm reader to know that."

He shook his head.

"I'm really in love with him," she murmured. "But... I'm worried."

"Why?"

"The night that Andy died...I woke up, and he wasn't with me."

"Oh?"

She shook her head. "But there would be no reason for Nathan...I mean, it's silly, isn't it? There's nothing violent in Nathan. He liked Andy. Nathan is a good person. He walked out of a store once with a pack of gum, realized it twenty minutes later—and we had to go back to pay for it. I guess I just had to talk to someone. And you're trying to figure out the truth about Andy, aren't you? That's really why you're here."

He smiled, touched her hand. "No, I'm here for another matter, but...I think what happened to Andy has something to do with it."

"If I love him, I should have faith in him, right?"

"Blind faith isn't always a good thing."

"Oh, God! I can't imagine what he'd think if he knew I was here with you, talking like this," she murmured.

"Patricia, let me see what I can find out, if something is bothering him. How's that?"

She smiled. "You won't—"

"I swear, he'll never know we talked," Brent assured her.

Patricia rose. "I'm glad that Nikki has you," she said gently. "You really are something. Something good, I mean."

"Thanks."

She started to walk away, then turned back, frowning.

"She does have you, doesn't she? I mean, this isn't just a..."

The question took him by surprise, and it took him a second to answer. Then he said, "She has me. As long as she wants me."

He rose and joined her. As they walked out together, she studied him. "I hope that...well, I just hope that whatever you are...you don't hurt her."

"I would never hurt her."

Patricia looked away, then back at him. "Or cause her to be hurt?"

He felt a tightness around his heart. Could he cause her to be hurt?

No. He wouldn't allow it to happen.

"I would die myself before allowing her to be hurt."

Patricia smiled, then asked wistfully, "I wonder if Nathan feels that way about me. Never mind, don't answer. And ignore me. Go find Nikki."

He nodded and left her.

* * *

Marc Joulette sat at his desk, not working. He shook his head. Massey looked up at him. "What?"

"Nothing."

Joulette pretended interest to the file in front of him. He didn't know what the hell to do.

"Are you going to try to call Haggerty?" he asked Massey.

Massey lifted his hands. "We don't know what the hell we're in for tonight."

"Right."

"So what would be the point?" He got up and walked away. Marc looked back at the file, but the words simply spun before his eyes.

He got up, figuring more coffee couldn't hurt.

As he crossed to the Mr. Coffee, he saw his partner.

Owen Massey was standing in an alcove, talking on his cell phone.

Marc walked back to his desk, sat, hesitated, stared in the direction in which Massey, now concealed by a dividing wall, had gone, then reached for the phone on his desk.

He set it back into the cradle, and pulled his own cell out of his pocket.

He was still talking when Robinson came walking over to him. He flicked his phone shut without finishing his conversation. "What is it, Robinson?"

"Thought you might like to know—we were just called to the building where Andrea Ciello lived."

"Yeah?" Joulette said.

"Her place was torn apart."

"Torn apart? It was robbed?"

"Hell if I know. We're going to have to get hold of her friends or someone, try to find out if anything was taken." He shrugged. "You try to give people a little time, but we should have had her friends in there, cleaning out the place before now. She didn't have any family, but her rent was paid through the end of October, so we didn't rush things. It doesn't look like a robbery, though it looks like someone was searching for something. The crime scene folks are working it now. But there was a stereo, DVD player, jewelry—none of it touched."

"Who put in the call?" Joulette demanded.

"Mrs. Montobello." He rolled his eyes. "She thought that Andy had come back as a ghost, that she was tearing her place up looking for something."

Joulette sighed. "And I'm willing to bet the other tenants were out, right?"

"On the nail," Robinson said. "The report is on my desk. Just wanted you to know you guys are welcome to it."

"Thanks," Joulette said. Robinson walked away, and Marc Joulette waited for Massey to return from his call.

When he left Patricia, Brent hopped on the streetcar and headed for the Garden District. When he arrived, it seemed at first that the cemetery was oddly quiet and empty. He closed his eyes, felt the mist sweep around him.

He opened his eyes, searching.

Here, there…a ghostly form, none of them Andy, and none of them Tom Garfield.

He hoped that Nikki hadn't left and felt in his pocket for his cell phone, thinking he would just give her a call. As he pulled it out, he wandered past her family mausoleum, hoping to find Andy Ciello.

She wasn't there.

On a hunch, he headed toward his wife's grave.

As he neared it, he dropped his phone.

Nikki was there.

But she was obscured by a strange man in a long black coat. He was tall, with long dark hair, and he looked like one of the weirdos who roamed the parish, like maybe he was convinced he was a vampire or something.

He looked as if he was threatening Nikki.

"Hey!" Brent yelled.

Nikki turned. The man reached out, as if to grab her.

Brent raced, adrenaline kicking through him, remembering his words to Patricia. He would die himself before he allowed Nikki to be hurt.

He tackled the stranger, and they fell to the ground together.

He heard Nikki scream, "Stop!" But the sound didn't filter through to the rational section of his mind. He flipped the man and straddled him. "Who the hell are you? What are you doing?"

To his amazement, the man—lean, with sharp, narrow features—stared up at him, not fighting and looking at him with something almost like amusement.

"Brent!" Nikki cried.

But he still ignored her, watching in confusion as the man started to smile. "Nikki, you didn't tell me that you'd hired a bouncer."

"What?" Brent said.

"I'm Max Dupuis." The man cleared his throat. "Your employer, I believe."

Brent remained very still for long seconds, feeling like an idiot. Then he rose, reaching down to help the other man to his feet.

He had definitely overreacted.

"Brent. Brent Blackhawk," he said.

Nikki was still staring at him as if he'd lost his mind. He gave her a grimace with a quick, almost imperceptible shrug of his shoulders that asked, How the hell was I supposed to know?

"I guessed you were Blackhawk," the man said. He still seemed amused, rather than offended. "I hear you're a natural."

"I know the area. A lot of facts and a lot of legends."

"Good to meet you."

"Yeah, um, sorry about that. I guess I'm a little tense. Nikki was mugged the other night."

"She was telling me," Max said, eyeing Nikki. Brent had to wonder if he'd hurt the guy. He was almost painfully thin, which made him appear even taller. If he were a teenager, he would be a Goth, but Max was no teenager. He appeared to be in his early to mid thirties. "I hear you ran the fellow down."

"No, I didn't catch him."

"You got him away from Nikki, that's what counts." He smiled. "So, got some time? How about some coffee?"

Brent kept from groaning aloud by glancing toward the ground. "I have some time," he said, looking at

Nikki. Then he looked back at Max, and realized that suspicion was already creeping into him. So this was Max. Where the hell had he been all this time?

Out of town? Or lying low somewhere? Dressing up in a dark mask and attacking women in the street? And if so, why? Then there was the information he had just received about Nathan. There was only one thing to do, and that was check them all out one by one. He was certain of one thing, though: Madame's place was involved somehow.

He wondered about Max's arms. Was he a junkie? The man was thin enough. Scrawny, but he didn't look wasted. Then again, if you were selling drugs, and making a mint, you might well be smart enough not to sample your own wares.

Max, apparently oblivious to Brent's assessment, glanced at his watch. "Hell, not coffee. It's well past cocktail hour. Let's have a drink. On me. I've got my car, so we'll head back into the Quarter, if that's all right with you two?"

Nikki shrugged, frowning as she watched Brent. She seemed concerned, he thought, shrugging as he looked back at her. "Fine with me," he said.

Max started walking; Nikki did the same.

Brent held back for a few seconds. He touched the tomb, feeling that little stir of pain and nostalgia.

And he noticed the flowers that someone had brought. Nikki?

"Brent?" Nikki had turned back.

He smiled. "I'm with you. Right with you."

Max's car was a Lexus. The inside was clean—a surprise, since the outside of the car looked as if he had been driving through a swamp.

"Sorry," Max apologized. "I had her down to the bayou country. I was meeting with some shrimpers."

Nikki laughed. "Max, it looks as if you took the car straight *into* the bayou."

Nikki sat in front; Brent in the rear. Max was a good driver. He dexterously made a U-turn to head back to the Vieux Carré.

He caught Brent's eyes in the rearview mirror. "The shrimpers are having a rough time. They need legislation to stay afloat. We're shipping in foreign-caught, frozen shrimp, and families that have been in the industry for years are going to go down if new laws aren't passed. And the thing is, fresh shrimp, caught in our own waters, taste better. That's why you get some of the finest seafood you'll ever have right here in New Orleans. The thing is, I think folks would be furious about what's going on and they'd change things themselves if they were a bit more educated. If restaurants had to tell them where their seafood came from."

"Max, I thought you were in Colorado," Nikki said, mystified. "Don't get me wrong. I'm delighted that you're fighting for the shrimpers."

"What's the deal with the politicians?" Brent asked.

Max flashed him a rueful smile. "They all lie?" he suggested, then shrugged. "Who really knows? I'll say this, Harold Grant has done a lot of work for the industry, but...not enough. Billy Banks claims he's a powerhouse, and that things will get done when he's in office. Are you a local?"

"Yes, and no," Brent told him, leaning back. They had reached the Vieux Carré.

"Oh my God!" Nikki gasped suddenly.

"What?" both men asked.

"I forgot Julian."

"You forgot him?"

"He was in the cemetery with me for the tour," Nikki explained, pulling out her cell phone. Just as she did so, it rang.

"Julian?" Nikki said.

He and Max could vaguely hear the agitated sound of Julian's voice. Then Nikki said, "Okay, okay… okay… *okay.*"

She clicked the phone closed and looked at Max. "Can we take a run back to the cemetery?" she asked.

Max laughed, and turned the car around.

"We have a meeting, a must-have meeting, because Max is back," she said.

"We do?" Max asked.

She frowned at him. "Please?"

"Sure. I'm a vicious boss, huh?"

"For today," Nikki said.

"Are you two speaking another language?" Brent asked.

Nikki turned, grinning. "Julian got himself too entangled too quickly. His sudden roommate found him in the cemetery. He told her that he has an important meeting."

"Ah," Brent murmured.

Julian was waiting at the cemetery gates. Susan had her arm looped through his.

Julian quickly introduced her to Max and Brent. As soon as they reached her hotel, Julian saw her out, disentangled himself quickly, slipped in next to Brent again and said, "Max, step on it."

Making a tsking sound in his throat, Max did so.

Julian leaned back in the seat, closing his eyes. Then they flew open again. "Nikki, how could you do that to me?"

"Julian, I didn't know where you were."

"But you didn't look for me."

"Honestly, Julian, I'm so sorry. Max showed up, and then Brent came and nearly decked Max, and—"

"What?" Julian said, puzzled.

"I didn't know who he was," Brent explained. "I thought he was hitting on Nikki."

"I wasn't almost *decked,*" Max protested.

"I tackled him," Brent said diplomatically. "He was with Nikki, and after what's been happening, I just jumped to conclusions."

Max shook his head. "Nikki is probably more at home in any of these cemeteries than anyone I know. If she thought she was in danger, she'd know just where to go. She knows which crypts have been abandoned. I bet she could hide out in any one of our cemeteries for a week and not be found. I've been around with her. I know a few of her little secret spots."

"I'm sure you're right—unless Nikki didn't know she should be hiding," Brent said.

"Where are we heading?" Julian asked Max.

"Wait a minute," Nikki interjected suddenly, glaring

at Max. "You were in the bayou country, not far away, and you didn't come to Andy's funeral?"

Max shot her a quick glance. "Nikki, I'd only met her twice. And I was out on a shrimp boat."

"You were on a shrimp boat?" Julian demanded, stunned.

"Max, you were her boss," Nikki said, aggravated.

"Nikki, I gave you credit. You hired her." He hesitated for a minute. "You said she was clean."

"She *was.*"

Max let out a sigh. "Oh, Nikki...one of your greatest virtues is your belief in people. Your insistence that the rest of the world is open and honest and good."

"Max, I'm not a blind idiot," Nikki said.

"Max," Brent interjected evenly, "even the police feel that Andy might well have been helped into the grave."

Max gave Brent a startled glance in the rearview mirror. "Why?"

"Because of another similar death," Brent said. "Even if you were in the bayou country you must have heard the news. An FBI agent named Tom Garfield—a man who was definitely as clean as a whistle—was found with enough heroin in his veins to kill an elephant."

"What would Andy have had to do with an FBI agent?" Max demanded, scowling.

"We met him at Madame's," Nikki explained. "Well, we didn't exactly meet him—we ran into him. I thought that he was a bum."

"She gave him a twenty," Julian said.

"Nikki, I'm sorry," Max said. "To tell you the truth, I was aggravated with you. I thought you made me hire a woman who ended up causing major problems."

"I'm sure she's sorry that her death inconvenienced you," Nikki said sharply.

Max let out a sigh. "I didn't mean it that way."

The tension in the car was thick, worrying Brent. He was supposed to meet Massey outside St. Louis Number 1 later, and he really didn't want Nikki with him.

But he wasn't sure he wanted to leave her with either of the men in the car.

"So," Julian grumbled, "where are we going? Max, are you buying your hardworking employees a drink?"

"Sure. I'll park at the office, and we'll walk over to that French place on Canal."

Brent glanced at his watch. It was after five o'clock.

As Max pulled into a spot in a narrow alley next to a door that advertised "Legends and Myths of New Orleans," Brent realized that he'd yet to see the office. The guides pretty much never used it, he realized, because they met one another and their groups at Madame's.

"When's the last time you were in here?" Max asked Nikki.

"I don't know. About two weeks ago, I think."

"Then I guess I should check the mail," Max said.

He parked the car, and as they all got out, he headed for the door with his keys out, calling over his shoulder, "Just a second. I'll grab the mail, toss it in the car, and we'll be on our way."

He opened the door and went in, turning on lights. "I guess I should check the answering machine," Nikki said.

She stepped past Max, who was busy picking up

piles of mail from the floor where it had fallen in from the slot.

Hovering near the door with Julian, Brent studied the office space. It was small and attractive. There was only one desk, and the walls were filled with prints by local artists. There was a comfortable-looking chesterfield sofa by the wall, and scattered chairs were casually set near the desk. There were several file cabinets, and a computer.

Nikki hit a button on the machine and the message kicked in, Nikki's voice saying, "Press one for a description of our tours. Press two for times…."

Her disembodied voice went on to say that no reservations were required, that potential tour-takers should arrive at Madame's fifteen minutes before the tour, or, in the case of Lafayette Number 1, arrive at the cemetery fifteen minutes ahead of time.

Nikki listened to the few messages, all of which had been forwarded to her cell phone, then reset the machine.

She was disturbed, and trying not to look it, Brent thought.

"Come on, Nikki. We're ready to go here," Max said.

She nodded, and came out from behind the desk, smiling far too brightly.

"You haven't been in the office yet, I take it," Max said dryly to Brent. He glanced at Nikki. "The government will be on my ass if we don't fill out those papers."

"It's been busy, Max," she said. "And with Andy… Besides, it's *your* company," she reminded him a little sharply.

Max only shrugged, looking at Brent. "Tomorrow,

if you like the job and plan on keeping it, you'll have to fill out some IRS forms."

"I'm not sure how long I'll really be hanging out in New Orleans."

"Oh?" Max inquired.

Brent shrugged. "Let's see how it goes, all right?"

He managed to fall back with Nikki as they walked. He waited until Max and Julian had entered into conversation, then took the moment to catch Nikki's arm and draw her close as they walked. "What's bothering you?" he demanded.

She looked at him, eyes wide. Then she shrugged. "Oh…a friend died, I think she was murdered, I'm seeing ghosts…conversing with them, actually. And I'm beginning to be glad that I can talk to them. Max is weird, Julian is weirder…and…" She glanced at him seriously. "I really don't know who you are."

"You know all you need to know. This has nothing to do with me."

She smiled. "You couldn't care less if Max keeps you on or not, because it isn't really your job."

He frowned. "Nikki, you're not worried about your job. Max has a gold mine in you, and he knows it. What's the truth?"

She let out a sigh. "I don't know. But…you know how it seemed like someone had been in my apartment? How I just had a feeling? Well, once I started to talk to Andy, I figured it had to be her. But…I just got that feeling in the office, too. If I wasn't in there, no one should have been. Except for Max, of course, but he hasn't been here."

"Was anything missing?" Brent asked.

"No."

"Changed around?"

"No." She flushed. "But I'm one of those organization freaks. I know exactly how I left the papers on the desk, and they were just a little askew."

"Rats?" he suggested lightly.

She frowned at him.

"I'll check into it, Nikki."

"How?"

"Trust me. I'll find a way."

She studied him seriously. "You will, won't you?"

He nodded. She watched him closely then. "Your turn. Why are you so keyed up and tense?"

"I'm not."

She laughed. "Not usually, but you are now. You've glanced at your watch about ten times."

"I need to go out at dark."

She still watched him intently. "Again?"

He nodded.

"And you're not going to tell me where, are you?"

He shrugged. "Nikki, even *I* think I might be on a wild-goose chase tonight."

"But why are you so tense?"

"I don't want to leave you alone."

"I'm not alone. Julian is desperate to stay with someone he works with, and Max is back now."

He was silent.

She groaned. "I've known Julian all my life. And I keep Max's business running while he trots all over, doing whatever he wants."

He let out a soft sigh. "Nikki, I know you're going to get angry, but…"

"But what?"

His clenched his jaw. "I can't betray a confidence that may have no bearing whatsoever on what's happening. But I'm not the only one wondering about your group, okay?"

She stared straight ahead. "I'll go home alone then."

"But—"

"I was afraid because of Andy. But I'm not afraid of her anymore."

"I shouldn't go. I should just let the cops—"

"No!" she said sharply, her beautiful eyes full of resolve. "I want you to go, to do what you have to. Do you understand? I'm comfortable in my own home. I'm kind of hoping for a visit from Andy."

His eyes narrowed. "Nikki…you're up to something."

"Shh," Nikki said.

Their path through the Quarter had taken them past Madame's. The woman was outside with her coffeepot and stopped dead when she saw Max, smiling. "As I live and breathe. The master is returned from parts unknown."

"Hi, Madame," Max said, planting a kiss on the woman's cheek.

She smiled, patted his face and said, "Looks as if you've been roughhousing a bit." She glanced at the others. "What's going on?"

"Brent tried to beat him up," Julian said lightly.

Max laughed. "Do I really look beat up? How embarrassing."

"No, there's just a smudge of dirt on your chin," Madame said.

Max looked at the others. "Thanks for telling me, guys."

"I didn't see it, honestly," Nikki said.

"Why did you try to beat up Max, dear?" Madame asked Brent. She turned to Max before Brent even had a chance to answer. "You could fire him, you know."

"I don't think he'd care. Besides, I hear nobody does a cemetery tour like this guy. He's as familiar with them as Nikki is. Maybe he slides into the tombs at night and gets to know the ghosts, huh?" Max teased.

"There are no such things as ghosts," Madame said with a wave of her hand.

Madame's buxom figure had been blocking the table directly behind her. A familiar voice suddenly sounded from around her derriere. "Ah, Madame, you are mistaken. Many things exist that we don't see."

Contessa rose, having finished her coffee. Her marble eyes touched Nikki with warmth and concern. She spoke very seriously. "But spirits are seldom evil. The cemeteries, when they are locked down and it is deep and dark and mists rise…they are safe, sad places. But when they are used by the living, that's when evil reigns."

"Contessa," Madame said with a laugh. "You're good, you're really good. No wonder I send people to your shop all the time. And, of course, you send your customers to me." She looked back to Max. "Well, have you come for café au lait? In celebration of your return, I'll bring it out for you, on the house."

"Very kind, Madame," Julian said. "But Max is buying—and we're going to find a different kind of spirit, if you know what I mean."

"Sure you don't want coffee?" Max asked.

"No, you're not going all cheap on us. Alcohol," Julian insisted.

"We're heading out, I guess, but thanks for the offer, Madame," Nikki said. She smiled warmly at both Madame and Contessa.

Contessa stared at Nikki oddly. "Cemeteries are no place for the living at night," she murmured, then walked away.

"Strange lady, even for New Orleans," Madame said.

"Well, we'll see you later," Max said, and they started walking again.

Once again Brent made a point of lagging behind with Nikki. "Out with it, what the hell is going on? And why did Contessa say that to you?"

"No reason."

"Nikki, don't be an idiot."

She hesitated, eyes searching his, apparently deep in a mental dilemma. Then she blurted, "I'm going to the cemetery tonight. I saw Tom Garfield today, and I think he said I should come there tonight. He tried to talk to me, but I couldn't hear the rest of what he said. I believe he knows something about what happened to him—about what happened to Andy. I have to go."

"What?" Brent nearly shouted, he was so astounded. She'd planned on him leaving, because she meant to head to the cemetery herself.

"Are you insane? Do you know how dangerous going

there is under the best of circumstances? You weren't going to tell me about this? And you saw Garfield? You talked to him? Nikki, you swore you'd tell me—"

"I haven't exactly had a chance, have I?"

"You were going to go to the cemetery alone?"

"I just meant to see what was happening. Don't you understand? For some reason he trusts me. I have to find out what he was trying to say, what he was trying to tell me. He doesn't trust anyone else. I didn't have any intention of becoming a one-woman assault team. I wasn't going to attack anyone. I was just going to be there, hidden. Max was right. I do know where to hide in that cemetery. I'm willing to bet I know it better than you do."

He started to answer her, still furious that she hadn't realized her own personal danger, then bit his tongue.

Julian and Max had paused, waiting for them to catch up. Max was assessing him anew, Brent realized, which meant that Julian had probably been describing his relationship with Nikki.

"Something wrong?" Julian called sharply, sounding like a wary older brother.

"No, we're with you," Nikki called, and sounded perfectly casual.

She looked at Brent. It was a very regal look. She simply didn't intend to be frightened, victimized or dismissed. She intended to fight.

"We'll talk later," Brent said beneath his breath.

She gazed at him, judging the distance between themselves and Max and Julian. She smiled as she walked, but her words were biting. "And where were you going? The cemetery?"

"The cops are going to be there, Nikki. You don't have to be."

"Yes, I do."

"*No.* Nikki, dammit, I'm trying to keep you safe."

"I'm not going to sit around and wait. I saw Tom, and he's trying to tell me something. And I'm not waiting. I'm not going to be like Andy."

"Nikki, you can't be there."

She glanced his way sharply. "You need me there."

"Nikki—"

"Dammit, you need me there. I'm the one Tom Garfield trusts, remember?" And with that, she hurried on ahead of him, smiling as she linked arms with Julian.

18

Nikki was startled when Brent suddenly declined to join their group.

He was really angry, and he had no right. She really hadn't had a chance to tell him that Tom Garfield had appeared again.

She herself felt furious at being afraid, at feeling she was a target, that someone might come after her.

But before Brent took off, he looked at her and said, "I'll pick you up just before eight, okay?"

So she nodded and listened as he told Max that it had been a pleasure to meet him, sorry about the way it had happened, he would get his work papers taken care of, thanks for the drink offer, but he had a few things to attend to.

Then he was gone.

But his eyes touched hers before he left, more eloquent than any words. *I'll come for you. Be there.*

So she walked into the bar with Julian and Max, who said simply, "Interesting guy," as they were led to a table.

"Yeah, very interesting," Julian agreed. "I didn't trust

him at first." He was watching Nikki as he spoke. "But my judgment about people doesn't seem to be great."

"Nikki, where does this guy come from?" Max asked after he'd ordered a dirty martini.

She opted for a beer, wondering if she was going to be paranoid the rest of her life. Before she could answer him, she found herself looking around the bar. But she didn't see anyone who looked suspicious, or even anyone she knew.

"New Orleans."

"Really?" Max said. "I'm sure I've never seen him before."

"I'm sure there are a lot of people here who never cross our paths," Nikki said. "And he hasn't lived here, not for a while."

"So he just kind of appeared at the right time, huh?" Max asked.

Julian started to speak. Not at all sure why, Nikki kicked him. He managed to keep quiet, but he shot her a look that said it was time she saw the psychiatrist again.

"He definitely appeared at the right time," Nikki said.

Julian added, "I'll tell you this, Max, he knows his stuff."

"So, Max, tell us more about the shrimpers," Nikki said, anxious to turn the conversation in some other direction.

Max warmed to his cause so much so that Nikki found herself drawn in, despite the fact that she'd expected to be unable to think of anything but the coming night. As she listened, though, she found herself growing indignant for the people who worked so hard, and decided that from now on she would eat only home-caught shrimp.

Even so, at the back of her mind raced a single question.

Where had Brent gone now?

And why?

At his bed-and-breakfast, Brent put through a call to Adam.

He would never know how the man managed to do it, but within twenty minutes he was able to report that Haggerty was a bona fide agent, and yes, he was known for being a loner.

Adam also managed to access the recent expenditures of Max Dupuis.

Brent ran over his expenses during the last two weeks.

There hadn't been a single charge made in the parish of New Orleans for over two weeks. He moved on, pulling up the dossiers that Adam had managed to acquire on Julian and the others. There wasn't a criminal record in the lot.

Well, except for Andrea Ciello. She had been busted and jailed several times. But she had cleaned up and made it through school. And there hadn't been a mark on her record in several years. She had attended rehab, and since then, she'd been clean.

He'd expected nothing else.

Studying everything that he had, albeit quickly, he couldn't find anything to suggest that any of Andy's close circle might have gotten involved in a major drug operation.

Julian and Nikki had indeed attended the same schools; Julian had been a year ahead of her. He'd been a theater major, an honor student. He'd done his share of work as a bartender, spent a few months in Europe, and he had performed a one-man show at a small local theater before working with the tour group.

Nothing there.

He stared at everything, shook his head and called Adam back. "Get me what you can on the two cops, Marc Joulette and Owen Massey. Oh…and anything more you can find out about the FBI agent, Haggerty. And a café, a place called Madame D'Orso's. Check out the woman who owns it, while you're at it." He thought quickly, then asked for whatever Adam could get on the voodoo shop that Nikki liked. "Contessa Moodoo's Hoodoo Voodoo."

"I can get you some records pretty quickly. Getting anything deeper on the cops and especially the fed may take a little longer."

"Do what you can," Brent said, and thanked him.

A few minutes later he was studying the newest records Adam sent, but, as Adam had warned him, there wasn't much there. Brent looked at the grainy images of the men as they appeared on his screen. In a hundred years, he would never have recognized Massey in the youthful picture he had. Joulette's image was pretty good; Haggerty must have had a hair-and-makeup artist for his official picture.

Madame D'Orso, née Debra Smith, had come from the North about fifteen years ago. She'd gotten financing through a local bank, and was apparently paying back her loan in a timely manner.

The voodoo shop had previously been a toy store. Before she took over the location, Contessa had operated in downtown New Orleans. Having become extremely successful, she had moved to her present location, with its high overhead, nearly four years ago.

Frustrated, he logged off. He strapped on his ankle holster and snub-nosed Smith & Wesson, grabbed the packet he had acquired on Archibald McManus and hurried out.

He had to pass Marie's hotel, so he figured he would just leave the material with the concierge. But Marie exited the elevator just as he was approaching the desk. She came running toward him, took the packet and thanked him profusely.

"You're doing all right?" he asked her.

She was still bruised, but she flushed and smiled. "I'm fine. I was lucky, and you know what else?"

"What?"

"I think there are ghosts."

"Oh?"

"I think the ghost of that old slave may have saved me, and I'm going to try to do something for him."

"Marie, he's dead. He's been dead for over a hundred years. Don't go near that cemetery."

She laughed. "I know, but I'm still going to find something to do for him. And when I have it figured out, I'll call you first." She hesitated. "You know, there's something bad going on in that area."

"Don't go back at night. In fact, don't go back at all without a ranger or a group."

"I won't. I swear."

He wished Nikki would be as careful, but in a way, he understood. There was no way *he* would refuse to fight back if he knew that someone was after him.

He glanced at his watch and hurried on.

On a sidewalk just a few blocks away, he waited in the shadows. In time he saw Patricia and Nathan leaving her apartment, heading for Madame's. He followed them, keeping a discreet distance, doing his best to listen in on their conversation.

It was casual. Patricia said that she wanted to lead the tour that night, and Nathan said she was more than welcome to, because he was exhausted.

When Patricia went into Madame's for coffee, Brent slid into the chair opposite Nathan.

Startled, Nathan began to greet him, then went silent when he saw the look in Brent's eyes.

"I'm running out of time," Brent said flatly.

"Excuse me?"

"I've seen you at night," Brent lied. "But I haven't quite figured out where you've been going."

Nathan immediately flushed a deep red. "I—I don't know what the hell you're talking about."

"It won't take Patricia long to buy coffee. And I'll be happy to ask the question with her here."

Nathan stared at him, his color deepening even further. Finally he leaned closer over the table. "If you're suggesting that I would have hurt Andy in any way, that I would deal in drugs—"

"I'm not suggesting anything. I want the truth. And I hope it's something you can prove."

Brent glanced toward the windows. He could see Patricia at the counter. Madame wasn't there; a pretty young girl was taking Patricia's money.

"Ticktock, she'll be here any second."

Patricia had paid. She was heading toward the door.

"Good God, yes, it was another woman," Nathan blurted quickly. "But it's over. Really over. Please…I don't know what I was doing. I'd rushed into this living-together thing, and I was feeling trapped and—"

"Not good enough," Brent said.

"I met her at the bar," Nathan said, looking over Brent's shoulder. "Her name is Varina White. She's from Chapel Hill, North Carolina, and she's gone, but I have a phone number. For the love of God—"

"If I find out you're lying…" Brent said softly, letting the threat hang unspoken in the air, then he jumped up. "Patricia," he said, and pulled out a chair.

"Brent, I didn't know you were here. I would have gotten you a coffee."

"It's all right. I just saw Nathan and thought I'd say hi. I've got to get going. Hey, I didn't even tell Nathan yet. Max is back. Got to meet him today."

"Cool," Patricia said, looking slightly anxious.

"Strange guy, huh?" Brent said.

"Strange, definitely. But he's a good guy. Into different causes all the time," Nathan said. He looked shaky as he poured sugar into his coffee.

"Sure you won't join us?" Patricia asked.

"No, I'll leave you two lovebirds alone. Stick close, okay?" he said. "After what happened to Nikki..."

"I intend to stick to Nathan like glue," she said.

"Good thing. See ya."

He turned and walked away. He'd learned to be a pretty good judge of character. He would bet his life that Nathan had been telling him the truth, but at the same time, he was wondering how he had managed to bully the man into doing it quite so easily.

He glanced at his watch. It was growing late. There was nothing more he could do this evening.

Swearing, he hurried toward Nikki's.

"Well, kids, stuff to do," Max said, yawning. "And sleep. I haven't done much of that lately." He turned serious suddenly, looking at Nikki. "Thanks. And I'm sorry. I guess I've dumped a lot on you lately. And I should have come back for the funeral. I'm more selfish than I knew. You've been great, keeping everything going for me."

Nikki shrugged. "Hey, you always said that you were the moneyman, that you believed in delegation."

"You should make her a partner in the business," Julian said.

Max frowned. "Hey, I just bought you drinks and a session at the raw bar," he protested. He kissed Nikki on the cheek. "Okay, major meeting tomorrow, for real," he said, looking at Julian. "I'm going to actually do some work myself. I promise," he said.

"Right," Julian called after him. He grimaced, looking at Nikki. "Want another drink? Wait, you didn't actually have a first one. That was iced tea, right?"

Nikki slid off her stool. "I have to get home, Julian."

"I'm coming with you," he said firmly.

"Julian, you don't have to come with me. Brent will be there."

"I'm not letting you walk back alone."

She sighed, growing nervous. She didn't want Julian with her tonight. Brent would probably be unhappy to see him. She was sure Brent didn't want to explain what they were up to.

"I'm fine, Julian, honestly. You've been the best friend in the world. I appreciate everything you've done."

"And that's why you have to be a friend back tonight," he told her. "Nikki, I can't go back to my place. Please don't make me go back there."

"You're not a kid, Julian. Tell her how you feel. It's your place. You've got to get her out of it."

"All right, but I'm still going to walk you home first."

When they reached her place, she opened the gate, and he followed her in. "Hey…I can go hole up in the guest room. I'm sure Brent isn't sleeping there."

"Julian, go home. Explain nicely that you're just not ready for the kind of commitment she seems to need."

He nodded, but he still stood there at her front door.

"Julian? What's wrong?"

"I just…I'm not leaving until Brent shows up."

She groaned and opened the door wide. "Fine. Come on in."

Nikki had a strange look when she opened her door again a few minutes later. Brent arched a brow, hoping that Andy Ciello, or her spirit, had stopped in once again.

But Andy wasn't there.

Instead, he found someone very much alive.

Julian.

"Julian didn't want me to be alone," Nikki said.

"Thanks, Julian. But I'm back," Brent said pointedly.

Julian stood up and looked at them both, suddenly serious as he stared at Brent. "I don't know what you two are doing," he said flatly, "but you're not doing it without me."

Nikki laughed softly, and though she tried to speak teasingly, her nerves were apparent in her voice. "Julian, I'm sorry your love life is more than you could take, but mine is going great. I don't need a chaperone."

"You two aren't headed out on a hot date," Julian said flatly, staring at Brent.

Brent crossed his arms over his chest, intrigued. Why the hell would Julian suddenly be so suspicious of their movements?

"Nikki was behaving strangely at the cemetery this morning," Julian said. "I don't know what she thinks she saw, but I watched her during the afternoon."

"You were sleeping all afternoon," Nikki said.

"That's what you think. Nikki, I know you. I know you better than this guy," Julian argued.

Brent clenched his teeth. Time was ticking away. This was his chance to discover the truth about Julian.

But at what cost?

Massey and Joulette would be there. Maybe he should take this opportunity to test the man.

He lifted his hands. "Let's go."

"What?" Nikki demanded.

"Let's go. But get out of that shirt, Julian, into something black. When you're trying to meld with the dark, you need to wear dark clothing."

Julian seemed startled to have won so easily. He jumped up, stared at Brent, then headed for the stairs. He paused halfway up. "Listen, you're not going to run out while I'm changing…?"

"No," Brent said.

When Julian had disappeared, Nikki stared at Brent, baffled. "You're letting him come?"

"I think he's going to be at the cemetery whether we let him come with us or not."

"But you don't trust him," Nikki reminded him. "You don't trust anyone."

"Like I said, I think he intends to go, with us or without us. If he's with us, we'll know where he is."

"For our own safety, right?" Nikki said a little tightly.

"And his," Brent assured her.

Julian raced back down the stairs then, anxiously looking at them as if he was afraid they'd been lying to him.

"Let's go," Brent said.

They saw to it that Nikki's door was locked, then started down the street. As they walked, Julian said, "Shouldn't we be slinking along or something like that?"

Brent stared at him, trying not to laugh; it had sounded like a serious question.

"I don't think we need to slink around on this part of Canal—there are a lot of people out."

"Uh, right."

But when they moved away from the center of activity in the Quarter, Brent did start to walk in the shadows, and when they neared the cemetery, he had them walk single file by the wall.

"There's a good place to hop over," Julian whispered.

"The gate will be opened," Brent said.

"How do you know?"

"Just a feeling."

It *was* open. Either someone had come before them, or Huey had managed to get the gate open. They slipped in. The graveyard was heavy with the sound of silence.

Brent inhaled.

Closed his eyes.

Opened them.

And Huey was there. "Not yet. Maybe not at all, but not yet," the old haunt said softly.

Brent nodded, indicating that they needed to find hiding places. He knew a few, but he wasn't surprised when Nikki lifted a hand, pointing. They hurried past a society tomb and on to one with classic Greek columns and a wrought-iron gate.

The gate was open, and they slipped inside.

Coffins lined the walls. Dust lay heavy on the concrete flooring. Broken stained-glass windows looked out onto the rest of the site. A slender thread of moonlight dusted the angels, cherubs, tombs and mausoleums beyond.

"What now?" Julian mouthed.

"We wait," Brent said.

Julian nodded. He sat against one of the inner sarcophagi in the small space.

Outside, the heated earth met the cooler air of the night. A soft ground fog was swirling.

As Brent stared through a ragged break in the once-beautiful glass, he saw forms of thicker mist moving within the fog.

An eerie light drifted toward the mausoleum where they waited.

He held his breath, praying that it would not disappear.

It came closer, closer….

He felt Nikki at his shoulder. He could hear the pounding of her heart. It was a drumbeat, loud and staccato.

"Oh, God," she whispered.

And he knew. She didn't want to be afraid. She didn't want to fear the fog.

But it was growing….

And a sense of cold was forming all around them.

"Man, what the hell are we doing out here?" Joulette demanded.

He was in the passenger seat. Massey had driven.

"Staring at a cemetery," Massey said.

Joulette looked at his watch. He shook his head, then sipped at the coffee in his hand. "What the hell is wrong with us?" he asked. "Why don't we work normal hours?"

"We're cops," Massey said.

"Shit!" Joulette said, straightening.

"What? Where?"

Joulette pointed with the hand that held his cup. And Massey saw that a figure, dark as the night, was moving along the fence.

"Shit," Massey repeated.

He started to get out of the car. As he opened the door, it slammed back at him. Stunned, he looked up.

There was another figure in the night.

And that one was right at his window.

The form began to materialize in front of the mausoleum. Julian, still seated against the tomb, suddenly seemed frozen there.

"What…what…?" he whispered.

Nikki ignored him. She touched Brent's shoulder.

"It's him?" Brent asked quietly.

"I think," Nikki said.

The terrible sense of cold was filling the tomb. Nikki felt it seeping down her spine. She closed her eyes for a moment, then turned.

Andy was with them.

"Andy, we need you," she said, her voice light as the air.

Brent turned, too, looking at Andy. "We need his help, too," Brent said. "For justice. For him *and* for you."

Andy nodded, frowning. "It's difficult…difficult to be here. I don't know why. But I'll try…I'll try."

"His name is Tom Garfield," Brent reminded her. "Tom Garfield. I need him. I need his help."

"I'll do what I can," Andy murmured.

Julian spoke up from his place against the tomb.

Shivering, lips chattering, he said, "You're both... you're both crazy. Talking to the air. Oh my God, it's cold in here. Cold, in New Orleans, at this time of year. It's the stone, of course...all the stone." There was no conviction in his voice.

Andy looked at Julian and shrugged. "He's still a good guy," she murmured.

Then she walked out of the tomb, a moving trail of light, mist and cold. The somber spirit of Tom Garfield stood dead still, wary as ever as he watched Andy approach. But she reached him. And as her astral hand touched his shoulder, she spoke softly, then turned to face the mausoleum.

"You go first. You're the one he's trying to reach," Brent said.

"Crazy, both crazy," Julian said, shivering still.

"Julian, you've got to be quiet," Nikki said.

"Maybe spending the night with that sexual barracuda would have been better," Julian said, arms clenched over his chest.

"Julian," Brent said in a low voice, but sharply. Julian looked up at him. "You've got to shut up. The ghosts in this cemetery are not the danger."

Julian stared at him, nodded, and seemed to find some resolve. "Right." He only mouthed the word.

Nikki looked out. Tom Garfield was standing next to Andy, not moving, looking from her to the mausoleum. He seemed faint and pale at first, made of narrow light and nothing more. Then his form became more solid. At first his feet weren't there, and then, slowly, they were, and he appeared as much alive to Nikki as he had in the street, as he had every time she had seen him.

Alive, and strong, and determined.

"He's trying," Brent whispered. "And he's..."

Nikki moved quickly then, exiting the mausoleum. She shuddered at the creaking sound the gate made in the night, seeming incredibly loud.

"Tom," she said, walking forward. "You've tried to talk. I haven't known how to listen."

Brent was at her side. "My name is Brent Blackhawk. You have no reason to trust me, except that Nikki trusts me," he said. "But I'm here to help. We're both here to help. To find the people who murdered you."

Julian had promised to be quiet. He had seemed to understand, but maybe it was all a little bit too much for him. They could hear the soft echo of his voice from within the tomb.

"Oh, God, oh, God, oh, God. They're at it again. They're talking to ghosts. And asking for help. Talking to ghosts," Julian murmured. But there was no mockery in his voice.

Nikki glanced back. She could see the shadowed form of her friend hunkered down low in the mausoleum.

Julian had his hands over his face. "What am I doing here?" he groaned.

She turned back to Tom Garfield. He was staring at Brent. Judging him. He seemed to take a long time in the chill, charged atmosphere of the mist-shrouded graveyard.

Then he spoke. His voice sounded grating, harsh, like the scrape of heavy equipment.

As if he were learning to talk all over again.

But he spoke. And the sound was clear on the air.

"Soon…the rear…the ovens. They come here… there's a stash. I'm not sure where. They're always masked."

"Let's go," Nikki said.

"No. You stay here, in the tomb with Julian," Brent said.

"I have to go with you."

"No. Please, Nikki. I'm not alone. The cops are out there."

Just then, like a strange thunder in the night, they heard a series of soft thumps from the rear of the graveyard.

Brent shoved Nikki toward the mausoleum. "Please?" he whispered desperately.

All around them, the mist seemed to swirl.

There were more and more forms around them.

And the cold brought on shivers.

"It's easier for me to fend for myself, Nikki. When I know you're in danger, I'm not as sharp," he said, and she knew that his words were sincere.

Tom Garfield had turned. The ghost of Andy Ciello watched, then slowly began to fade.

Brent followed the earthly remnants of the soul of Tom Garfield.

Nikki exhaled slowly, then turned and quickly found a place inside the tomb again. Julian was on the ground, still shaking, teeth chattering. He looked at her miserably and winced. "And I'm protecting you?" he said wryly.

"Ghosts do exist, Julian," she said, taking his hands,

holding them both to reassure him and for the warmth they provided.

He didn't agree, but he also didn't deny her words. He just stared straight ahead, through the wrought-iron gate of the mausoleum.

"Nikki?" he said on a breath.

"What?"

His eyes seemed fixed on the gate.

She looked out herself. And saw, even as Julian spoke again.

"Nikki...someone's coming." He looked at her tensely and added, "And it isn't any ghost."

"You!" Massey exclaimed.

Joulette was swearing. He'd spilled his coffee.

"What are you two doing here?" the man at the window asked harshly. Haggerty! Of all the damn times for him to show up.

"You're in our way," Joulette said.

"I rank, fellows, and I repeat, what are you doing out here?"

"We heard a rumor about some hooligans being in the cemetery," Massey said. He looked at Joulette with a frown that demanded, Did you call him?

Joulette was looking back at him just as suspiciously.

Massey looked back at Haggerty. In his customary suit, he was standing by the driver's door, staring down at them as if they were errant schoolboys.

"A girl was attacked out here the other night," Massey said.

"Yeah? And that's a big deal these days?" Haggerty asked.

"She might have been killed."

The darkness suddenly seemed to close in. Haggerty looked up. "Clouds over the moon," he said.

"Yell, well, there's someone in the graveyard, too," Massey said, angrily forcing his door open. "I am an officer of New Orleans, sworn to uphold the law, and this is my territory. Excuse me, will you?"

Joulette, too, exited the car. Before he could close his door, they heard the explosion as a shot was fired in the night.

19

Ghosts were invisible to most people.

Brent was not.

He had moved carefully among the tombs, even as he followed Garfield. But the shot that was fired out of the mist was fired at him.

Instead, the bullet hit the nose of a winged angel at his side.

He dove to the ground, and rolled, finding safety behind a society crypt just as another shot rang out.

Then there was the sound of thundering footsteps from all directions. In the swirl of fog, he saw a dark-clad figure running back in the direction from which he had come—toward Nikki's hiding place.

He pulled his Smith & Wesson and got to his feet, following. He dodged between the crypts and sarcophagi, angels, cherubs, broken stone and masonry, damning himself. He had known that something was going to happen. Come hell or high water, he should have found a way to keep Nikki out of the cemetery. How in God's name anyone could know she was hidden in a crypt…

Tom Garfield was ahead of him.

And ahead of Garfield was a figure, staring into the tomb where Brent had left Nikki and Julian. And he had a gun.

A gun that was aimed into the tomb.

A series of shots from the rear wall of the graveyard sounded, sharp like the bark of thunder in a fierce storm, exploding in the night.

The figure paused briefly, but not for long. It took aim again.

"Stop!" Brent shouted.

The figure turned.

"Put down your weapon."

The figure took aim at Brent.

With no other choice, Brent fired. He aimed for the wrist. And he aimed true. The gun went flying.

But before the figure could do more than scream in agony, another shot was fired in the night.

From behind Brent.

Nikki's would-be assassin fell to the ground. Even as he did so, sirens sounded in the night, so loud that the noise seemed to dispel the mist. Brent looked behind him. In the fading mist, he could see the shooter. The gun was pointed at him now.

He lifted his own weapon again.

"Drop it," came the command.

Brent held his ground, blinded in the night.

"FBI! Drop it!"

"Haggerty?"

"I just saved your life. Now drop your weapon."

Footsteps pounded behind Haggerty.

"Blackhawk? That you?"

It was Massey, shouting.

"Yeah, it's me."

He lowered his weapon. Haggerty did the same. "God above us," Haggerty swore. "It's not bad enough you two clowns are running around in here, we have to bring in the Indian ghost buster, as well. Shit. You ruined it. Ruined the sting. You guys keep out of my way from now on, do you hear? And the fuckin' paperwork is yours, too!" Haggerty bellowed in disgust. He turned and walked away, disappearing in the mist.

Both Massey and Joulette pounded quickly toward Brent. "You all right?" Joulette asked.

"I'm fine. The one in front of me..."

Nikki. Nikki and Julian...

Brent broke off and hurried to the mausoleum, throwing open the iron gates. His heart leaped into his throat and lodged hard.

There was no one there.

Nikki fell over the wall, right behind Julian. He caught her, breaking the distance to the sidewalk.

"This is insane. This is all insane," he said. He glared at her. "Nikki, for the love of God, what the hell are you into? You know, I like Blackhawk, but he's a wacko, and he's dangerous. What in God's name was going on in there? We could have been shot!"

Nikki stared at Julian. "I told you not to come."

The sound of another siren tore through the night.

"Let's get the hell out of here before we wind up involved in all this."

"We are involved," Nikki protested.

"No, we're not. We're outside the cemetery."

"Brent is in there somewhere."

"And you think he can't take care of himself? He's like this with the cops." Julian raised his hand, showing entwined fingers.

"Julian, someone's shooting in there and—"

"And we're lucky as hell the guy about to kill us was shot, and that we were able to escape unseen. Nikki, if we go back in, if we get involved, what would we do? What would we say? You had a feeling that you needed to go to the cemetery. You talk to ghosts. Oh, they're going to believe that. We'll wind up under arrest ourselves, if we're not killed first. Nikki, please, let's get away from here."

"Julian, I can't just walk away while Brent is in there."

"There are a million cops in there."

"And it sounded as if there were a million shots fired. How do I even know he's all right?"

"Because he is who he is," Julian said, and his voice sounded just a touch bitter. "He'll be fine. I'm willing to bet he's CIA or FBI or some kind of alphabet-agency person. He's tough as nails. He'll be fine."

"I can't leave him."

Julian stared at her for a minute in exasperation. Another police car went past them, its lights flashing, its siren blaring. He grabbed Nikki, dragging her into the shadows.

"I've got it," he said.

"What?" she demanded.

He reached into his pocket.

* * *

"Blackhawk!" Massey called. "What the hell are you doing?"

Brent shoved past Massey, anxiously scanning the nearby crypts. His veins felt as if they were filled with ice.

"Blackhawk?"

He barely heard Massey speaking. "Nikki!"

There was no answer. He started to run down the nearest path, searching the shadows and mist, shouting her name.

"Blackhawk?" Massey was chasing him.

Brent stopped dead. Huey was standing before him. "They got out of here, Injun boy. Jumped the fence."

"What?"

"Blackhawk, what the hell...are you talking to me?"

"She got out of here. It's all right," Huey said.

"Blackhawk, sweet Jesus, but you're giving me the willies."

Staring at Huey, knowing he was hearing the truth, Brent felt such a surge of relief that he nearly sank to the ground.

"She's all right," he murmured, closing his eyes. "I was so afraid that I'd find corpses!"

"There *are* corpses. Three of them," Massey thundered. "What in God's name are you doing?"

At that moment, Brent's pocket vibrated. He reached for his cell phone.

"Nikki?"

To his relief, he heard her voice.

"We're outside, Brent," she said quickly. "Julian

thinks we should get the hell out of here as quickly as possible. He says we don't know anything. But I had to make sure you were all right."

"I'm fine."

"What should I do? I wouldn't know what to say to the police. They already think I'm crazy. They must *really* think you're crazy, but at least you're 'officially' crazy—sorry, an official of some kind who's crazy—and…oh, God, you are all right?"

"I'm fine."

"Blackhawk," Massey protested. "Are you listening to me? We've got three corpses in the cemetery. We've got hours and hours' worth of paperwork, and you'd better have some kind of explanation for all this. And what are *you* doing? Romancing your girl on the phone."

"I'm fine, Nikki. Listen, go—" He paused, in an agony of indecision. He was almost positive that Julian was innocent of any wrongdoing. He would be willing to bet that neither Patricia nor Nathan was involved, either.

The problem was, there wasn't going to be just one guilty party in this.

And he didn't know just who *was* involved, or how deeply.

"Go to the police station, Nikki. Tell Julian to walk you there, and if he doesn't want to hang around, he can go home. Just tell them you're waiting for me, all right?"

"You're going to be here for hours," Massey told him.

"Fine," Brent snapped back at Massey, who began swearing.

"Let's go," Massey said.

"Go to the police station, Nikki," Brent repeated.

"All right," she told him.

And they hung up.

Brent turned and stared at Massey. "Three corpses?"

"Yeah, we had help tonight," he said dryly. "Haggerty. Well, hell, none of them got away, anyway."

"Who are they? Do we know any of them?" Brent demanded.

"How the hell do I know? We haven't gotten the ski masks off the stiffs yet," Massey said. "Let's go. The ME is on his way. Oh, man, this is going to be bad."

At the station, Nikki and Julian were told that they had to sit and wait.

Hours passed.

Julian grew so restless that he was annoying. His phone rang countless times, and he winced every time.

"Why don't you just answer?" Nikki demanded.

"Because she might figure out where I am and come here," Julian said.

"You've got to deal with it," Nikki told him.

He sighed. "Yeah, I know. How do I get into these things?"

"By being cute and irresistible?" Nikki suggested.

He glared at her and began to pace. "Man, we're a pair, aren't we? You're into a guy who sees ghosts, and I…man, I used to think I was all that. Then I met the nympho of the century. Nikki, do we have to wait here forever? What if we went to Harrah's or something? Someplace safe?"

"Brent said to wait here."

"It's going to be morning soon."

"And when it is, I'll just call Max and tell him that he's got to deal with his own business for a day, because I'm going to sleep. And I'm giving you the day off, too. How's that?"

"Great," he said, taking a chair again.

The desk sergeant gave him an aggravated look.

It didn't quell Julian, who was quickly up again, pacing.

"Can I go to your house?" he asked plaintively.

"Go," she told him.

He sat again.

She stared at him, and he sighed. "No, I'm not going to leave you here alone. We'll wait. We'll just wait."

Two men were dead by the wall. Brent was certain that he'd never seen either of them before. Naturally, they carried no identification.

The third corpse, the one by the tomb—the one who had been taking aim right where Nikki and Julian had been hiding—was just as much a stranger.

Massey swore.

"A shoot-out, and all three of the perps dead. This is not good, not good. There's going to be some serious explaining to do. The higher-ups are going to be going crazy."

"I shot this one," Brent said. "In the *hand*."

"You sure?"

"They can check the bullets," Brent told him.

Massey shook his head. "I went after the two coming in from the rear after I heard the first shot. Joulette was right behind me. I don't know if I killed one of the other two or not. They started firing away at us, and I fired back."

"Well, this one was killed by Haggerty," Brent said. "And ballistics will prove that."

"Haggerty was right behind us, but I couldn't say what he was doing. I warned him, but they were already firing at us. Who knows if he heard me." He swore again.

Brent kept silent but clenched his teeth. "We should have gotten some answers from these guys," he said. "They shouldn't all be dead."

"We've got answers," Joulette said, walking tiredly toward him. "There's a stash of drugs in the oven tombs that you wouldn't believe. Apparently this has been a dispersal point."

"Well, I guess that's it then," Massey said. "This is what Tom Garfield was on to. This is why he died. He got in with these guys somehow, and then they made him, knew he was an agent, and that's why he died."

"That's not it. Or not all of it. Come on, Massey," Brent protested. "There was something wrong with Tom Garfield when he was in Madame's that morning."

"One of these guys must have been around," Massey said.

Brent shook his head. "That's not the end of it, and you know it. No one shot him up with heroin in the middle of Madame's," Brent said.

"No, but...someone could have slipped him something at Madame's, enough to mess him up. Then they got him out of the Quarter, shot him up and dumped him," Joulette said.

"And how does that explain Andrea Ciello?" Brent demanded.

Massey swore. Joulette looked down at his feet. "Maybe we'll have something when we get identities on these guys."

"So you believe there is a connection?" Brent demanded. "And that we're not done, that finding these guys isn't the end of it?"

Joulette looked at Massey. "No. Right after you were in today, we got a report. Andrea Ciello's place was torn apart."

"What?" Brent said sharply.

"It looked like a robbery, except that our fellows don't think that it was. Nothing obvious was missing. We figured we'd get Nikki DuMonde in tomorrow, find out for sure. But there was too much valuable stuff still left there."

"So someone was searching for something," Brent murmured.

"That's what it looks like," Joulette agreed. "Anyway, let's get to work. We need to finish up here, leave it to the crime scene team, and get the paperwork done." He sounded exhausted and despondent. "Dead, dammit. All dead."

"Rather them than us," Massey said, trying to sound more optimistic.

"Yeah, well, there's that. But this isn't going to look good," Joulette said.

"You did make a major drug bust," Brent pointed out.

"And how are you going to explain it?" Massey asked. "The papers will have a heyday with it. 'Psychic warns police on drug deal.'"

"How about we don't tell the papers that?" Brent said. "Tell them that you talked to the girl who'd been attacked, and that your conversation led you to believe it was more than just vandals or schoolkids pulling pranks?"

"The reporters and the television crews are already assembling," Joulette said. "This mess isn't going to look good for Harold Grant. It will be like, wow, look at the city under him."

"It depends what spin you put on it," Brent said. "Look at what the police officers did during his term. It could give him a boost. Go make your statement. I'll meet you at the station," Brent told him.

Joulette looked at Massey, who shrugged. "What about Haggerty? What if he gives some kind of a statement, too? Knowing him, he'll claim he was the one who caught up with these guys."

"Hey, he didn't want to be in on the paperwork. He doesn't get to be in the papers," Joulette said. "Blackhawk, you know a way out of here...?"

"You bet," Brent said.

Brent was glad of the time it took to walk from the cemetery to Royal Street. It was time to think. Oddly enough, though it was sad to see anyone dead, it wasn't the fact that the drug dealers had been killed in the cemetery that disturbed him the most.

It was the knowledge that Andrea Ciello's place had been ransacked.

He doubted the culprits had been any of the thugs in the cemetery.

Nor had it been Max, Julian, Patricia or Nathan. Not given the timing.

Three hoods were dead. But he knew damn well they hadn't been the limits of the operation. There had to be someone else behind it.

If he took Max, Julian, Patricia and Nathan off the list, that left Mitch. But he had seen Mitch during the day, when the apartment had been ransacked.

Something else was odd. One of the gunmen had known exactly where Nikki was hiding. And if Nikki were there, it would have been a likely guess that he was with her.

What about Julian?

Odd man out?

Or the one to give Nikki away? Julian had known her since childhood. Knew her better than anyone else. Knew the cemetery. Had he come with them as a setup, knowing that the gunmen would hunt them down but not harm him?

His mind raced. Julian had excelled in theater arts. But he was Oscar material, beyond a doubt, if he had pulled off the fear he'd shown that night.

If not Julian, then who?

He remembered walking by Madame's, and Contessa, the weird old marble-eyed seer, coming up to Nikki, giving her a warning.

Was the woman in on it and trying to keep Nikki alive?

At that moment it had been Nikki, Max, Julian, himself…and Madame D'Orso.

His footsteps quickened.

He hurried toward the station, anxious to find Nikki, and even more anxious for Massey or Joulette to make it back.

"Hey," the desk sergeant called. "You Nikki DuMonde?"

Nikki nearly tripped over Julian as she hurried over to the man. She didn't get to answer. "She's Nikki. Yup, that's her."

The sergeant frowned at Julian, shaking his head. "I got a call from the brass at the cemetery. Seems that the Blackhawk guy you're waiting for is going to be tied up with them for hours yet. He says to go home with Julian." He arched a brow as he looked at Julian, who had evidently driven him nuts with his pacing. "I take it you're Julian."

"Just go home, with Julian?" she said.

"Yeah, I'll have a couple of uniforms drop you off." He called out to two cops who had just come in. One was stirring a cup of coffee, looking worn-out.

"Stevens, Hurst. Need an escort for these folks. See that they get to the lady's apartment safely."

One of them nodded, looking tired but willing. "Thanks," Nikki said. "We could just walk. I don't live that far."

"I said I'll arrange a safe escort home, and that's what's happening," the sergeant said firmly.

Rather than argue, Nikki nodded. "Thanks."

"Yeah, thanks, we're outta here," Julian said.

One officer, whose badge identified him as Hurst, opened the door. Nikki and Julian thanked him and walked out.

"We're right there," Hurst said, indicating the car almost directly in front of the station. The second officer opened the rear seat for the two of them, and in seconds they were headed for Nikki's place.

"Pretty cool, getting an escort," Julian said.

"I guess. I'm tired, too, but…I want to know what happened," Nikki said. "We don't have any answers about Andy."

"We will," Julian assured her. "If there are answers to get, your buddy will get them. He's the real thing—a real what, I'm not sure, but he's real, all right."

"This it?" Hurst pulled up in front of Nikki's place.

"Yes, Officer, thank you."

Nikki and Julian exited the police car. The officers did the same. "We'll make sure you get inside safely," Hurst said.

"I could probably take it from here," Julian said.

"Hey, we were told to see you inside safely," Hurst said.

He fiddled with the latch to the gate.

"I'll get it," Nikki said, smiling.

Both officers came into the yard and watched as Julian followed her toward her door. Feeling definitely guarded, Nikki walked up to the porch, inserted her key in the lock and twisted it, then turned to wave to the officers and let them know her door was open.

She never made it. She was dimly aware of something long...metallic...flying toward her head.

Then it struck.

The pain was searing, white hot.

She crashed to the ground, white hot gone to cold and ebony as the entire world faded away.

Brent reached the station and hurried in. The sergeant at the desk looked up and greeted him.

"Massey and Joulette back yet?" he asked.

The sergeant shook his head. "Not yet. Got the call, though. I sent your friends on home."

"What?" Brent said sharply.

"They called from the cemetery. I could hear all the commotion. He said I should send your friends home. Said you would be all night, probably."

"*Who* called?" Brent demanded sharply.

"Well, it was Massey. Or Joulette." The man flushed. "I couldn't hear. There were sirens, but it came in on police band. Had to be one of them."

"And you let them go—you just let them go?" Brent demanded.

The sergeant looked flustered and defensive. "I was told to. They're safe, don't worry. I gave them an escort. A police escort."

"By known cops?" Brent demanded.

The sergeant looked at him as if he were absolutely crazy. "Of course they were known cops."

"Where are they now."

"I don't know, but I'll give them a call."

Staring at him hotly, the officer tried the radio. He looked slightly uneasy when he didn't get an answer. "They're probably watching them…maybe checking out the apartment. I'll try Hurst's cell phone."

"Never mind," Brent said sharply. "Send a car out."

"Hey—"

"Send a car!"

Brent turned and burst back out of the station. He probably knocked over tourists, musicians and locals alike as he raced through the streets. As he ran, he heard a siren; the desk sergeant had finally called for a car.

He reached Nikki's.

A police cruiser was parked in front.

He wrenched at the gate, threw it open and nearly tripped over one of the officers. The man was clammy, but had a pulse. He left him and hurried to the next guy. He could see blood on the man's temple, but he, too, had a pulse.

The door was standing open. Brent raced for it. "Nikki?"

He ran through the house, but he knew it was empty. A misty figure was trying to form.

Andy.

"Gone…they got her!" she cried.

"Who, Andy, who?"

Andy shook her head…then cocked it. "That car… that car…they have her…in that car."

He heard the revving of an engine then and raced back out of the house. Another cruiser was pulling along the street and parking. Two uniformed officers slipped out of it. "Hey, buddy!" one cried.

"You've got two officers down," Brent said. "They're alive. Call 911."

"Halt or I'll shoot," one warned.

He stood still, gritting his teeth, knowing that if he told them what to do with themselves and ran, they would shoot.

The sound of the freshly revved engine faded as the car took off.

"Look, call your sergeant. I'm Brent Blackhawk."

Another car jerked up in front of the house. It was Massey and Joulette. Massey stepped out. "What the hell happened?"

"Two officers are down, Nikki and Julian are gone," Brent said. He still had his hands raised. "Tell them who the hell I am!"

For a moment there was silence. Could Massey be in on it? Or Joulette? Or both? If so…

"Get in the car!" Massey called. "He's with us. Get help out here!" he shouted to the officers.

Brent raced to the car. He had no choice but to take the chance.

Joulette was driving. "Now what?"

"Get around the corner. Nikki's in a car."

"What car?" Massey asked.

Brent stared at Massey. "You tell me. You called the desk sergeant, sending her home."

"The hell I did," Massey insisted.

"Joulette?" Brent said evenly.

"I didn't call anyone. And I told that to the desk sergeant," Joulette snapped. He was moving, starting to flip on his siren.

"No," Brent said quickly. "Just get around the corner."

Joulette did so, muttering beneath his breath. "This is nuts. Follow that car. What the hell car, are you going to tell me?"

"I don't know," Brent grated between clenched teeth.

Joulette went around the corner. There were a number of cars on the street. Brent groaned inwardly.

"Go out…get on I–10," Massey said. He picked up the radio and called for backup.

Brent turned and stared at him. "That's where we found Tom Garfield," Massey said.

Brent leaned back in the seat, praying he was right.

He closed his eyes for a minute.

The car grew suddenly chill.

Brent opened his eyes.

He was no longer alone in the backseat.

Tom Garfield was next to him.

The ghost was looking straight ahead, his eyes fixed on the road.

"I–10?" Brent said softly.

Garfield nodded.

Brent leaned back again. "I'm going to suggest, gentlemen, that you call the station and have Madame D'Orso, née Debra Smith, picked up."

"For what?" Massey demanded, looking back at him with a frown.

"Conspiracy to commit murder."

At his side, Garfield looked at him and cocked his spectral head.

This time it was Brent who nodded.

20

The pain in her head awakened her.

She opened her eyes, and the world was dead black. And still. She started to shift, trying to figure out where she was.

At first she was completely disoriented. For several seconds she was aware only of pain and confusion. And then she remembered. She had opened her door. She had started to turn.

And been hit.

Who the hell had hit her?

Julian? God, no. Please, not Julian.

But if not…

Then someone had been inside. Someone had been waiting. The police officers…they must have been hit, too. Unless they had been in on it. No. Then the entire police force would have had to have been in on it.

But someone had called the desk sergeant—from the cemetery—to say she should go home.

She shook her head, feeling a renewed stab of pain. She gritted her teeth, trying to move. She was confined. She wasn't tied up, just confined in a tiny space. She could hear commotion from beyond. Voices. Arguing.

"Shit! How do we explain more bodies in the swamp?" someone demanded. A chill swept through her. She suddenly knew why Andy hadn't known what happened to her. This killer struck from hiding with swift determination.

The blow that took her out had come from behind. Andy had probably been asleep. She had never seen whoever had come at her.

That kind of thinking wasn't going to help. She had to get out of whatever she was in.

Determined, she began to feel around. And then she knew. She was in the trunk of a parked car. Did they—whoever they were—think she was already dead?

It better not be you, Julian, she thought, madly searching in the total dark and stifling confines for a latch to pop the trunk. *It better not be you, because so help me, I will haunt you into eternity. I will learn how to move things. I will drive you insane.*

She swallowed a rising sense of panic and concentrated on her task. She didn't know what kind of car she was in. If it was a fairly new model, there had to be some kind of a release.

She would never find it, she thought, her panic rising.

Not if she let herself be consumed by fear. She had to get control of herself. She had to go slowly, methodically. She had to search.

She began to sweat, but somehow she forced herself to be calm. It felt as if hours went by, though she knew only minutes had passed. She could hear the rasp of her own breathing. She had to find the latch. Had to. If she didn't, she would die.

She wasn't sure how long it took her to find it, and when her fingers hit it at first, she couldn't make it work. Again, she warned herself not to panic. To just press and pull until the latch released.

And then…it gave.

She was sure the sound would alert her attackers.

She didn't dare pause, no matter what. If they were going to shoot her, better it should happen with her at least making a dash for freedom.

She grabbed the rim of the trunk, hauling herself up, cursing the dizziness that spun in her brain with her sudden movement. She crawled out, falling into thick grass and slime. She could still hear the voices, but realized they were a slight distance away, by the road. She had gotten out of the car on the bayou side.

She staggered halfway to her feet, and looked toward the foliage and the water. She knew they were there, though she couldn't really see either. Didn't matter. She half crawled, half ran into the welcoming damp, gloom and darkness.

"There," Brent said.

There was an old-model Ford with a huge trunk on the side of the road.

The trunk was open.

There was no one by the car.

Joulette pulled off the road. Another car pulled off directly in front of them, jerking onto the embankment.

"Haggerty," Joulette said with a sigh.

Brent leaped from the car; the detectives did the same. "How the hell…?" Massey was muttering.

"I got the call from the station," Haggerty said. "Let's spread out. That way we can follow any possible tracks. Let's hope she's not already dead."

Brent didn't need instructions. He had already started running.

She had to be found quickly. And by him. One of the men on the road was involved.

He just wasn't certain which one.

"Nikki?"

She had reached the water and was carefully trying to keep to the trees as she hurried along the edge. There were boats here and there along the bayou, shrimpers' boats. She had been just about to step onto one when she heard her name.

Julian.

She wasn't certain if the sound had come from the boat or from the water…or even from the group of trees ahead of her.

But he had seen her.

She slipped back into a grove of trees.

Then she saw him. He hadn't been on the boat; he had been just steps ahead of her.

"Nikki!" he called again.

She turned and tore in the opposite direction, racing as fast as she could.

Away from him.

Blindly, she tore through the foliage. She didn't know whether to return to the highway and pray an innocent driver would stop for her or simply find someplace to hide. She paused for a moment, breathing hard, knowing that her decision might well mean her life.

A branch snapped behind her. She hunkered down into tall grass that rimmed the bayou. Her hands fell on a thick branch. Her fingers curled around it.

In the darkness, she heard him approach. Julian. It was Julian. He was almost on top of her. She got to her feet, the branch in her hand.

She swung out with it, striking as hard as she could.

He moaned and started to fall.

She didn't wait to see him go down. She ran.

Massey headed westward along the water. He didn't know whether to call out or not. He gritted his teeth, listening.

What the hell had happened? How had it all gone so wrong?

He heard the sound of foliage rustling behind him, and he turned. As he did, his peripheral vision showed him the dock to his side and the ramp leading to a shrimp boat.

Haggerty was coming down the ramp.

"Massey!" Haggerty shouted raggedly.

Massey stared back at him.

Then he made a beeline for the man, catching him on the ramp, gut-punching him with his shoulder and bringing him down.

They struggled on the ramp for a moment, then both men crashed into the water.

The sound of many footsteps and thrashing sounded behind her. Nikki looked over her shoulder but kept running. There was another shrimp boat ahead. This one was large, with a dock and a ramp.

Was it a safe place to hide? Better yet, was there a weapon of some kind aboard?

She started to run toward it, then came to a dead halt, nearly crashing into a man. Soaked and staggering, he got to his feet directly in front of her. She couldn't halt her impetus and crashed straight into his arms, nearly sending both of them down again.

He righted himself, groaning.

"Nikki…Nikki…I'm Haggerty…FBI. Massey…is a rogue cop. He attacked me. Come on…come with me…I'll get you out of here. You'll be safe."

She stared at the man, stunned, pulling back, not trusting anyone.

"Jesus, we've got to hurry—"

"Let her go!"

Nikki jerked around. A second man was coming from the water.

Detective Owen Massey.

"Nikki, that man is a liar. He claimed to be an FBI agent. I don't think he is. I think he lied to us. I don't know how, but he killed Garfield, and he killed Andy."

"How the hell could I lie about being an FBI agent, Nikki? Think. Massey has been on the take, covering up while he's been pretending to investigate."

Nikki looked from one man to another.

Massey slowly raised his gun, aiming at Haggerty. Haggerty, a firm grip on her, thrust her behind him, taking aim in turn.

* * *

"Help!"

When he heard the cry, Brent spun around, then dimly saw through the darkness that a figure was rising.

Julian. He staggered toward Brent.

"Nikki...she must think that I...Brent, she...went that way." Then, even as he pointed, he fell, groaning.

Brent hunkered down by him, grabbing him by his lapels. "You were with her."

Julian groaned again. "Yes, and the cops were with us. And they got hit, too. They had me in the backseat, her in the trunk...they started arguing about who should kill us. Jesus, help me, I hurt all over—oh, God," he gasped.

"What?"

"I'm on...I'm on a corpse. Look," he demanded.

Brent did.

But it wasn't the sight of the decaying corpse that caught his attention.

It was the spirit that rose from it...

Someone he recognized from a picture he had so recently seen...

There were sirens in the night again. Nikki could hear them. More and more. The police were coming.

Would they come in time?

Even now, she didn't know which man to believe.

She looked from one man to the other, knowing that the guns would fire any second, that the explosion would be deafening, that one would die...

And if it was the wrong one, she would die, too.

"Drop them. Both of you." It was Brent. Brent's voice, deep and furious in the dark of the night.

Haggerty's hold on Nikki tightened as the sharp command grated out. He and Massey both turned, firing wildly. She was still in Haggerty's arms. Was he protecting her?

Or was he about to use her as a shield?

"Blackhawk!" Massey cried. "Thank God—"

"Blackhawk!" Haggerty echoed. "Take him, for the love of God. I've got the girl. She's all right. Get Massey before he shoots her for the hell of it."

"Put your weapons down, both of you," Brent commanded.

"He'll shoot me," Massey protested.

"*He'll* shoot *me*."

Brent moved down to the marshy embankment near the shrimp boat. He appeared entirely casual as he came between the two men.

"Drop your weapons," he said again, quietly, with grim determination. Then he turned and faced Haggerty.

"Drop it," he repeated.

But Haggerty shook his head. "I'll kill her."

"I don't think so," Brent said calmly. "Don't you see them? Garfield is there, to your right. And the real Haggerty—who you left in the muck and brush, as well—is there, on your left. Both good men, and you killed them."

"What the hell are you talking about? They're both dead!" Haggerty shouted.

But he must have felt it. Nikki did. Cold. Like ice. She didn't dare move, but she was certain that Brent was right.

"Drop the weapon, because if I let them take you… well, they'll make you die slowly…and in agony," Brent said. "Hey, why not? They were good men. They had everything in the world to live for, and you…come on, surely you can feel them by now?"

"Holy…oh, holy…" Massey whispered suddenly.

"You're a raving lunatic," Haggerty said. But he suddenly jerked around, as if he'd been struck from behind. Nikki felt herself miraculously freed.

Brent didn't wait. He didn't use his own gun. With a flying leap, he went for Haggerty's knees.

The man fell. Brent rose, ready to slam a knee against him, but it didn't seem necessary. Haggerty was on the ground, screaming, bringing his arms up, flailing…

Nikki didn't see the ghosts of Tom Garfield and the real Agent Haggerty that night. She was in Brent's arms too quickly.

But she heard the screams….

And then the shouts. Light flooded the darkness, and the bayou country came to brilliant and vivid life as cops swarmed in.

The man on the ground kept screaming, and screaming, his voice rising, shrill with pain, even as he appeared to struggle with himself.

Then he began to confess.

Nikki was confused…then shocked.

In the end, she still didn't know exactly what had happened. She only knew that she was being led from the swamp.

And that she was with Brent.

And that she was alive.

* * *

The following evening, she let Brent explain to the others.

They weren't meeting at Madame's—they would never meet at Madame's again. Of course, it wouldn't be Madame D'Orso's anymore anyway.

She had been in on the conspiracy. Her café had been a meeting place for the drug dealers, too.

"I'm so lost," Patricia said, sitting in the curve of Nathan's arm. "Madame was the head of the whole thing?"

Brent shook his head. "Madame was merely the go-between, and a source of news and information. She put buyers and sellers together, and helped find the little guys who sold on the streets. Like those who got killed last night," he added.

"So..." Patricia pressed.

"I still don't know how you knew that Haggerty, not Massey, was guilty," Nikki told him. "You found a body when you stumbled on Julian—"

"No thanks to you," Julian muttered, rolling his eyes.

"Julian, you weren't in the trunk with me, so I thought..."

"They had me in the backseat. I did the same thing you did. I wasn't out. When I heard the arguing going on by the road, I ran."

"Explain to me who was arguing," Mitch said. "I'm still confused."

"I knew I should have stayed with the shrimpers," Max moaned.

Brent smiled ruefully. "I should have seen it all before. Hell, someone should have seen it. But Robert

Greenwood—that's the real name of our false Haggerty—played it with raw nerve. He had been the henchman for a long time. He was the one who made Tom Garfield and then killed him—with a little help from Madame D'Orso. She had seen Tom in the café a few too many times. She knew he had picked up on something and was getting closer and closer to the truth. She hit him with a tranquilizer right before he stumbled into Nikki and Andy, and he was picked up right after, stumbling in the streets."

"Then Greenwood killed Andy…but why?" Max demanded.

"I can explain that." It was Owen Massey who spoke, coming up behind them where they sat at Sarah's, a different café on a different street. "Garfield had something, and Robert Greenwood knew it. But it wasn't on the body. And they couldn't find it at Madame's. It had to be on either Nikki or Andy."

"So why Andy and not Nikki?" Mitch asked.

Brent took over again. "Robert Greenwood knew everything about the group, since Madame kept him up on what was going on. He knew Andy had been a junkie, because he knew he could make her OD and it would look believable. So he started with her. He knew once Tom Garfield was killed that there would be a number of agents working the case, but he also relied on the fact that there's often poor communication between agencies. One man would be assigned to liaison with the New Orleans police. He found out who with little difficulty—lots of cops came to Madame's, too—and killed the real Haggerty, dumping his body deep in the bayou.

Once he'd rid himself of the real agent, he turned himself into the man. It wasn't hard for him," he explained.

"He was a con, used to being a chameleon. He and the real Haggerty were the same in size, they were lean jawed...he cut his hair, bought contacts—and counted on the fact that most ID pictures suck," Massey said. He shook his head. "We should have known. Our boss would get calls from the FBI, complaining that they hadn't heard from him. Then he'd call in saying he was onto something, and that he needed the others to back off. Eventually, if he'd played it long enough, he would have been caught. But he didn't intend to play it that long."

"When did he intend to stop?" Patricia asked, puzzled.

"When Billy Banks was elected," Brent said.

"What?" Max demanded, suddenly sitting up straight and looking completely puzzled. "How the hell...?"

"Massey and Joulette hit it on the head in the cemetery," Brent said. "Billy Banks wanted to be big in politics, and he also needed money to bankroll his campaign. He found Robert Greenwood and the world of illicit drugs. Banks could move all kinds of deals, get the stuff in, and pretend in the meantime that he was going to be hard on crime. He made money, and he tried to make Harold Grant look inept."

"Great," Max groaned. "It was a massive conspiracy. Banks at the head of it, Madame as a liaison, and this pseudo-Haggerty fellow, Greenwood, running all the dirty work. His underlings all used ski masks. I assume that meant they never knew one another and never knew Haggerty? Or Greenwood, I mean."

"That's pretty much how it went," Brent said.

"And you suspected all of us," Julian said with a groan.

"It had to be someone close to Nikki and Andy...and that was you all," Brent explained.

"I wasn't even here," Max complained.

Brent offered an apologetic smile. "Billy Banks never got his hands dirty—he was above it all. He was just the financing."

"My money is legitimate," Max protested.

"I know," Brent said.

Max stared at him.

"I checked you out, of course," Brent said.

"The thing I don't understand," Julian said, puzzled, "is how you knew from seeing a decaying corpse that Haggerty was fake."

"Or," Massey added with a shudder, "why the man was struggling as if there were a gator chewing him apart while he was lying on the ground. Why the hell he admitted everything...ratted on Billy Banks in seconds flat."

Brent smiled at Massey.

"I think you do," he said softly.

Massey looked away. "Hell! All I know is that thanks to you, Blackhawk, I need a vacation. One hell of a vacation. And I'm going to get it. So is Joulette. Shit. You had the two of us suspicious of one another, sneaking around to check up on our own leads. We both thought the other guy was ratting to Haggerty. Meanwhile, it was Madame giving him information."

Mitch cleared his throat. "There's still another question. What was Haggerty—sorry, Greenwood—looking for? What did he think Andy had? And once he'd trashed her place and hadn't found it...was that why he went after Nikki, as risky as it was?"

"My purse is at a forensics lab," Nikki told him. "Whether it was true or not, we don't know yet. But Robert Greenwood believed that Tom Garfield had kept information on a chip—that he'd filmed some of the comings and goings and dealings he'd seen, and that, knowing he was about to be a dead man, he'd passed it on."

"I'm sure they'll find it," Brent said softly. "It's either caught in the lining of Nikki's purse—which is why a girl who looks a lot like Nikki was mugged, and then Nikki herself—or it's on the clothing she was wearing that day. We pretty much know everything." He glanced at Massey wryly again. "Thanks to Greenwood's mysterious confession."

Max sighed and stared at Nikki. "You do realize that we're about to have the most popular tour company in the entire parish, don't you? We'll have to hire a lot more people. Of course, given the terrible circumstances we've recently lived through—"

"*We?* You just got back," Julian protested.

"*We.* We're just one big happy family, right?" Max said. "I've canceled all tours for the next week. I believe we go on having customers meet here, but I'll have to work out the financial end with the owner." He stared at Brent with a sigh. "I guess you're not really working for me, are you?"

Nikki stared at Brent. He glanced her way with a dry smile. "Now and then. When I can. And Nikki won't be around for a while, either."

"Nikki?" Max said.

"You're going to have to work yourself for a while. I'm going with Brent to see the Wild West."

"Ah, the Indian thing," Max said sagely, then quickly amended, "Sorry, Native American."

Brent laughed. "We're going on a honeymoon, to the Grand Canyon."

Max congratulated them; Julian rolled his eyes; Patricia shrieked, saying the wedding had better be in New Orleans. Massey promised them a police escort if they wanted one.

The talk and the explanations went on for a while, until it seemed they had talked themselves out and silence fell, but it was a pleasant silence.

Then Brent excused himself and Nikki, and asked Massey to accompany them.

"Where are we going?" Massey asked.

"The cemetery."

Massey groaned.

"No, no, it's all right," Brent told him. "You just need to wait outside."

"Then why are you taking me?"

"It's illegal to be in there, of course," Brent told him. "Unless we have official permission."

"I owe you. But don't you go conjuring up any ghosts. I didn't see what I thought I saw last night. You've just got something in your voice, and that's how you made Greenwood believe those fellows he'd killed were next to him."

Brent put a hand on his shoulder. "It's all right, Owen. Really."

Massey groaned again.

At the cemetery, he stood guard as day ended and dusk fell.

Hand in hand, Nikki and Brent entered. "Huey?" Brent called.

Nikki saw the old man as he came out to greet them. "Hey, there, Injun boy. And you, miss," he said to Nikki.

"I came to thank you, Huey," Brent said. "And I hope that, if I need you, you'll be around."

"Well…I don't think I will be. I've just been waiting on you comin' around again," Huey said.

"Oh?" Brent said with a frown.

Huey gave a broad grin. "You wouldn't believe… that pretty young gal came around again. Marie."

"Old McManus's descendant?" Nikki asked.

Huey nodded. "She done found that I have a great, great…well, I don't know how many greats. But I got me a pretty descendant, too. A little girl just as sweet as can be. And Miss Marie McManus, well, she brought the girl to the graveyard with her momma, and she showed her about where I'm supposed to be, and they were talking, and the momma, she's pretty poor, but that Marie girl wants to be her big sister and pay for piano lessons."

"That's nice, Huey. That's really nice," Brent said. "But…"

"Well, you see, late at night, after the ruckus, I was

pretty proud. Felt like I'd stopped some bad stuff from hitting the streets. And I reckon I was right enough to feel proud, 'cause I saw this passage—prettiest passage I ever done see, living or dead. It was like I was beckoned to follow, only it just wasn't right yet. Today, after seeing those girls…it's right. I'm going to be looking for it. Looking for the light." Huey tilted his chin, indicating that they should look behind themselves. "I'm thinking as how your friends there are ready, too."

Nikki spun around, as did Brent.

She knew, however, who she would see.

Andy. And Tom Garfield. She wasn't surprised, and she wasn't frightened. She wasn't even disturbed by the cold when Andy came over to her and she felt the strangest hug. There…but not there. Cold. And yet so very warm. Andy kissed her cheek. "Thank you," she whispered.

"Andy…"

She felt tears rising in her eyes. "No," Andy told her. She winked. "That passage Huey is talking about… well, you can't imagine. And…"

She flicked her hair back, wickedly winking. "I don't have to go alone."

The ghost of Tom Garfield reached out a hand to her.

Andy took it.

Nikki never actually saw any of them go down their magnificent path.

They were just there, and then they were gone.

And then Brent whispered to her softly. "It's time for us to go now, too. We have a different path."

She took his hand, and they left the cemetery together.

They took Massey and Joulette for drinks that evening, then went back to Nikki's. Alone in the house, they made love, then made love again, the act made special by the simple fact that it was so physical. They couldn't help but feel so grateful and so alive.

Later, Brent rose while Nikki slept. He walked out on the balcony.

New Orleans. Home.

It was a great place. A wonderful place. It was his heart. Nikki had become his heart.

Um, yeah, it was full of ghosts. But they were great ghosts.

It was also full of history, art, music, and wonderful memories of the past.

And with Nikki in his life, it held a future full of hope.

* * * * *